"I Just Want to Feel Better About Me . . .

I'm not without scruples, and I'm not a jerk, out looking for quick tumbles. But you made me feel like one last week."

She drew a breath to argue, but he cut her off.

"Hey, it wasn't a setup. I drove you home because I didn't want you to kill yourself. When you told me how much you'd put into the project, I felt bad for you. It made it much harder to tell you that I was the one who . . ." He stood up and pushed the chair away.

"It was just an impulse when I took you in my arms. It wasn't loaded with base motives."

He paused, searching her face for some sign of yielding, but she kept her eyes expressionless and said nothing.

His hands passed over his jaw in a gesture of chagrin. "I may as well put the other foot in it . . . I feel an impulse to kiss you now."

Dear Reader,

When two people fall in love, the world is suddenly new and exciting, and it's that same excitement we bring to you in Silhouette Intimate Moments. These are stories with scope, with grandeur. These characters lead the lives we all dream of, and everything they do reflects the wonder of being in love.

Longer and more sensuous than most romances, Silhouette Intimate Moments novels take you away from everyday life and let you share the magic of love. Adventure, glamour, drama, even suspense— these are the passwords that let you into a world where love has a power beyond the ordinary, where the best authors in the field today create stories of love and commitment that will stay with you always.

In coming months look for novels by your favorite authors: Maura Seger, Parris Afton Bonds, Elizabeth Lowell and Erin St. Claire, to name just a few. And whenever you buy books, look for all the Silhouette Intimate Moments, love stories *for* today's women *by* today's women.

Leslie J. Wainger
Senior Editor
Silhouette Books

IMRL-7/85

Soft Touch

Möeth Allison

Silhouette Intimate Moments

Published by Silhouette Books New York

America's Publisher of Contemporary Romance

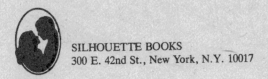

SILHOUETTE BOOKS
300 E. 42nd St., New York, N.Y. 10017

Copyright © 1985 by Möeth Allison

Distributed by Pocket Books

ISBN: 0-373-07111-6

First Silhouette Books printing September, 1985

10 9 8 7 6 5 4 3 2 1

America's Publisher of Contemporary Romance

Printed in the U.S.A.

Silhouette Books by Moeth Allison

Love Everlasting (IM #8)
Russian Roulette (IM #43)
Every Other Weekend (IM #102)
Soft Touch (IM #111)

MOETH ALLISON

was born in England and came to the United States in 1960. Before she started writing fiction, she was an editor and copy editor in London, New York and California. Although she is a compulsive writer, in between manuscripts she takes time out to fix gourmet meals for her family.

Chapter 1

SHE IS ON THE CATWALK OF THE BRIDGE, POISED A hundred feet above the East River. She can jump now, before she loses her nerve, or she can contemplate eternity for a moment, and let a sudden gust or the rumbling of a heavy truck throw her off balance and rob her of the last conscious choice she will ever make. Chalice York closed her eyes for three seconds, teetering on the brink, then crumpled the sheet of paper in her hand and tossed it into the wastebasket.

"Baloney," she muttered. This was *The Snipe*, not *Antigone*. She'd just have to talk Walter out of it, that's all. She had already tried once; she'd just have to try harder. She had simply wanted Millie to walk unheeding into the path of a westbound bus.

But Walter Ryan was the director, and he balked at shooting a traffic scene in midtown Manhattan.

"A dive stunt will cost a fraction of the time and money," he kept insisting.

Sure it would. Because all but a few seconds of it could be faked with stock footage right here in a Hollywood studio. And they could trim back a day or two on location shooting in Manhattan.

Chalice pouted and glared at the keyboard of her typewriter. She knew how it went. Walter was eager to save money. About seventy thousand, she guessed. But why here? What was seventy thousand in a fifteen-million-dollar movie budget? When the star would be offered a cool three million in return for about twenty-six days of work? Why were they always so chintzy with the things that really mattered? And it *did* matter. Jumping off the Brooklyn Bridge just wasn't Millie.

Chalice flexed her shoulders and slid her typing chair back from the desk. She took a fistful of typed sheets from the dogeared stack and threw them into the wastebasket. The entire bridge sequence. So much for a full morning's work.

Rising in response to the doorbell, she gave a soft groan. Her tailbone was sore from sitting. She didn't even know if the Brooklyn Bridge *had* a catwalk, come to think of it.

Luke stood in the hall looking the way he always did when he rang her bell, as if he had some nerve intruding on the creative process.

"Sorry if I'm bothering you, but I've got an hour before my class," he said. "I'm just going out for some air. Thought you might want to take a break."

Chalice rubbed the stiff muscles in her neck and glanced at her watch. It wasn't midday after all, she discovered. It was almost five.

"Sure, Luke. Why not?" She gestured over her shoulder at the living room with an expression of disgust. "Sitting here all day hasn't done much for me."

They drove down to the municipal beach, and she managed to squeeze the Honda into an empty curb space on California Street. Fifteen minutes after leaving home, they were crossing Ocean Park Boulevard.

It was a cool, overcast day, and the beach was deserted. Still wearing the gray warm-up pants she'd been working in, Chalice began to jog slowly over the damp, packed sand left behind by the tide. Luke politely paced himself to her speed.

She felt sluggish after so many sedentary hours, but the moist slap of a salt breeze on her face was blowing the cobwebs away. It felt good. As they drew level with the Sheraton, Chalice pulled away from Luke and sprinted the last few yards to the Santa Monica pier in a mad, flat-out dash.

Moments later she collapsed on the sand beside the pilings, huffing and puffing.

"Gosh, Chalice, take it easy," Luke said, not even warmed up yet as he hunkered down beside her.

She knew he wanted to say: "Don't overdo it. You don't get enough exercise to really stay in shape." But Luke wasn't a preachy type. It was one of the things that made him so endearing . . . that, and the fact that his strongest four-letter word was "gosh."

Chalice struggled to her feet and brushed off her pants. "I'm just fine," she panted and grinned. "Come on, I'll buy you a triple dip from Franny's. You deserve it, for getting me out from under." He had fixed her desk lamp that week, and he was forever running little bitty errands for her.

Franny's was just across the road, and Luke's idea

of heaven was one of their huge scoops of vanilla, lodged in a sugar cone, then custom-dipped in warm caramel, crushed nuts, and melted chocolate.

"Aren't you going to have one?" he asked when they got to the counter.

She smiled. "Of course not."

They emerged from Franny's and headed back along the boulevard to the car, Luke admiring the gourmet confection in his hand while it was still intact. "Are you sure you don't want a taste before I start?"

Chalice shook her head.

"You hardly eat at all, Chalice. Even sitting at a desk all day has to burn up calories."

"Sure feels like it sometimes," she said. "Today, for instance, I feel I've been digging ditches for eight hours, but it doesn't burn up real energy." She saw his anxiety, and added, "And I do eat, Luke—very wisely as a matter of fact, for someone who sits for a living."

Sweet Luke, she thought, what is Hollywood going to do to you? So far he hadn't changed, but it was only five months.

She had first met him in the hallway of her building on the day he moved in with his cousin Billy. All she knew of Billy was that he was a dental student.

"Are you at the dental school too?" she had asked him.

"No, ma'am," he had told her with the respect due to an older woman. "I've just finished a two-year youth mission for my church, and I'm staying on here to try my luck as an actor."

Chalice had been on the West Coast for six years, locking horns with the movie industry. She was still on the fringes of the action, and at twenty-seven, she felt like a babe in the woods more often than not. But listening to this tall, angel-faced youth with his backpack and his bicycle clips, she had felt like a woman of the world. It was a heady sensation. She had adopted Luke on the spot, pointing his nose toward a good drama class, and a job at Chickeeburger, a local fast-food joint.

Since then, Luke had netted a couple of walk-on parts in television, and one tiny guest role on *Little House on the Prairie* where he got to speak. Seven words. He might even make it, she thought, but more likely he would give up after a couple of years and go back to Provo. He was incredibly attractive, of course, but all the young hopefuls were incredibly attractive.

As Chalice saw it, Luke had two things going for him. The first one was a thoroughly-wholesome-kid quality that was quite genuine. The second was a very savvy talent agent. And that was Chalice's doing.

Robert Shankel had once been her own agent, and although he was an incorrigible womanizer (a fact she had discovered in the most painful way possible), he was a top professional.

She glanced up at Luke as they crossed Second Street. He was tackling his ice cream as if he were a child as he loped along beside her. He was twenty, and no dummy; and at six-three, he loomed twelve inches above her. But all the same, she had a ridiculous urge to hold his hand at the crosswalk. If Luke had been a girl, she would never have sent him to see Robert Shankel, not knowing what she did now.

But she hadn't known anything about Hollywood

when she arrived six years ago. She had been a virgin like Luke, in every possible sense of the word. Robert Shankel was just the name she saw most often in *Variety*, linked with mind-boggling film deals, famous names, and seven-figure contracts.

Her opinion of Robert's professional skills hadn't changed, but as a human being, the man was a twenty-four-carat jerk. Just like all the others she came across in Hollywood. It was par for the course in these parts. It was why she spent more leisure time in innocent outings like this than she did on dates.

When she did accept a date, she kept to public places and never allowed her romantic interest to stir. It showed, she supposed. She rarely got asked more than twice. Icicle York, one date had called her. It didn't matter. Only her writing mattered. For emotional support, what she needed much more than a man was a network of friends she could trust, friends like Luke, a surrogate kid brother. Rachel, her role model, confidante, and best friend. And oddly enough, Robert Shankel.

No, Robert would never be a close friend exactly; it was more the kind of situation that occurs with some strains of virus. One Shankel attack gave you lifelong immunity. As an ex-lover, even as an ex-agent, he was a useful guy to know.

It was Robert, she remembered, who had gotten her story idea off the ground by introducing her to the right director.

Walter Ryan was certainly the right director, young enough to take chances, and successful enough to be in demand. Walter had been so taken with *The Snipe*, he'd even paid her a little out of his own pocket to develop the idea into a thirty-page treatment. Then he really got turned on and urged her to write a full script. Then rewrite it and rewrite it until she hardly recognized her original story line. She'd been working on it ever since. It had become an obsession almost. *The Snipe*. Millie, Sal, the whole cast of characters . . . the project had been going on so long now, she couldn't quite imagine life without it.

But still, as Walter pointed out frequently, they'd come a long way with it, and would probably go all the way. At last, it was all falling into place. They had a producer now, Lou Hosner of Pacifica Studios. Money was waiting in the wings, and as soon as they had a bankable star for the lead, it would be a "go" project. Then she'd be paid handsomely for all these months of reworking the script.

Luke had finished his ice cream by the time they got back to the car.

"Want me to drop you off at class?" she asked him.

"No thanks, I'd better go home and check the answering service first," he said. "I can get to school in fifteen minutes if I run. That's better than I can do on the moped when the lights are against me."

Chalice grinned as she pulled away from the parking meter and took the back streets toward Carlyle. Robert issued the same order to every new client. *If you don't have an answering service, get one today. And check in with them every hour, including weekends.*

Luke only had to be told something once.

He turned to her now as they stopped at the Seventh Street light. "What are you going to be doing tonight?"

"What I've been doing all day. Reworking the latest draft of *The Snipe*."

Luke gave an audible groan. "Gee, it seems like you've been working on that movie ever since I met you."

"Longer," Chalice said. "Sixteen months, to be exact."

"Holy smoke!"

"And it's not a movie yet, Luke."

"Then what is it?"

"It's a package." She scowled through the windshield as they cruised past short residential blocks. Stucco-fronted houses slid by, spray-painted in pastel colors so familiar that she no longer registered them.

It was a package all right, but it wouldn't be more than that until they had a top box-office name signed up to play Sal.

"Don't you ever get discouraged?" Luke asked her.

She laughed. "Never on Fridays. Seriously, Luke. If you get discouraged in the movie business, then . . ."

"I know, I know." He folded his arms over his chest and recited his line. "Then you don't belong in the movie business."

"Right."

"So how do you handle the big disappointments?"

Out of the corner of her eye, she saw his ingenuous sky-blue gaze, and chuckled. "I go absolutely crazy for a day or two, then I pick myself up, have a session with my agent, then get right back to work."

"You go crazy?" he said, shifting restlessly in the passenger seat. "What do you mean, crazy?"

Chalice tapped her index finger on the steering wheel and smiled, remembering. "Well, once I took up skydiving. One jump was enough. I usually have to psych myself up to jump into a swimming pool."

"Skydiving!" Luke looked impressed. "No kidding?"

"No kidding. And another time, I blew every penny on a one-way ticket to Rio, to see my mother. She lives there."

"Well that's not so crazy," he said, disappointed.

"It is if you know my mother." They turned on Carlyle, then nosed into the alley alongside the apartment building. "I was twenty-five at the time, and Kyla works hard at looking twenty-nine. Her new husband was under the impression I was away at boarding school. It wasn't the most joyful reunion."

Luke's interest revived. "So what happened?"

"She promptly gave me airfare back to Los Angeles, and by the time I got here, the crazies were over and I was ready to buckle down."

"My mom's forty-seven, and she wishes I would come home and apply to Brigham Young," he said, awed as usual at the vast variety of the human condition.

"I can understand that, I guess," Chalice said as they walked up the steps from the garage.

Luke thrust his hands into the pockets of his jeans, shaking his head. "I can see how you'd go crazy, Chalice. Sixteen months working on a job and it still hasn't come together," he said. Wow! Still, if it's been going on for all this time, I guess it's going to make it." He spoke with as much conviction as he could muster. "It must be a good sign, huh?"

"Oh yes. There's no question about *The Snipe*,"

she said brightly. But it wasn't quite true. You were always on quicksand in this business, even in midproduction.

"So when do you think you'll know for sure, Chalice?" Luke asked, as they walked along the second-floor corridor.

Very soon, she thought, with a rush of energy.

Walter Ryan would be back from New York next week. Maybe with Brad Alexander in his pocket. That's all they needed to get the green light. Brad Alexander was so hot, he'd gotten three million dollars plus for his last two films. So hot, in fact, that he never had to work again if he didn't want to. But he'd been idling for a year now. He had to be bored. Oh please, God, let him be bored. And the way she'd rewritten the lead, Brad Alexander just had to find the part irresistible.

"Chalice? How long will it take, do you think?" Luke lingered at her front door while she fiddled with her keys.

"It's like this, Luke," she said. "Any moment now, the director will be signing a star for the lead . . ."

Then she'd be rolling, with her first original film. Not a thirty-minute sitcom based on someone else's stock characters, not a blatant rip-off like *Return of the Killer Bees*, not an adaptation of a book or a play where seventeen other writers got in the act before they went through the revolving door. No, this was her very own brainchild, destined for the big screen. And when it showed; every print would carry her credit line up front.

ORIGINAL SCREENPLAY BY CHALICE YORK.

Luke was right. *The Snipe* would make it. It had stayed alive too long to die now.

"So, *then* will it be a movie?" Luke asked.

"When Walter Ryan signs up a star, the investors will commit the money," she intoned in a faraway voice. "And when the money's in the bank, the studio will be committed. And when the studio's committed, then we're in preproduction, Luke . . . *then* it's a movie."

He was still in New York, Joe Verdi reminded himself, still on home ground. But seated in the lounge bar, he could feel his solar plexus tighten as he traded opening civilities with Walter Ryan. The blond young man facing him was a prime example of the new movieland breed. To Joe, they all looked alike—preppy WASPS, all graduates of the Film School of the University of Southern California. All still in their twenties, and all, dammit, brilliant. It wasn't the brilliance or the early success he resented so much. It was that supreme Ivy-League confidence.

At thirty-five, Joe still had all his dark hair. He was a muscular five foot nine, and he kept every inch in good shape at the gym. But the tall, golden boy across from him made him feel like an aging, swarthy runt. It reminded him of what he could expect for the next few months.

"I saw *Summer Days* last night," Ryan was saying.

Summer Days was currently playing at the Shubert. Joe had written it under financial pressure, the most consciously commercial effort of his career.

"Just great, Joe. I loved it."

"The critics were kind," Joe said. "But no one's getting trampled to death at the box office."

"The Shubert's a big house to fill. It'll pick up."

"Possibly," Joe muttered. Ryan might be a whiz

kid when it came to the silver screen, but if he
thought *Summer Days* was going to pick up, he
didn't know a thing about Broadway. Joe had sat in
the half-empty house through three evening perfor-
mances, and he could smell doom. The play might
just make it through the month, but it would never
solve his money problems. Only a miracle could do
that, or another film job. It was the sole reason he
was sitting here tonight.

"Get me a movie, George," he had told his agent
a few days ago. "Why aren't you getting me some
schlock movie to write before *Summer Days* folds
and my name is mud?"

"Finish your manuscript for Scribners first. You're
too much of a writer for the film market, anyway.
You told me never again. You said Hollywood makes
you ill."

"So for a hundred thousand, I'll suffer a few
weeks. You're not listening to me, George. The
wheel turns. I need the bread. Talk to Norman on
the Coast. Promise me. The first thing that comes
along, and to hell with artistic standards. I'm talking
need here. Dire need."

George Nadel was the agent to have in time of
need; he had come through so fast, Joe's head was
spinning. Just a few hours ago, George had thrust a
synopsis into Joe's hands.

"Go home and read this. Pacifica Studios has an
option on it that's running out in a couple of weeks.
They're ready to move. Walter Ryan wants to talk to
you about writing the script. The Sherry Netherland.
Six tonight. Actually, all you have to do is nod your
head."

Hey presto. Just like that.

Joe knew it wasn't magic of course. He knew

perfectly well why he was being wooed at this
moment by Walter Ryan. George Nadel just happened to represent Brad Alexander. George was the
only man who could persuade that overpaid and
undermotivated superstar to get off his behind and
work again. It was a trade-off.

Pacifica Studios wanted Alexander for the lead.
What studio didn't? Joe grinned to himself, imagining George's encounter with Walter Ryan. George
always laid his cards right out.

*Hire Joe Verdi for the screenplay, and I'll deliver
Brad Alexander for the lead.*

They'd go for that. He knew their thinking. *Joe
Verdi's not exactly chopped liver. If that's what it
takes, let's go.*

Brad Alexander was gilt-edged insurance. Put his
name on the marquee, and the public would line up
in the rain to see any piece of garbage.

Joe had no illusions. But surprisingly enough, the
treatment he'd read just a few hours ago wasn't the
usual garbage. The story was promising. Moving
even. *The Snipe* had substance to it.

Walter Ryan was starting his second vodka, and
still carrying on about the imperatives of the live
theatre as if he knew a thing or two. At the moment,
Joe was more concerned with the imperatives of the
live playwright. It was time to cut short the bull.

Joe reached for the envelope that lay on the
vacant seat between them, lifted out the slim binder
inside, and pointedly riffled through the typed pages
of the treatment.

Ryan responded immediately, sitting tall in his
armchair. "You had a chance to look at it? Good.
What d'you think?"

"Haven't done a whole lot of thinking yet," Joe

said neutrally. "George just gave it to me today. It's a good story line. Well structured. A bit mawkish toward the end, is my first impression . . . but it could be toughened out in the writing."

Joe closed the binder and looked at the author's name on the title label, noticing it for the first time. "Who's Chalice York?" he asked idly.

"Jeffrey York's daughter. She's a television writer, but she has some good ideas." Ryan flashed polished teeth. "I agree with you about the mawkishness. For the script, we've got to have raw, gut-level impact to make it work. I need you, Joe."

In a pig's eye. What you need is Brad Alexander. Joe returned a modest smile, dismissing the compliment. "You mean the late Jeffrey York? Pinewood Studios and all?"

Ryan nodded.

So there was a daughter who worked in Holly-wood, Joe reflected. That explained the baloney first name. As a film director, Jeffrey York was one of the greats. His name lived on because of half a dozen real classics, *The Chalice* not included. *The Chalice* was mediocre sword-and-gauntlet stuff, an Arthuri-an epic that lived on the late late show. Joe had stayed up to watch it once, simply because it was a York movie. *The Pits* would have been a more appropriate title.

Joe glanced again at the typed label on the folder. Chalice York. If he was in her shoes, he'd change the first name and just hang on to the York part. But then, she was Hollywood. They all marched to a different drummer out there. He dismissed the inter-esting tidbit and brought his mind back to business.

"I can give you a first draft in three weeks," he said.

"So you'll do it then?" Ryan looked as if the good fairy had just granted him the princess of his choice.

"Yes, I'll do it."

Joe took a quick gulp of his bourbon, then almost choked when Ryan said, "Lou Hosner's prepared to offer you a hundred and fifty. Plus a hotel per diem, of course, because he wants you on the set until we finish shooting. There'll be about ten days of location work in Manhattan, but the rest will be shot at the studios."

A hundred and fifty thousand dollars. It was fifty percent more than he'd expected, and it would go a long way to putting out the fires in his life. Joe cleared his throat and said, "Sounds fair to me."

"George thought so too." Ryan glanced at his watch. "Good. I'll call Lou right now and he'll have the contract waiting for you when you arrive. George is flying out Monday. He can look through the paperwork and sew up the details on the spot."

Ryan leaned across the table. "We're really anxious to move on this. I realize it's not much notice, but can you be ready to leave on Monday with George?"

"I'm sure I can."

"I can call Hosner and tell him it's a deal then?"

Joe smiled and shook the hand that Ryan was holding out with such boyish enthusiasm.

"It's a deal."

Chapter 2

CHALICE HAD LOOKED FORWARD TO THIS LUNCH WITH her agent. First, she was getting a check, and that was always good news. And second, Sam Firestone could always be relied upon for a delicious line of patter: tongue-in-cheek industry gossip, the latest Hollywood agent jokes, the freshest scandals. But today, he seemed to have run out of chitchat. In fact he looked tired and unusually ill-humored as he placed an envelope on the white tablecloth beside Chalice's wineglass.

"Your check," he said.

"You okay, Sam?" Chalice asked, lifting out the contents of the envelope.

"Sure."

The gross amount on the statement was seventeen thousand dollars. Less Sam's ten percent. The check clipped to the statement was made out accordingly.

But Chalice was expecting only seven thousand for developmental work on *The Snipe.* Not seventeen . . . She was almost afraid to ask. Nothing had made sense this week.

Stalling for time, she bent her head to examine the check more closely, one hand reaching up to stop her overgrown bangs from flopping forward and obscuring the view.

Across the table, her agent sipped a club soda. It was all that kept him from an ulcer on a day like this. And most days were like this, come to think of it.

"Doesn't all that hair drive you nuts when you're working?" he asked her crossly. He was entitled to be crabby, he decided. He was seventy-six years old, and this noon, he felt every day of it.

Chalice just kept staring at the pale green check drawn on the Bank of America. On the memo stub was typed, "Pacifica Motion Pictures/The Snipe." No clue to account for the extra ten thousand dollars. A clerical error? She didn't believe that. She didn't know what to believe anymore.

Walter Ryan had been due back in town last weekend. Half the week had gone by, and still no word from him. She'd heard a rumor that he was staying on in Manhattan to look over suitable shooting locations. She couldn't get anyone at Pacifica to confirm or deny it. Lou Hosner wasn't returning her calls to the studio. But if the rumor was true, it meant they were already preparing to go into production. Walter wouldn't be looking at locations unless *The Snipe* was a "go" project. And if it was a "go" project, why would they want to keep the screenwriter in the dark about it?

Chalice tried to drown out the warning signals in

her head. Sam hadn't hinted at any bad news. In fact it was Nora who'd called. "Can you meet Mr. Firestone for lunch at Lowry's?" was all the secretary had said. "He has a check for you." That in itself was odd; Sam always called her personally.

Maybe the extra money was an advance on the final script. But if so, where was the script contract? Sam certainly didn't have it with him at the restaurant.

Calm down! They were just bending the rules a little because they loved the script so much, and because sixteen months was a long time to be kept dangling this way. Even in Hollywood. Sam wasn't volunteering a word.

Chalice took a deep breath and made a conscious effort to sound casual. "What's the extra ten grand for, Sam? Don't tell me you squeezed a few more drops out of Hosner?"

Sam tried to smile, but it was hard looking at her eyes. They were huge and very vulnerable as she waited for his answer. Dear God, she was actually holding her breath. This one was going to hurt.

"Chalice, honey . . ." He heaved a sigh. "I got you a little heartache money, darling. I'm afraid they're hiring someone else for the script."

If he had to do this bit one more time, he was going to quit the business, he thought. For good, this time. He'd renewed that resolution almost every working day since World War II started. This time he nearly meant it. This wasn't just any young talent sitting here while he did the studio's dirty work for them. This was Jeffrey York's child, with the same desperate yearning in her eyes, the same creative flair, and the same astonishing naiveté when it came to Hollywood. *The last battleground between artistic integrity and Mammon,* her father had once called it.

Sam had represented Jeffrey York for the last five years of the director's life, the Hollywood years. The Englishman had seen himself as St. George, capable of slaying the dragon. And three times he actually had. Jeffrey's triumphs had been the high points in Sam's career. High points were in short supply these days. Times had changed. They were making so few movies now, and memorable ones were rare.

"I'm sorry, Chalice. I know what you were expecting; I'm truly sorry," he said, watching her take it in. She was sitting still as stone, as if she were absorbing a blow to the body.

Jeffrey had died too soon, at the height of his powers. Now Sam realized there was such a thing as living too long. He'd played this miserable scene too many times.

"How can they hire someone for the script, Sam?" she said softly. "The script's already written. About a hundred times."

Her face was almost as colorless as the white tablecloth. She was young, he reminded himself. She'd get over it in a week or so, "I got you a credit line, of course," Sam said, rubbing his midriff, where sharp knives seemed to be at play. "Based on a story by—"

"Based on a story my foot!" Her voice was no longer soft. A few heads turned at nearby tables, but she ignored them. "It's my movie, my screenplay! Sixteen months of my life, Sam! Anyway, Ryan loves the last version. Hosner loves it too. You can talk them around."

They both knew there wasn't a hope in hell. Sam

said nothing. What was the use? Hadn't he told her a hundred times not to write this script on spec? Speculative work was okay in moderation, but she'd gone way overboard on *The Snipe*. He knew why, too. This one was special to her. An original. And those sons of bitches kept holding out the carrot to her.

Sam leaned forward. He was in considerable pain now, but he brushed it aside. "You know it has nothing to do with your writing, honey. It never has."

She also knew words were pointless now, but they kept spilling out. "I stayed up nights reworking the Sal scenes. Just to tempt Brad Alexander with an irresistible role."

"And you succeeded," he said. "They got him for Sal." Would she feel any better if she knew the details? he wondered. She had a right to know anyway.

"You want to know why you're off the project? It's just a courtesy to George Nadel for getting Alexander to . . ."

"I don't want to hear it!"

Sam's mouth was still moving, but Chalice clapped her hands over her ears. She could hear nothing but the crazy rhythms drumming through her nervous system. She didn't want to hear another word about their crummy commodity trading.

"I don't want to hear it. I don't want to hear it," she repeated over and over as she left Sam at the lunch table and hurried out of the restaurant to her car.

She drove recklessly along La Cienega, racing amber lights, passing buses as they pulled into her lane, and on the freeway, playing chicken with the speeding cars like a hell-bent teenager.

At the bank, she began to make out a deposit slip. There were six customers in line, and only one teller on duty. Anger lumped in her throat as she waited an interminable three minutes. The line didn't move. If she had to stand here one more second, she'd explode. Impulsively, she thrust the check and the deposit slip back into her purse, marched out of the bank and drove home at lunatic speed.

Various drafts of *The Snipe* were stored on the living room bookcase in an assortment of boxes and folders. She glared at the shelves, turned on the stereo, then looked at the latest version of the screenplay, still lying beside the typewriter. She pounced on the topmost sheets and ripped them in half, throwing the ragged white fragments up in the air and letting them flutter down on the carpet, the desk, the furniture. She stopped only to turn the radio dial, tuning in the most raucous AM station she could find. Blaring teenage rock. Raising the volume up to earsplitting maximum, she went back to her shredding, as though it had top priority. Tearing each sheet in two wasn't enough for some reason. She grew industrious, reducing each strip to pieces the size of postage stamps.

In half an hour, the only evidence of *The Snipe* was a living room white with confetti. Over a thousand sheets of notes, takeout scenes, false starts, revisions, all reduced to minute scraps that coated every horizontal surface of the room. No tenants had complained about the radio noise; no one had even thumped on her wall. She didn't feel any release, only a splitting headache.

She silenced the radio and wept for a few moments, then dialed Rachel's number.

Rachel Lorrimer heard her out in appalled silence, then tucked the phone under her chin, and glanced at her watch. "Stay where you are," she said. "Don't move from the apartment, and try not to break anything you'll regret. I'm coming right over."

Everyone had their own way of coping with the hard knocks, Rachel thought, as she drove along Coast Highway. Chalice's way was just less predictable than most. Losing *The Snipe* was going to be the worst.

As a serious actress, Rachel wasn't a stranger to the injustices of show business, but once she'd been naive enough to think that there was a stage in life where you could say you'd paid your dues and from there on, it was clear sailing.

She had believed herself to be at that envious stage seven years ago. She was understudying the lead in her first Broadway play. In addition to being understudy, she had a small speaking part. The play was being well received, and her husband had just flown to Hollywood for an important screen test.

They had only been married three months, Rachel and Al Braddock. They were desperately in love, and they were obviously bringing each other luck. Al was offered the film role three days after his screen test. It was almost too good to be true. Naturally, she had left the play to join Al on the coast, and give him moral support. She remembered thinking that Marianne Frieze was carrying the play, and she was as strong as a horse. As Marianne's stand-in she was never going to take over the lead. Not even for one night. But Al, on the other hand, was at a turning point in his career. This movie could make him a star, and he needed all the help he could get. He was her husband, for God's sake. With understudy for Marianne Frieze added to her acting credits, there would be other opportunities for her.

It had been the right move, for Al. For fifteen weeks she devoted her days and nights to soothing his nerves, boosting his morale, and coaching him in his delivery. It was his first movie and he was mortally afraid of failure.

"What would I do without you, darling?" he had breathed adoringly through those tense days of shooting. "What would I do?"

Rachel still wondered sometimes. There was no way of finding out. Al Braddock had become a phenomenal success. He had become Brad Alexander, a synonym for superstar.

For Rachel, though, the move hadn't been too smart. She hadn't known that Marianne Frieze was pregnant. Three weeks after Rachel quit, Marianne actually retired from the cast, and her new understudy inherited the lead for the run of the play.

Enjoying the privileges of stardom, Al had gone on to younger, glossier wives. Women who had gladly changed their names to Mrs. Brad Alexander. He was working on his fifth, she believed.

It wasn't something that bothered Rachel anymore. After all, it was seven years in the past, and they hadn't been bad years really. She made a very good living in wimpy television roles, and even more in shampoo commercials . . . Nowadays, the whole fiasco only came to mind when she was nursing

Chalice through one of her crises. Chalice wasn't quite young enough to be her daughter, but she did get the urge to mother her once in a while.

Rachel slowed the car when she got to Chalice's block and began to look for a parking spot at the curb. Yes, everyone had their own way of coping, but Chalice's way was a bit disconcerting. Like a cyclone. It was usually over in a day or two, but she sure did go crazy while it lasted.

She breathed a sigh of tentative relief when Chalice let her into the apartment. The living room was littered with minute fragments of white bond. Snipe confetti, Rachel presumed. Chalice looked a bit weepy, but if she'd contented herself with tearing up the script, it wouldn't be too bad this time. Half an hour with a vacuum cleaner, and the room would be back to normal. So would Chalice, with a bit of luck. The housecleaning would be the last part of the therapy. Rachel knew better than to offer to help. Instead, she asked, "Is the worst over now?"

"I haven't even begun yet." Chalice's voice was ominous as she paced the living room, kicking up little clouds of paper scraps with her feet.

Rachel sighed, and noticed the manic gleam in her friend's eye. She couldn't possibly leave her alone tonight. There was some kind of rampage brewing inside her. Rachel had been looking forward to an evening in Bel Air tonight. Glen was picking her up at six-thirty.

As a lover, Glen Suffian was refreshing—not a flaky, temperamental artist, but a successful tax attorney. Movie people were his business clients, not his rivals. It was a nice change for Rachel to be with a relaxed, noncompetitive man who was thoroughly attentive.

"Chalice, Mort Shaffer's throwing a party tonight," she said.

"Yes, I know." Chalice continued to rustle her feet along the carpet from the front door to the window seat.

"You got an invitation? Wonderful! Then why don't you go take a nice hot bath, doll yourself up, and come with Glen and me."

Chalice looked at her as if she'd lost her senses. "What on earth for?"

"For one thing, because it's better than going into one of your infantile tantrums," Rachel said, then immediately regretted it. "For another thing, I'm supposed to go with Glen, and I don't want to miss it."

"So what's stopping you?"

Rachel jumped up from the window seat and grabbed Chalice by the shoulders, stopping her in midstride. "You know damn well. I'm not about to leave you here alone in this mood. Besides, you'd enjoy it too," she called after Chalice, who had turned away to resume the pacing. "I'll bet Glen and I will be the only guests who aren't members of the Writers' Guild. You know that bunch. All card-carrying fellow sufferers. You really should be with fellow sufferers tonight."

"I really should get drunk tonight," Chalice muttered.

"Then you might as well do it on Shaffer's booze."

"No way."

Chalice had an unusually low tolerance for alcohol. One glass of wine was her limit, as far as Rachel knew. In her present mood, she'd get into far worse than harmless mischief if she started exceeding her limit.

"I'm not leaving you here alone tonight, and that's that." Rachel took her stance, arms folded and feet slightly apart. As unmoving as a cigar store Indian. "Blow your evening if you must. Just bear in mind you're blowing my evening too. My whole future with Glen, as a matter of fact. I can't even call Glen and warn him. He's coming to my place straight from a meeting. I'll try to patch it up, of course. But when I explain to him that I stood him up in order to watch a girlfriend drink herself silly, I don't think it'll ever be the same again for us . . ."

Chalice stood under the shower, scrubbing her skin until at first it glowed, and then it hurt.

It was two hours before Rachel agreed to leave, and not before she extracted a promise from Chalice. She would show up at Shaffer's, and she would drink nothing before she arrived. Chalice agreed to go, but only on the condition that she arrived under her own steam. She was in no mood to drive to Bel Air with a contented, cooing twosome.

By the time she had slithered into a silky green jumpsuit and was curling her long red bangs around a hot iron, she was beginning to regret her promise. The jumpsuit was too tight for comfort. She gnashed her teeth. Sixteen months of almost continuous work on *The Snipe*, and all she had to show for it was some Judas money and the five extra pounds she'd just squeezed under the zipper.

More like ten, she thought, examining herself in the full-length mirror. She was definitely looking rounded about the hips and thighs and bosom.

She thought about changing to something less clingy and reached back for the zipper, then dropped her hand. Everything in her closet was going to be

tight now. She hadn't worn anything dressier than
jeans or sweats for ages. Well, who needed a Bel Air
party tonight anyway? She didn't have to go.

Visions of Rachel skittered through her mind.
Rachel would be frantic if she didn't show up.

Chalice stepped back from the closet mirror and
gave her reflection one last detached glance. Some
people might think her extra inches did something
decidedly sexy to the jumpsuit. She didn't, but she
knew she looked all right. Her hair was a casual
tumble of springy curls, and her makeup was all in
place. Three tones of eyeshadow, mascara, blusher,
highlights and shading. The works.

What the hell? She wasn't the first writer to get
kicked in the teeth, and she wouldn't be the last one.
Rachel was right. Maybe she did need to be with
fellow sufferers.

Rachel was wrong, she thought an hour later,
when a uniformed waitress opened Mort Shaffer's
imposing front door. Rachel was dead wrong.

"Hi, honey. Glad you could come," Mort said
vaguely. He wore a bow tie and an expensive
burgundy dinner jacket. His bald head was moist
with perspiration. It was apparently strenuous, being
a convivial host. He gave her a Hollywood hug,
pointed out the bar, then slipped away without ever
calling her by name. Perhaps he couldn't even
remember it.

She walked past a huge catered buffet. Beluga
caviar, Nova Scotia salmon, and six covered chafing
dishes. The place was swarming with people, every
one of them smiling and having a wonderful time.

What on earth am I doing here? she wondered,
avoiding the enormous platter of hot hors d'oeuvres

that was being circulated by a tuxedoed waiter.
French windows opened on to the patio where she
noted outdoor heaters, which were hardly necessary
on this mild night. The small portable dance floor
was packed with bodies gyrating to the sounds of the
live trio.

Mort Shaffer was a screenwriter who'd played by
their rules and made it big, Chalice reminded herself. Fellow sufferer indeed. What did he know
about suffering?

She caught sight of Rachel across the room and
grimaced to her. Rachel's face lit up with relief, and
she started to break away from the group she was
with, but Chalice shook her head, gesturing for
Rachel to stay right where she was.

She could leave, or she could numb her senses and
just tough it out. A sudden flash of dogged defiance
made her decide to stay. She had skipped her lunch
with Sam, but the way this jumpsuit felt, maybe it
was just as well. Anyway, she wasn't hungry. She
just needed a strong drink to soften the hard edges
of success flashing all around her. Then maybe she'd
stumble into a party mood.

Ignoring the calorie-laden buffet table, she made
for the bar and worked seriously on a vodka tonic,
revving herself up.

By the time her glass was empty, Tim somebody
was fetching her another. She was deep into an
outrageous flirtation with him, only the first of
several, she decided. Tonight, all men were fair
game.

Joe Verdi chewed on another Di-Gel, then took
himself and his club soda off to a dim recess of the

playroom, or the rec room, or the family room, or whatever the hell room it was. It hadn't been such a hot idea to come tonight.

But yesterday George had finally sewn up the contract for the screenplay, and Joe had been feeling good about it—as good as he ever felt when he was on the West Coast. He'd been out here three days, and he still hadn't given Morty a call. He and Morty went back a long way. All the way back to Philly. So yesterday, after he'd signed the contract, he had called Morty and found himself agreeing to come to this bash.

He had forgotten how much he hated Hollywood parties, and tonight he'd discovered that Morty himself had turned very Hollywood. He'd lost his appetite these last four days, but still his stomach churned with excess. The overrich blend of pleasure was more than he could take. There were just too many leggy blondes, shoulders tanned and moisturized, noses caliper-perfect. A relentless feeling of hyped-up celebration in the air. It was suffocating. Indoor-outdoor living in houses designed for perpetual sunshine. Well, at least it was dark outside now. He comforted himself by finding the dimmest, quietest corner of the room.

Through a window he could look across the patio to the other right-angled wing of the house. Behind a wall of glass, the beautiful people were swirling around the living room bar. Like ornamental fish in an aquarium, he thought.

And there she was again. The little redhead.

She had first caught his eye because she was the only woman in the room who wasn't sporting a perfect tan. She had luminous white skin, and her cheeks were flushed. The delicate flush of body heat, he decided. Not that brick-colored powder that bloomed on the other women's faces.

And she wasn't ten feet tall like the rest of them; she was little, but stacked. Perfect proportions. She held herself defiantly, an upward thrust to her chin, as if she were proclaiming her self-worth in this world of tall people. And she sure was having a good time.

He watched her for a few moments, his jaundiced outlook giving way for the first time to mildly sexual interest. She had very shiny eyes. He could see them gleam from where he was standing. Which one of these men had she come with? he wondered, as she disappeared from view with some guy's arm possessively clutching her waist. It was hard to tell. She seemed to be flitting and intimately acquainted with everyone. Hollywood kiss-kisses and hugs all round.

A woman on the sofa behind him said something. Joe turned, and for a few minutes, got caught up in conversation with a trio, all concerned with some momentous dispute that was dividing the guild. Only Joe didn't know which guild. There was one for screenwriters, of which he was a member, because he was obliged to be. There was also SAG for screen actors, and for all he knew, a dozen other guilds besides. "Guild" was a favorite buzzword out here. He didn't want to make an idiot of himself, so he nodded politely to show that he was involved, and made what he hoped were the appropriate noises.

He gave up all pretense of listening when the redhead came through the open doorway. She was with a different man again. There was a pool table at the far end of the room, and she perched on it, laughing, while the guy rubbed noses with her.

Joe leaned down toward the ivory sofa. "Who's the small redhead?" he asked the woman who sat on the end, and he gestured to the pool table.

"Chalice York," the woman told him, and dove right back into the all-important special meeting scheduled for next Tuesday. "Hope you can make it," she told Joe. "It's essential that we have a quorum on Tuesday, or the whole issue's going to slip away from us."

"I'm sure going to try," he said, and slipped out onto the patio, through the French windows.

So that's who she was. He hadn't given Chalice York a second thought since the Sherry Netherland. She had written the *Snipe* treatment and sold it to Ryan . . . but if she was a child of Jeffrey York, maybe she hadn't planned on selling just the treatment. With her background, he'd lay a bet she'd had the screenplay pegged for her own. Ryan had described her as a television writer. But that's what they all did out here, Joe remembered. They plugged away at writing for the tube while they struggled for the big screen credits.

The musicians were taking a break. Joe descended the five flagstone steps to the decking, then skirted a kidney-shaped pool, heading for the furthest reaches of the patio. Tucked in the shadows, he leaned against the low stucco wall that defined the property line, and stared across the floodlit water, watching the action inside the house from a safe distance.

Edging into the corner where the south and west walls met, Joe discovered he could see the pool table inside the room. Chalice York was still sitting on it, swinging her legs. He studied her more carefully, and wondered whether she was really having such a wonderful time, or whether she was just working hard at it. There was something peculiarly intense about the way she held her shoulders, and she was drinking too much for damn sure. Every time he'd turned around he'd seen her at the bar, or receiving a fresh drink from one of her fetch-and-carry admirers. But there was something very amateurish about the way she was gulping it down. Maybe she always hit the bottle that way. Or maybe she was really upset about the movie, and determined to deaden the pain with booze.

Stop imagining things, he told himself. He slipped back into the living room while the bar was quiet, got a refill of club soda, then took up his post again in the patio corner. Chalice York had disappeared from his line of sight. It occurred to him that maybe he should introduce himself and say something friendly.

You wrote one helluva treatment, Miss York. I'm really going to enjoy working on the script . . . ?

No way. The more he thought about it, the more he sensed that somehow she'd gotten a raw deal. He'd better lay low. The woman was definitely hyper. If she knew he was here, she might even make a scene. Anonymity was smarter when in doubt.

For no reason at all, he began to feel decidedly shoddy. Hell, what did he have to feel shoddy about? Somebody with her connections must have it made in this town. She probably had trust funds from daddy coming out of her ears. But he couldn't help feeling remiss, as though he were neglecting to do the decent thing. But there was no question of doing the decent thing, because he hadn't done anything wrong in the first place. He'd been offered a job, fair and square, and he'd accepted it. She probably had no intention of writing the screenplay anyway. He was just playing with situations in his head. Scenarios. He never did know when to quit writing.

He looked at his watch, then moved toward the nearest lamp to see the dial. It was almost midnight. He could decently call for a cab when he'd finished his club soda, and go back to the hotel.

"Hi. What are you doing, lurking in the shadows?"

Chalice York was right in front of him as he turned, so close that, in a startled gesture, he spilled ice-cold soda on his shirt.

His answer to her greeting came out as a smothered yelp.

"Don't you know you're supposed to mingle and laugh a lot at these things?"

You're doing enough of that for both of us. Jeez lady, you're higher than a kite. He brushed off his shirt and took an instinctive step backward. "I don't know anyone here except Morty Shaffer." It was halfway between self-defense and an apology.

"I'm Chalice York. Now you know two people."

"Joe Verdi," he said, then winced, and almost bit his tongue. Would she throw her drink in his face and soak the rest of him? He tried to stop himself from ducking.

"Joe Verdi who wrote *Not If I Can Help It*?" Instead of aiming the glass at him, she tipped it back and drained it to the ice cubes. "I saw the L.A. Stage Company's production in January. I was wowed."

She tucked her arm in his and began to lead him around the pool towards the French windows of the living room. The trio was at it again, with the amplifiers blaring.

"I missed *Summer Days* when it tried out here, but the critics sure gave it a big boost." She was yelling above the din as she walked him toward the living room bar.

Relief flooded him as she let go of him. He didn't have to say anything else about himself. At the bar, a tall blond prince received her with open arms, lifting her on to a high stool as if she were a little girl. She flirted outrageously with him while the bartender poured her a vodka gimlet, but as soon as she had the glass in her hand, she climbed down from the stool and scanned the room.

He had backed away somewhat, but he should have escaped altogether while the going was good. He was cowering in the shadows at the far end of the living room, hoping he was invisible, wedged between a love seat and a wall of bookshelves.

She perched beside him on the back of the love seat and touched her glass to his. "You're one helluva playwright, Joe Verdi."

"Thank you," he said in a strained voice.

She straightened her spine, and he couldn't help noticing how the dark silk of her jumpsuit flowed over her breasts. They would be milk white, he thought, like the translucent skin at her wrists, emerging from the long sleeves. Her fingernails were unpainted. He could see pale half-moons above the cuticles as she raised her glass to him. In this room flashing with bare shoulders and golden arms and legs, to glimpse her naked fingernails had a strangely weakening effect on him. He took a slow, nervous gulp of soda.

"So what are you doing on the West Coast? A movie?"

"Yes, a movie," he mumbled.

She didn't know he was doing *The Snipe*. That was a lucky break. But he was pushing his luck. Supposing she asked him which movie?

Instead, she pursed her lips. "Movies are my least favorite subject tonight," she said after a moment's reflection, and set down her glass on a bookshelf. "Shall we dance?"

"Yes ma'am."

Chapter 3

JOE VERDI THE PLAYWRIGHT. SHE'D ACTUALLY STUM-
bled over a Broadway lion. It was a sobering
thought. But unfortunately not quite sobering
enough.

Chalice had been working on unscrambling her
wits ever since he'd mentioned his name. Of all the
extravagant compliments she'd been handing out
this evening, only the one she'd given him was true.
Joe Verdi was a brilliant dramatist. She'd admired
his work for quite a while.

Out on the dance floor, she tried to put her body
on automatic pilot to conform to the rhythm boom-
ing out from the bass. No need for conversation
here, but it was still hard to think clearly.

Somewhere she'd read a profile on Joe Verdi.
Long time ago. There was something about him
working as a longshoreman, and a prison term

. . . or was it Vietnam? Anyway, it was a tough-guy kind of background, and it showed in his work as a breathtaking reality that could set an audience back on its heels. Some critic had said that. Gritty, that's what it was. And how she envied that ability, and all the raw material he had to draw on. Impressive. And here she was dancing with him. More or less.

If she wasn't so tipsy, she'd probably be in awe of him, and a bit tongue-tied. But tonight was different. She was feeling no pain. She'd always wondered what that really meant. Now she knew. It meant exactly what it said.

Over the evening, she had developed a pattern of behavior. She would come on provocatively to the nearest available man, then when he made the inevitable proposition, she would duck out and attach herself to the next man. About an hour ago, Rachel had bullied her into eating something. She had nibbled at a piece of melba toast with something greasy on it, and washed it down with black coffee. Almost immediately, she'd felt terribly queasy and bolted for the bathroom. She was better now, fuzzy, but better.

She concentrated on looking at Joe Verdi; it took some discipline to get her eyes to focus properly, just as earlier it had taken effort to shape her thoughts into speech. She couldn't possibly do both at once. His features were coming clear now. Ah, there he was! Hey, he was cute. She'd always thought of him as venerable. Maybe in his fifties. But he was quite young. Very fine brown eyes under untidy brows, thick dark hair, walnut-colored skin, and a smooth hard jawline that gave him a really neat chin.

"You have a neally reat chin," she told him, and

knew it hadn't come out right. But she wasn't sure what was wrong with it.

"Thank you."

He certainly wasn't the greatest conversationalist. Most writers were more verbal than that. He was shy, maybe. He wasn't the greatest dancer either. His feet kept getting in her way. It wasn't that easy to keep your balance in these strappy, slender-heeled sandals, anyway. No wonder she never wore them.

"Don't you think you should have something to eat?" he said.

"No, I tried that already." She giggled and stumbled again.

He tightened his grip on her, holding her against his body until she was steady again.

It felt absolutely marvelous. *I don't have to write ever again,* she thought. *I could make a career out of going to parties and falling against dark, unaggressive men like Joe Verdi.*

"Well, how about if we sit this one out?" He began to edge her away from the tiny dance floor. "I could find us an empty couch in there," he said hopefully.

Chalice heard the frank purr in her voice from a slight distance. "I should *laahve* to sit on a couch with you."

But every seat in the house was occupied, and she wound up leaning against a wall, while he gave desultory replies to her questions. She was trying very hard to draw him out now, but he seemed desperately awkward with her. With a sense of surprise mixed with sharp disappointment, she realized that Joe Verdi had no intentions of making a pass at her. Well, she wasn't going to quit until he did. Tonight she was collecting passes. Like a ticket inspector. She giggled again.

Pass please. Where's your pass? Can't travel on this train without one.

"Where's your pa—date?"she asked.

"I came alone."

"Isn't that incredible? So did I."

He cleared his throat. "As I said earlier, I don't know anyone here except Morty."

"That's sad." She shook her head. "So . . . very . . . sad."

"Tragic," he said.

Chalice narrowed her eyes and pointed her index finger at him shrewdly, just to show him she wasn't as drunk as all that.

"Good word, for a playwright."

His face cracked. It could have been a smile. Then again, it could have been a wince. Why was he so gloomy?

She was getting absolutely nowhere with him. What she needed was another drink. With that in mind, she pushed herself away from the wall, and turned to Joe to announce her intention. Joe's head looked funny. It was beginning to swim around, and the rest of the room with it. She clutched at his lapel as it passed by for the third time, so that she could get on the carousel with him and keep her balance. She closed her eyes for a moment, swaying, and when she opened them, the room had settled down to a slow waltz. This was not good. People waltzed; rooms did not. The last thing she needed was another drink.

A shudder of prim disapproval seized her. She was

drunk and probably embarrassing this reserved man.
Something in her shrank from the knowledge in
self-disgust.

"I think I'll go home now," she said abruptly, and
headed towards the front door.

Only it wasn't the front door. She was back on the
patio again, and a firm hand at her waist was guiding
her back into the house.

"No, no," she protested, slapping his hand away.
"I really ought to go home."

"I think so too," Joe said, steering firmly.

She had a small purse dangling from her shoulder
by a skinny strap, but no coat or wrap.

"Do you have everything you came with?"

She frowned. "I came alone. I thought I told you
that."

She was suddenly very dignified. "It was nice
meeting you," she said, and minced down the front
steps in those ridiculous heels.

He watched her from the doorway, hypnotized by
the twitch of her round little buttocks under green
silk as she wove her way across the front lawn to the
street. Then it suddenly occurred to him what she
was doing, and he darted after her.

He fell into step, companionably following her
zigzag route, and spoke as casually as he could.
"You're not um, er, driving a car by any chance, are
you?"

She stopped in her tracks and gave him the frozen
look of an Edwardian duchess. It lacked nothing but
the lorgnette.

"Of course I'm driving, you cretin. How else
would one get to Bel Air?"

He held her elbow as she wandered up and down
the street, looking for her car, and tried to coax her

back into the house with all the tact he could muster. The only sane thing for her to do was stay at Morty's and sleep it off. She wouldn't hear of it.

She was impervious to tact, so he tried the direct approach. "Look, lady, you're in no condition to drive. There are at least eighty people in there with cars. If you won't stay over, then someone has to drive you home."

She turned duchess on him again. "Young man, don't be impertinent," she said with plummy, garden-party vowels that rang up and down the block.

"Okay, okay. Forget it. Just come on back inside and I'll call you a cab."

"A cab? *Cab*? Have you quite lost your wits, fellow?"

This was crazy. He was being bullied into weaving up and down the block by a ninety-eight-pound shrimp with an accent right out of *Masterpiece Theatre.*

The street wasn't sheltered like Morty's patio, and the brisk night air on the open hillside was hitting her hard.

"I don't even know what we're looking for," he said as they retraced their steps for the third time.

"A car," the duchess informed him. "An automobile."

"What *kind* of car?" he said wearily.

"A red one."

It turned out to be the Honda Civic right outside the driveway. But by the time she recognized it, she seemed to have lost her keys. Joe fished them out of her purse for her and figured there were only two reasonable courses of action. He could physically restrain her, or he could take the wheel of her car and drive her home. He couldn't possibly let her take off alone.

She sank into the passenger seat without comment when he opened the door for her. The driver's seat was adjusted for a midget. Wedged behind the wheel, Joe groped around, looking for a lever to adjust the position. It wasn't easy with his knees shoved up against his chin.

"I can't possibly drive from here," she complained. "My arms aren't long enough."

At last he got the seat to slide back, and put the key into the ignition. "You're not going to drive. All you're going to do is give me directions." He waited. "Please?" He watched her head relax and slip sideways. Her eyes closed.

He shook her shoulder. "You can't go to sleep yet. I don't know where you live. Where are we going? I need some instructions."

Half asleep, she instructed him. "Home, James. And don't spare the horses."

Joe dropped his head to the steering wheel and wondered where all his heroic patience was coming from. He knew exactly what he should do now: take the keys back into the house and just leave her in the car to sleep it off. But something in him resisted, pinning him to the seat.

Why did he feel so responsible for her? He was probably the only one of Morty's guests who didn't know his way around this town. He'd lay a *bet* he was the only one who'd come by taxi. Why him? She was a total stranger, and he didn't owe her a thing. Besides, he'd never driven in Los Angeles, and he had no intention of starting now. He could feel a cold sweat breaking out at the very thought of a freeway . . .

He made the fatal mistake of turning his head. Blissfully sleeping beside him, she looked enchanting. Like a precociously curvy little girl.

Ah well, maybe she only lived a few blocks away and he wouldn't have to take a freeway.

He leaned over, and gently shook her awake.

The dashboard clock showed three-fifteen by the time he killed the engine. He had driven to the far end of the civilized world. For a few moments he leaned back in the seat, recuperating. There had been freeways, all right. Three of them the wrong ones, and two of them, as she'd explained to him earnestly, definitely the right freeways, but going in the wrong direction. His worst nightmares were less harrowing than this.

He had taken it in small stages, waiting at each rest stop for the fog and sleep to clear from her brain so that she could spout the next set of garbled directions.

After the first ten minutes of the trip, he had been ready to give it up. But it was too late. He had no idea how to get back to Morty's place.

What was it about this woman that she could soften him by the mere act of falling asleep like a tired child? His will had turned to putty. He was a chocolate candy with a sticky soft center.

He pulled out the ignition key, and looked past her curled-up body through the passenger window. It was a large stucco building. He hoped to God it was the right one this time. He was completely unnerved.

Joe heaved himself out of the car, and fished her out from the passenger seat. Her limbs were spongy with sleep, so he carried her, grateful that she was small, and coaxed directions out of her until they were actually at an apartment door on the second floor. When it opened to her keys, he could have wept with joy. All his resources were drained, and small as she was, she was beginning to feel like a dead weight in his arms.

There was a large bed in one room. He laid her on it and breathed a deep sigh of relief. She didn't make a sound as he walked out of the bedroom.

The next step was to find a phone and call a cab, but he was past it now. He couldn't even give a cabdriver an address. Where was he anyway? Somewhere east of purgatory and slightly to the south of hell? He saw a sofa and forgot all about looking for the phone. He brushed off a cushion that was covered with shreds of paper, and crashed.

Sunlight poured over her closed eyelids like molten metal. Chalice groaned softly and turned her head on the pillow. The movement started a hammering behind her eyes, and she struggled to a sitting position, whimpering from the internal blows. Her tight jumpsuit was twisted under her, binding her crotch and half strangling her. Gingerly, she unzipped the jumpsuit and peeled it off, trying not to wriggle. Every movement of her head was torture. She needed to get under the covers, but the effort set off those terrible hammers again. Huddled under the blanket with her eyes squeezed shut, she pleaded with the hammers to stop.

Her eyes watered with pain. So this was a hangover. She could have lived her whole life without knowing this.

At last she could feel the hammers subsiding. The pain in her sinuses yielded to a cool, numbing sensation taking over . . . An ice pack. When she opened her eyes, a disreputable figure leaned over her. Rumpled shirt, tousled hair, and dark unshaven face. Seconds passed, then the face crystalized into someone slightly familiar. Joe Verdi. Alarming memories filtered into her consciousness. Exactly how crazy had she been last night?

Panic furred her throat and harshened her voice. "What the hell are you doing here?" She struggled to sit upright, then winced, reached for the ice pack and clutched it to her forehead.

"I drove you home," he said. "Somebody had to. You shouldn't drink so much. You just don't have the body weight to absorb all that alcohol."

At the mention of body weight, she let go of the ice pack, grabbed for the sheet and pulled it up under her chin, remembering she was half-naked.

"And drive you home was *all* I did," Joe said, addressing the look of pure horror on her face. "I was sleeping on your sofa until your cries of pain woke me." He took the ice pack off the bed before it soaked through the blanket. Melting chips of ice were seeping through the thin kitchen towel. "There's one more tray in your freezer. Shall I fix a fresh one?"

She was okay now, as long as she kept still, but she'd kill for some hot coffee. "No thank you," she told him, her lips barely moving, "but a cup of coffee would be nice."

He turned and left the room like an obedient flunkey. "Jeez, she's even a duchess when she's sober," he told the coffeemaker.

He threw the ice pack into her kitchen sink, hunted through the cabinets for cups, coffee, and filters, then started a brew. He kept thinking about her illustrious father. She wasn't a duchess exactly, but Hollywood royalty, for sure. The realization carried a slight sense of awe. He fought it off resentfully. He had three critical successes on Broadway behind him. And a movie that had grossed thirty-five million including cable sales. He had no cause to be intimidated by this little snip, no matter who her father was.

"How do you take your coffee?" he asked her, poking his head through the bedroom doorway.

"Just cream, please."

He ground his teeth. *Just cream, please.* She was sitting back on the pillows in the same position as when he'd left her. But she had a peach-colored robe on now. That annoyed him. If she could get out of bed for the robe, she could have made her own coffee and spared him that damn treasure hunt.

"What I did for you last night was no small favor, I want you to know." He took two steps into the room and folded his arms as he spoke. "I don't drive."

Her eyes grew wide with astonishment, and he noticed they were an odd honey-mustard color. "You don't drive?"

"Not on Los Angeles freeways. They scare the hell out of me. I've driven jeeps through Saigon and a supply truck in Danang. I've even motored through New England and around D.C. But what I did last night was pure heroism as far as I'm concerned." He turned on his heel and went for the coffee while she chewed that one over.

When he came back with two mugs, there were tears rolling down her cheeks, and she made no effort to hide them from him.

"Whatever I put you through last night, I'm sorry. I don't usually carry on like that. In fact I have no head for liquor, and I hardly drink at all. I've never been drunk before."

"Hey," he said. "It's okay. Don't cry. It's okay, really. Just, for your own sake, don't ever do that again, okay?"

"I won't." The tears came faster. "It's just that, well, I was trying to work off the very worst day of my life. It was awful. I got bumped from the movie I was working on."

He set down the coffee, reached for the box of tissues on her bedside table and handed her a couple. Suddenly he was feeling like the worst kind of jerk, and those tears were working on his insides like battery acid. He was eroding away to mush.

When she'd mopped her face, he handed her a mug of coffee and sipped at his own, trying to shake the wet-noodle effect her tears had on him.

His voice came out in a soggy whisper. "That's rotten luck," he said. "I understand it happens all the time out here."

"Not like this, it doesn't. I've been working on the screenplay for over a year. Hell, this was my very own movie."

"The screenplay?" His stomach flip-flopped. *Screenplay*? But it was only a thirty-page outline.

She dipped her head to the coffee, and waiflike, her bangs slipped forward to meet her wet lashes. Beneath them, her eyes were huge and tragic. "You didn't notice all that shredded paper in my living room?"

The paper snowstorm. He hadn't given it a thought last night. The weird decor just seemed to go along with the whole bizarre evening.

As she poured out the story, he felt himself deteriorate in progressive stages, from shocked, to appalled, to absolutely devastated. It was ruthless, the Hollywood system. Monstrous. She looked so vulnerable, so utterly betrayed, that he began to drown in fellow feeling. He knew what it felt like to get shafted. God, did he know! But how could he tell her he was in town to take over *The Snipe*? No way.

"Thanks for the coffee," she said, putting down her empty mug. She had stopped sobbing, but her eyes still brimmed with tears. "And thanks for listening, and for everything you did last night. I tend to go crazy when I get a letdown like this. But I've never gone as berserk as I did yesterday. I'm very grateful to you for seeing me safely home, and I apologize for giving you such a hard time. I really made an idiot of myself."

She knew he understood completely. She could tell from the sadness in his eyes. They were chocolate-dark and brimming with compassion.

"You look like someone who needs a hug," he said, and put his arms around her.

It was simple and generous, and better than any verbal sympathy he could have offered. She did need a hug. His arms were strong and caring. And his solid chest was such a comfort. She felt wrapped in his kindness, and filled with the clear agreement between them: The world was so rotten that the good guys really had to hold fast to each other, and cling.

After some clinging, she raised her head and looked at him, overflowing with gratitude. It was wonderful to communicate so much without a single spoken word. He was like a soulmate. Such a warm-hearted guy. She touched her lips to his and felt the rough stubble of his cheek. Even that felt good, but he avoided grazing her cheek with his beard, and instead, just brushed his lips over her face while he stroked her hair.

She responded with enthusiasm, and then with something more remarkable. Her sense of comfort gave way to a definite surge of excitement. After three years of avoiding this kind of thing, could she actually be turning on again? Not the phony playacting of last night, but a basic urge to make love to this man?

"You keep your romantic feelings in too much," Rachel kept telling her. "You only allow them out in your writing. It's not a healthy way to live."

But what would Rachel know? She was an actress. Emoting all over the place was the way she lived.

Chalice shrugged the robe off her shoulders because she wanted the feel of Joe Verdi on her skin, and her wanting was so insistent that it startled her. It's all part of yesterday, she thought, shivering at the touch of his fingers. Like the wild drinking spell. So what if she wasn't through with the crazies yet? She was entitled to freak out on this one . . . and Joe seemed more than interested in cooperating.

Tenderness and compassion were storming him. Then, as he felt her respond in his arms, lust stirred. The powerful blend of feelings began to hit him below the belt. He drew away to tear off his clothes, then an attack of sheer gallantry stopped him in his tracks. He wanted her fiercely, but he couldn't lay a finger on her until he'd told her the truth. And when he told her, of course, that would be that. He toyed with the idea of just not telling her. God, it was tempting. But he couldn't stoop that low. She'd been led on enough by the Hollywood jerks. He didn't want to become one of them.

"There's something you should know," he said. He sat on the edge of her bed with his back to her, twisting his shirttails around in his hand.

"You're married," she said flatly, and when he shook his head, she kept guessing. "Attached? Diseased?"

"No, nothing like that . . ." It was even harder to say than he'd imagined.

She turned him around and nestled back in his arms. "Then it can wait. I don't need to hear it now."

Without his permission, his hand slid under her bra strap and skated over the satin skin below her shoulder blades. He forced himself to speak. "Cupcake, you're going to hear it sooner or later. And I'd rather you heard it now. From me." *That's a downright lie. At this moment I'd rather do anything than tell you this.*

"*Cupcake?*" she echoed, and grinned up at him. "Where'd you get that from?" It was the crassest, sexiest thing anyone had ever called her. *Cupcake.* The very sound set the strangest vibrations pulsing along her nerves, goading her with desire. She wound her fingers in his chest hair, wondering why he was resisting his own clear desire to touch her. "Why cupcake?" she murmured, finding the word tantalizingly erotic on her tongue.

"I don't know," he mumbled distractedly. "Because a chalice is a cup I suppose. It just came out."

And because Chalice was an absurdly pretentious name that he couldn't bring himself to call her. Cupcakes were small and sweet and irresistible. But he had discipline, didn't he? He'd survived Marine boot camp and last night's trip. This should be easy.

He mustn't let himself get diverted. He called his wandering hands to order and sat bolt upright. "Sweetheart, I have to tell you this because . . . because . . ."

She captured his hand and tucked it under her chin.

"Because, er, it's . . ." With a mind of its own, his hand slid down her throat and curved around a firm full breast. He touched her nipple and drew back as if he'd burnt himself. "Because, the thing is—" Forcefully, he cleared his throat. It bulged with the right words, but they were stuck there, choking him. "The thing is . . ."

"Please Joe, not now . . ."

His voice was hoarse. "Look, it's something that might make you change your mind about letting me take your clothes off. I'm out here because . . . I'm out here t-t-to . . ."

She spread her hands over his chest and touched one of his nipples with her teeth. "Are you on the run from the law or something? Have you committed some unspeakable crime?"

"No, of course not, but—"

When she looked up, she couldn't help laughing. The mortification on his face was adorable, and beads of sweat were forming at his temples. She licked at them, tasted salt, then nibbled his ear.

"Then forget it. Please?" She didn't want to change her mind, didn't he understand? This was insane, gloriously insane. But sanity would strike again soon. It wasn't as if he was indifferent. At the moment, he was so turned on he was stammering, falling apart.

She wrapped her arms around him and drew him

down on the bed. "Whatever it is, Joe, it doesn't matter. Forget it," she whispered into his shoulder, and into the underside of his jaw. "Forget it . . ."

Honor and decency deserted him as her lips moved upon his.

"Forget it," she breathed.

And he did. His tongue, unshackled at last as it roamed the wet satin of her mouth, forgot all burdens, and his body began to drown in her downy warmth.

"That was incredible," she mumbled to his shoulder, as she lazed in his arms. She glowed with the feeling of having been stormed with love.

"Hmmm."

Her face lay against his chest, and she heard the deep resonance of the sound he made, like an appreciative purr.

What was more incredible was that it could happen this way, she thought. Not a slow, steady blossoming, but pow! A stranger and a thunderbolt.

She rolled over onto her side, raised herself up on one elbow and slid her hand over his torso. His texture was delicious under her palm. *Steady there, kid. You could be just wallowing in sentiment. This may not be the real thing.* Then again, she thought, maybe it was. Wouldn't that be wonderful? To have a permanent claim on this man who was so right, so perfect that she was tempted to pinch herself to see if she was really awake, and pinch him to be sure he wasn't a figment of her imagination. Warmhearted and sensitive Joe Verdi . . . and so sexy.

Had she actually thought he was unaggressive? She glanced at his face on the pillow. His eyes were closed, but his lips curved in a blissful half-smile. Whatever had held him back at first, it certainly wasn't a lack of sexual drive. She was feeling positively ravished at the moment, gloriously ravished.

His hand was trailing up her arm, so she knew he wasn't asleep.

"How would you like some breakfast?" she asked him.

"Ummm."

As she stirred, his muscles clamped and held her still. He pulled her down until her mouth was over his, and she let her weight rest on him again as their lips touched, grazed, pressed. The kiss deepened, and she forgot about breakfast. She was on her back, his weight pressing her into the mattress, and then he shifted and began to stroke her breasts awake.

Breakfast was the strange meal they mooned over at three in the afternoon. She had put a fresh blade in her razor for him, and he looked very handsome after his shower and shave, even though his dress shirt was limp and his pants looked as if he'd slept in them.

"I did," he explained.

She thought it was the most brilliant piece of wit she'd ever heard.

"So that's who lives under the party makeup," he said, caressing her cheek. "Hello, cupcake. It's nice to make your acquaintance." He smiled tenderly and kissed her earlobe. "I like you even better in your morning face."

"It's midafternoon."

"Yes, but you have a really reat nose."

She heard the falsetto caricature of her own voice and dissolved in laughter. "Did I really say that?"

His shoulders were shaking too. "Cross my heart."

They sat at the kitchen table and shared the last

three eggs in the refrigerator, and two slices of whole wheat that had been frozen for eight months.

"My God, how long does it take you to get through a loaf of bread?" he asked, fascinated.

She gave a sheepish shrug and patted her hips. "Once or twice a year I go on a binge and throw a one-pound loaf of Roman Meal into the grocery basket."

He nodded gravely. "I see, for the occasional Roman orgy."

The toaster was temperamental so the bread got burnt, but they ate it, and the black carbon all over it didn't seem to matter in the least.

She laughed all the way through his story of last night's trip. "You poor darling! Well, you won't have to face that again. No, don't call a cab. I'll drive you back to the Westmont." Her smile was sheepish. "You can trust me at the wheel now . . . I'm fully restored."

His eyes shone as he reached across the table and touched the tip of her nose. "You're fully . . . fantastic," he murmured.

She was enchanted with his humor and his tenderness, sensitized to every nuance of his voice and face, drinking it all in greedily. Over his last cup of coffee, he grew quiet. He must be so tired, she thought. The sofa was small and hard; he couldn't have gotten much sleep; and it really must have been an ordeal for him to get her home last night. Maybe she shouldn't have laughed quite so uproariously at his fear of the freeways.

She found her keys on the coffee table where he'd dropped them last night. She picked them up and glanced around at the litter of torn paper. How had she ever let a piece of work become so all-important? she wondered. No movie mattered that much. She let things get out of proportion. She'd clean it up after she dropped Joe off at his hotel. And she'd never let her life become so utterly unbalanced again.

Back in the kitchen, she dropped her keys on the table and sat down with Joe to finish her coffee. He was awfully quiet.

"What was it you were so anxious to tell me last night?" she asked, remembering suddenly.

The quality of his silence changed. She could feel it like a sudden shift in the weather before a storm. When he spoke, the words were slow and deliberate, as if he were under some severe handicap.

"The Snipe," he said, "is the screenplay I came out here to write."

Chapter 4

RACHEL BLINKED TWICE, THEN GAPED AT CHALICE slack-jawed. "I just don't believe this," she said. "I don't believe what I'm hearing."

"Neither did I, at first. You can imagine . . ." Chalice lay curled up on a sofa at Rachel's.

Four hours after Joe Verdi had detonated his bomb, the initial impact had worn off, leaving Chalice with a healthy level of indignation that was somehow invigorating. She could be objective in the telling now, she thought. In fact she was enjoying her stagey reenactment of the scene, and Rachel's gratifying response. Actors always made the best audiences, and Rachel's conversation pit was just right for Chalice's performance, a perfect little theatre-in-the-round, intimate and uncluttered. The room was all pale lavenders and soft whites, a calm haven in a turbulent world. Chalice had come instinctively, like a homing pigeon.

Glen was around. He practically lived with Rachel now, but he had retired to the kitchen with exquisite discretion as soon as Chalice arrived, to cook some time-consuming Armenian delicacy, he explained. The smell of it wafted by, subtly delicious, as he opened the kitchen door at that moment and looked at them from the dining area.

He was a slim, elegant man, his straight dark hair slightly silvered. "You'll stay and eat with us, won't you?" he asked Chalice.

"Yes, of course she will, darling," Rachel told him, and he disappeared again with a good-humored nod.

"Rachel, I don't think—"

"You're staying. Don't argue with me. I want to hear the rest of this. It's mind-boggling. You said you didn't believe him at first. So what happened then? What on earth did you say to him? Can you remember word for word?"

That was easy. It wasn't going to fade for a long, long time . . .

She didn't say a word at first. It was ridiculous, just too preposterous to take seriously. When she'd convinced herself of that, she smiled. "You're kidding me, of course, Joe . . . Joe?"

His eyes held to hers, sober and unhappy. Then he looked away as if the sight of her face was too painful. "I wish I was," he muttered, marginally audible.

"What? What did you say?"

"I said I wish I was. Kidding, I mean. I'm afraid it's the truth, babe."

This man, she thought, who had invaded her body and soul with the tenderest intimacies of passion,

who had just risen from her bed and who was at this
moment sitting at her breakfast table . . . *this man
was walking off with her screenplay.* Impossible.

Chalice shook her head, trying to take in the
enormity of it, retracing the day's events in the
strange new light of what he was saying in all
seriousness. Her morning hangover. Her tears. His
heartfelt compassion.

"Such rotten luck, you said. *I understand it happens all the time!"* The dazed quality in her voice
changed suddenly to a metallic rasp. "You understood, all right."

She hurled her coffee mug at the kitchen sink and
listened to it shatter. "Damn right, you understood.
You actually said I looked like someone who needed
a hug . . . Someone who needed a hug? *From you?*
And all that time, you knew that you were the one
who—"

Chalice broke off gasping, as the insult raced
through her bloodstream, along her limbs, until her
very fingers and toes radiated with outrage. That
two-faced, cheating bastard!

"My God, I've been had. Twice," she whispered.

"Honey, please! I tried to tell you before, and
well, you know what happened, cupcake. It just
got—"

"I know what happened, all right, you loathsome,
lying creep! Get out of my house before I scream
bloody murder and have you arrested for rape."

Color drained from his face. "For *what?"*

"You heard me. Get out."

Rachel leaned forward with a rustle of claret-
colored silk. "And then what?" she asked.

"And then nothing." Chalice sipped her diet soda

with relish. "He left without another word. I didn't even let him use my phone to call a cab. I like to think he had to walk home."

Rachel looked thoughtful as she topped up Chalice's glass. "Did it ever occur to you that none of it was his fault? He's just out from New York. How was he to know that you'd been screwed by the studios?"

"Oh, he knew all right. I spent the morning telling him about it. Apologizing left, right and center for my awful behavior. *My* awful behavior, mind you. I actually felt guilty. He made such a big deal about driving me home. Twenty lousy miles! You'd think he was bucking for a Distinguished Service Cross or something. I absolutely wiped the floor with myself, come to think of it."

Rachel turned away and began to set the dinner table, lingering over white porcelain dishes ringed with pale purple. Circling the dining alcove, she kept her back to Chalice, carefully hiding the amusement on her face. "You sound so serious about it," she said over her shoulder.

"You better believe I'm serious."

Rachel fiddled with the white linen napkins and silently played it again from the top. The whole anecdote according to Chalice, starting with her fuzzy recollection of leaving the party. "But you can hardly say he forced himself on you."

Chalice shuddered, remembering Joe Verdi in her bed, and couldn't decide whether the tremor was pure anger or remembered passion. Unfortunately that wasn't going to fade either, not for a long, long time. "He turned me on, sure. But under the most outrageously false pretenses," she muttered.

"Seduction, maybe?" Rachel suggested.

"As far as I'm concerned, morally it was rape. As much as he's raped my movie."

"That was Pacifica Studios," Rachel pointed out reasonably. "Walter Ryan, if you like, but not Joe Verdi. It's hardly likely he knew what was going on out here when he accepted the offer, is it?"

"He could have asked," Chalice said darkly. "My name was on the treatment. He could have damn well found out and declined the job."

Rachel tried to hold down her laughter. Turning down a job like that was outside the possibilities of the world they lived in. Besides, a treatment was one thing, a final script, another. More often than not, they were by different authors. She wasn't a writer, but even she knew that.

"Oh, come on, love! Don't tell me *you'd* have turned it down if you'd been in his shoes. That's absurd."

"It's also quite beside the point and you know it," Chalice said, her voice laced with wounded dignity.

"I do?" Rachel turned and glanced at her friend before she resumed the shuffling of knives and forks. "I met the man, as a matter of fact," she said. "Mort introduced him to us just before you arrived last night. Personally, I thought he was charming. How you can just dismiss a guy who has that much talent and looks the way Joe Verdi looks, I just can't figure. With a little encouragement, you could have something going there. Correction. Sounds like you already had something going."

"Do you need any help with that?" Chalice asked pointedly.

"No thanks." Rachel came back and perched on the arm of the sofa, rattling serving spoons in her hand, and watched Chalice removing nonexistent

lint from the sofa cushions. "He reminded me a bit
of Robert Shankel. A slightly more rugged version. I
thought you tended to go for that type."

"You must be out of your mind!"

Rachel bit her lip. It had been the wrong thing to
say. "I just meant to look at, that's all. Nothing else.
He doesn't have Shankel's glib manner with women.
No, he was a bit reserved, if anything. Personally, I
found that refreshing." She sighed and pushed herself up from the upholstery. Still playing the spoons,
she took a few steps towards the kitchen, then
paused and looked back, tall and graceful in the long
silk housecoat. Her face above the mandarin collar
was like a flawless pale bloom on a slender stem.

"What are we ever going to do about you, Chalice? Aren't you a bit tired of playing den mother to
sweet young things like Luke Benson? You couldn't
even *tell* him something like this. His ears would turn
pink and fall off."

Chalice cast a withering look in the general direction of her hostess. She had come to share the
supreme irony of all this. A classic, double-edged
betrayal if ever there was one. And all Rachel
wanted to do was turn it into a soap opera. The
woman was hopeless; with her bone structure and
smooth straight hair, Rachel could look as cool and
above-it-all as a Saint Laurent fashion model, but
under the svelte exterior beat the heart of a bored
suburban housewife.

"I'm going to see what Glen's up to back there,"
Rachel said, swirling graceful folds of floor-length
skirt as she moved. "Poor thing. I think he's scared
to come out. He's probably under the impression
that you're against any man who's over twenty-one."

Just in case there was any truth to that, Chalice

spent the rest of the evening being extra nice to
Glen. It wasn't hard. Glen Suffian was pleasant,
devoted to Rachel, and a superlative cook as well.

They dined on grape leaves stuffed with meat and
pine nuts, served with a thin yogurt dressing, bite-
sized flaky pastries filled with *kashkaval* cheese from
the Balkans, a tangy chopped salad he called *tab-
ouleh,* and *lahmajune,* a meaty Armenian version of
pizza, baked in crisp individual rounds and eaten
with a sprinkling of fresh lemon juice.

After second helpings of everything, Chalice
began to wilt. The unusually large meal, and the
cumulative effects of recent high living, prompted
her to bow out of Rachel's at eight-thirty, leaving
the couple alone.

"What was all that about?" Glen asked Rachel
when they were cleaning up the kitchen.

She stowed the last dish of leftovers in the refrigerator and grinned. "Now don't tell me you didn't
hear. You were only twelve feet away, and she
wasn't exactly whispering."

"I heard every word," he said, "but I'm talking
about you. Mort told us Verdi was signed to write a
Walter Ryan film. You knew he was Chalice's re-
placement, so why did you act so amazed when she
told you?"

"I wasn't about to ruin her story." Rachel gave a
Mona Lisa smile. "It was precious."

"Precious? The girl was screaming rape. She was
ready to strangle the guy." He cupped her face with
his hands and rubbed noses with her. "You never fail
to mystify me, thank God."

"Darling, there's nothing mystifying about it.
Chalice has spent far too long being soured on
men."

Glen rolled his eyes. "And this latest episode is supposed to change her mind?"

"It has possibilities, yes. I think those two could make sparks fly. She needs some grand passion in her life aside from her work."

Glen put his arms around her. "This, of course, was something entirely unrelated to her work," he said slowly.

"Absolutely."

"I give up. Even my mother tells me I'm stupid." He was nuzzling her neck and sliding his hands inside her long wide sleeves. "Never mind what Chalice needs, inscrutable one. The chef has needs too."

The living room debris was still waiting for Chalice the next morning, and she discovered she was out of vacuum bags. What with a trip to the store and various odd jobs, it was past noon before she checked her answering service. She had indulged her emotions for two days, she realized. It was time to get back to the business of making a living.

"Rachel Lorrimer was sure anxious to catch you," the service operator told her. "I've got six messages stacked up here. But they're two days old."

"That's okay," Chalice said.

Rachel had been frantic when she discovered Chalice was missing from Mort's party, and imagined her driving home in the state she'd been in. "Nothing else?" she asked.

"Yes, there's one that came in yesterday from Nora Toms. You want the number?"

"No, I have it, thanks."

Nora was Sam Firestone's secretary. Chalice was about to call Sam anyway. She had a sudden hunger to get back to work again; almost any work would look good right now.

Nora's voice sounded tired and harassed. "Miss York, I'm afraid I have awful news to break. It's Sam . . . he passed away yesterday. He had a heart attack on Wednesday, and they thought he'd pull through at first, but he didn't."

"Wednesday?" Chalice said, not quite believing it. "But I was with him Wednesday at Lowry's."

"He was on his way back here after lunch, I guess. He collapsed in his car."

"Oh, Nora . . . How terrible."

He hadn't looked at all well, Chalice thought. And she had flown off the handle. She had walked out on Sam in the last hours of his life, hopping mad about a movie.

Nora sounded awkward. "Mr. Meachum will be personally handling your affairs, Miss York. He says you're not to worry about continuity. We were just going through the files when you called. Would you like to come in and talk to him next week? Or would you rather he called you?"

Neither, she thought. Sam's son-in-law would definitely not be handling her affairs. She didn't like him, and she didn't care for the way he operated. She had a feeling Sam was never crazy about him either.

"When's the funeral?" she asked.

"Eleven on Sunday morning," Nora told her. "At Forest Lawn . . . What should I tell Mr. Meachum?"

Chalice had a vision of Harry Meachum leaning over Nora's desk while she spoke, gesticulating, mouthing words, and pressing Nora to get a commitment. He would pick up his ten percent of any residuals, of course. Aside from that, she didn't owe Harry Meachum a thing.

"Tell him I'll be at Sam's funeral," she said.

It wasn't a hysterical Rudolph Valentino funeral, and there was no lying in state. Sam Firestone was neither rock idol nor movie star. He was just an semi-orthodox Jew who had lived a long, useful life, and had chosen to be buried in a plain pine box, no flowers. But Hollywood was burying one of its own, and the large memorial chapel overflowed, because Sam was one of the grand old men of the industry. There were precious few grand old men left.

The famous faces at the grave site were the actors Sam had helped to stardom. There were others, equally distinguished, in attendance. But their names were known only to people like Chalice, who made their living in this tight little world of celluloid entertainment. Cinematographers, composers, writers, independent producers, directors, fellow agents, and the heads of three studios had come to pay their respects.

Chalice spent a few moments with Sam's daughters, but declined the invitation to go back to the Meachums' afterward for refreshments. She had only come to say a private good-bye to Sam.

She'd never been a model client, she thought. He had given her good advice, and as often as not, she'd ignored it. Particularly on *The Snipe*. Anxious to keep Walter Ryan happy, she had gone ahead with the script without a contract, contrary to Sam's strong suggestions. It wasn't the first time, but never once, in the five years she'd known Sam, had he said, "I told you so."

I think I've finally learned my lesson, Sam. I hope you can hear me. You were a very patient man.

Sam Firestone was also the last link to her father. As his coffin was lowered, she suffered the echoes of ten years ago, when she had stood, numb with grief, at another open grave ringed with mourners. It occurred to her that Jeffrey York would have turned fifty-seven this month. She looked up and saw Robert Shankel, standing across from her. He caught her eye for a moment and nodded solemnly.

On the way back to the parking lot, she fell into step with him.

"It's sad," he said. "He had a long life and a quick death, but still. Sam Firestone gone. It's like the passing of the old era. He came into this business as a kid, when the Sam Goldwyns and Louis B. Mayers were running the show."

"That era's been gone a while, Robert," she said. "Sam never had any illusions about that. He was seventy, but he was never old."

Robert gave her a sad smile. "He was seventy-six, as a matter of fact."

"I'd never have guessed," Chalice said. "He was ageless." She sighed. "I'm going to miss his agent jokes."

"We all will," Robert said. Then after a moment's silence, he added, "I'm sorry you lost control of *The Snipe.*"

So it was on the grapevine already. She supposed it was prime trade gossip, now Brad Alexander was signed up to star in it. "That certainly wasn't Sam's fault," she said.

"I never thought it was for a moment," Robert told her. "Look, none of us can stop the legal mayhem in this business. All we can do is hand out flak jackets." He studied her face. "How've you been, Chalice? You look kind of peaked."

He had walked her back to the Honda. She hesitated before she unlocked her door. "It's been a bad week."

He touched her shoulder lightly. "It'll get better. I'll see you around."

As she drove out through acres of sculptured lawns, she thought of Rachel's comparison. It was true; Robert Shankel and Joe Verdi were similar types, and it was more than a physical resemblance. They were both very gifted at what they did best. And they had both touched that deep-seated nerve in her, or chord, or weakness—whatever it was that could make her come unglued. With a conscious effort, she pushed the thought of Joe aside and made herself concentrate on Robert Shankel. There was no danger in that direction.

What Robert did best was monitor the industry, navigate fragile careers through the straits of Hollywood. These days, they were treacherous straits indeed. The passing of the studio system, rocketing production costs, television coming of age, and the mushrooming of cable and satellite channels . . . it added up to a confusing, unpredictable business. Agenting had become an art for the adept only. Robert Shankel was a high priest.

He sniffed out every signing, every merger in the wind, and trimmed his sails accordingly. He knew every shift in the balance of studio power, every producer looking for a property, and the kind of property they were looking for. He knew exactly when to push for more money or more artistic control, and exactly when to back down.

Agent expertise . . . now Sam was gone, she was

without it. And she had to have it if she was ever going to lick this town. It took a whole lot more than good writing skills to make it happen.

Who was there in Robert's class? she wondered. She could think of half a dozen high-powered agents, but they avoided all but the top handful of screenwriters. The real money for a Hollywood agent lay in representing star performers and a few of the top directors. Writers were way down on the totem pole.

Getting Robert Shankel as her first agent had been a fluke, she supposed. Only after leaving him had she discovered how hard it could be to find effective representation.

People naturally assumed that dropping her father's name was all it took. It got her through the door, all right. What it got her at most was a free lunch and some sentimental reminiscences about Jeffrey and the good old days.

Best of luck, kid. We're not taking on any more writers at the moment. I only wish we were. It'd be a privilege to represent Jeffrey York's daughter. Well! It's been wonderful talking to you. Got to run now, but if there's ever anything I can do to help you, don't hesitate to call. I really mean that.

Anything. But don't ask us to go to bat for you.

If it hadn't been for Sam coming out of retirement, she might still be knocking on doors with her two puny TV scripts clutched under her arm. Sam had been the only agent her father ever had, and the only one to say yes to her.

Except for Robert of course. She often wondered about that. Why had Robert been willing to represent her when she was fresh out of Bryn Mawr and so green? Surely not just to get her into the sack.

Hardly. She wasn't that special, and Robert was never desperate for a bedmate.

Had it been just that he was another Jeffrey York fan? So were most movie buffs over thirty. But they didn't stick their necks out for old times' sake. Sentiment went so far and no further in this town. Had Robert maybe seen something particularly promising about her early efforts? Thinking back on them, she doubted it.

Could it be that under all the slick, shallow pragmatism of his lay a buried streak of genuine human decency? It was a startling thought.

Joe rolled a second sheet into the typewriter and frowned at the blank page.

The furnished house in Brentwood had a good-sized study with a battered but serviceable desk, and a window that looked out onto a quiet canyon slope behind the backyard. The place was bigger than he needed of course, but the rent was more than covered by his per diem allowance. It was a whole lot better than trying to work in his suite at The Westmont and infinitely preferable to the office they provided on the studio lot. That had come complete with burgundy velvet upholstery and a phony Louis XV escritoire. The fact that Scott Fitzgerald had once used the suite hadn't helped a bit.

Joe had moved out of the hotel, taken the house for two months, and installed the studio typewriter in the study. He would complete the first draft right here, within these four nondescript walls.

The IBM sat humming at him, and the dried brush on the canyon slope outside was pleasantly drab. Six miles from Pacifica Studios, this was a safe, uneventful little corner of suburbia. There would be no more stargazing as he walked past sound stages wondering if that really was Barbra Streisand chatting with a grip. No more gaping at weird sets of moonscapes or passing the time of day with scaly creatures from outer space on their way to the studio commissary for a tuna fish sandwich. No distractions at all. He couldn't afford them.

He still hadn't recovered from the major distraction of his encounter with Chalice York. It was the first and definitely the last time he ever went near a woman in this crazy place. Why did he let it get to him like this? She was just another nutcake in lala land. He typed one more line, then stopped. Indignation was once again beginning to rob him of concentration.

God knows, he'd tried hard enough to tell her that morning, but she'd made it very clear what she was interested in, and it wasn't conversation. Everything he should have said to defend himself, all the rebuttals to her vicious attack paraded through his consciousness, powerfully eloquent, indisputable, and far too late. He'd grown out of revolving-door sex in his twenties. No one could call him promiscuous anymore, but what did she think he was made of? Flaunting those shoulders at him. Eyelashes still dewy with tears. Rounded thighs moving languidly under the sheet.

He went to the kitchen and poured himself some ice water from the refrigerator. Rape, she called it. If anyone had been raped . . . seduced . . . reduced to oatmeal, it had been him. He shook the last Di-Gel out of the vial on the counter and chewed on it. No use dwelling on it. He'd been seduced and then lambasted for it. He should never have driven her home.

In his typewriter sat the second page of his schematic for *The Snipe*—just a list of the principal scenes in narrative sequence. He liked to work from his own blueprint, but he could hardly call this progress. It was little more than was already laid out in the treatment. Her treatment, He opened it again to page twenty. It wouldn't lie flat. The red plastic folder kept closing, leaving him staring at the cover with her name on it.

He unlocked his clenched teeth. This wouldn't do at all. Three weeks, he'd told Ryan. One of them was gone already. He turned the folder face down, slid off the clips that bound it into the spine, then threw the cover in the wastebasket. He preferred to work from loose sheets anyway.

Chapter 5

THE DIRECTORY LISTING IN THE LOBBY WAS UN-
changed, Chalice noticed. J. GREEN & SHANKEL, it
read still, although the J. Green part had long been
out of the picture. Robert Shankel, sole owner of the
agency for twelve years, was not concerned with
such details. He was too busy making money to care.

And making money was exactly what he was doing
when he waved her into his office with his free hand.
She sat in the captain's chair drawn up to his desk
and watched him in action on the phone. Robert was
horse trading with some studio executive over a
client's contract.

"Jess," he was saying, "you take artistic control
from Oliver Cantrel, and you take Cantrel out of the
movie. We've been round and round on this one,
and . . ."

He broke off, rolling his eyes at Chalice, then
swiveled his chair toward the window, the receiver

clamped to his ear. Jess, apparently, wanted to go round and round some more.

Chalice waited for him, letting her eyes pan the room. The office hadn't changed much in five years. The same rosewood furniture and pale rust carpeting. The usual clutter of work in progress, folders, manuscripts, and correspondence on the credenza. The same faint odor of ancient cigar smoke in the air.

That fragrant scent of illicit Cuban tobacco . . . She smiled, recalling the green college graduate who'd once needed all her courage to cross this threshold.

It was her third week in California, and she'd done it; she'd actually gotten herself an appointment to see Robert Shankel, the wheeler-dealer she'd been reading about in the trades. She wasn't surprised to smell cigars. Mr. Showbiz would be five by five, paunchy and balding, and of course, chomping on a cigar. She knew it because she knew everything in those days. She would be twenty-one in a few months, and she was full of confidence.

The butterflies didn't start until the receptionist told her, "He'll see you now, Miss York. It's the room at the end of the corridor. Just walk right in."

He wasn't squat or balding at all. She still remembered the split second of stark surprise. Robert Shankel was a good twenty years younger than her mental image. He was lean and dark, and obviously brilliant. She was thrilled to the marrow when he agreed to represent her after reading her material.

Immediately, he became her guru and her god.

For three months, it was "strictly business." She wrote her heart out for him, following his specific suggestions. He critiqued her scripts, his comments ranging from brutal to encouraging. He made her rework everything she attempted. Then he asked her out to dinner for no particular occasion. She assumed she was being romanced, but she was only being staked out for the kill. She hadn't stood a chance. It was all over in three weeks. It wasn't even an affair, really; it was simply a stretch version of the one-night stand. A Shankel special.

She was crushed, heartbroken, but his prompt sale of two scripts to a network show had helped mend her feelings. Not even a broken heart could take away from the thrill of her very first professional sale as a writer. He really was a top agent, but she had still felt bound to take her business elsewhere after what happened. He understood. Incredibly, he even waived his ten percent of the deal.

Call it a parting gift, sweetheart. I'm a sentimental slob.

She was far too short of funds at the time to protest the parting gift . . .

She had sworn she would never go back to Robert, and here she was in this room again. But she was six years older, six years tougher. There was no longer any danger of her being swept off her feet.

It was still a kick to listen to Robert go to bat for Oliver Cantrel, two-time Oscar winner and director par excellence. But it was simply the thrill of a detached observer. She was no longer intimidated by Robert's power, no longer romantically susceptible to his personality.

He was facing her again, frowning into space.

"What d'you mean, between the lines? Columbia puts 'final cut' in the contract. Paramount never gave us an argument on 'Freeze.' I've got producers waiting in line for his services. He doesn't need this hassle, Jess . . . Jess, will you . . ." He broke off and turned his back again, propping his feet up on the window sill with a disgruntled sigh.

Chalice found herself staring at the back of his head, thick black hair tapering down to just above his collar. Yes, like Joe Verdi's. She was unmoved by it. After that jerk Verdi, she doubted she'd ever again have a weakness for dark, clever men. It was strictly business from now on.

Robert leaned his chair back and stared blandly at the ceiling.

"You know that, and I know that," he said. "But when a director's got that many awards, his ears tune out. No. No. Don't tell me points, Jess. It won't wash. For a lousy half point more of the profits, he's not going to give up the privilege of final cut." Suddenly his feet left the window ledge and hit the floor. He jerked ramrod straight in his chair as if he'd felt a cattle prod in his back.

"No! In the contract, Jess. Don't give me 'between the lines' crap. Black and white or forget it." He paused, then went on more calmly. "Yeah, he's in Brussels. I'll be calling him in the morning. You'd better make up your mind before then, or find yourself another director. Talk to you later."

Without missing a beat, he slammed the receiver down, smiled, and said, "Sorry, Chalice. What can I do for you?"

She didn't waste words.

"I want film contracts, Robert, and I want you to handle me. Professionally, understand. I'm looking to be on your client list again, not in your bed. Are you interested?"

He flipped the cards on his Rolodex file and laughed. "I thought you'd never ask."

"You'll take me on?"

"Sure." Robert rose, reached an arm across the desk, and shook her hand. "Welcome back to J. Green & Shankel. But if you ever do what you did to Sam on *The Snipe*, I'll drop you like a hot potato."

"I won't," she said. "I've learned." Chalice reached for her checkbook, thought for a moment, then made out a check for four hundred and fifty dollars, and handed it to him.

He stared blankly at the check. "What's this?"

"It's the commission you earned on my first sale. You once made a gift of it, but if we're going to work together . . ."

He didn't react beyond a mild lift of his eyebrows.

At a signing, Robert's lunch tab was often more than that. She wondered for a moment whether he'd laugh or protest.

"You're the client," he said after a moment. "Whatever makes you feel good." He shrugged and placed the check on his desk calendar.

Chalice relaxed. He knew what she was trying to say, and he was letting her say it. She'd been right; when it came down to business, Robert was his own kind of gentleman.

Before she left his office, he had fixed up three firm appointments for her. Two on Thursday with studio executives, and one in Malibu on Friday, at the home of an independent producer.

It was definitely the right decision, she thought that afternoon, watching Luke work on her car. She had grown up enough to deal with the Robert Shankels of this world on her own terms.

"How's it going, Luke?" she said, joining him under the hood of the Honda.

He straightened up and grinned, a regular grease monkey. "Fine. Your radiator should've been flushed before this, but it's all cleaned up now." Peering into the bowels of the car once more, he tightened the radiator cap. "And you're overdue for a tune-up."

Luke had taken auto mechanics in high school, and he loved being elbow deep in car grease. The Honda had never been so pampered as in the past few months.

"Haven't seen you since last week," Chalice said. "How've you been?"

"Good," he said. "Got a callback from Wolfstarn Productions. But I won't know for a while. Seven of us got callbacks. How about you, Chalice?"

"I got myself an agent. Robert Shankel again."

"All right! He's very smart. Just like you said." Luke removed two spark plugs and cleaned them off lovingly with a rag. "I never figured out why you left him in the first place."

Her voice became stilted. "Well," she said, "Sam Firestone was my father's agent. I felt that—when he came out of retirement . . ." She trailed off, then started again. "Robert is a bit of a ladies' man," she finished awkwardly.

"Got fresh, did he?" As he bent to replace the spark plugs, she saw the quick flush on the back of his neck.

"Sort of."

Rachel was right, Chalice decided. This kind of story was not for Luke's tender ears . . . they *would* turn pink and fall off. The thought led relentlessly back to Joe Dante, as so many of her thoughts had done since last week.

Long after the car was fixed, and after she'd turned out the light to sleep that night, the man kept nudging back into her mind.

Robert had sent her home with plenty of reading to do in preparation for her interviews, but she had put off starting until the morning because she was tired.

No, not tired, she admitted, still wakeful behind closed eyes, just overstimulated. Provoked. Joe Verdi was horning in on her concentration. No matter the distractions of the last few days, he kept on intruding.

Driving away from Sam's funeral, she'd thought of him. In Robert's office. Chatting to Luke while he tinkered with her car. He was forever butting in.

"Joe Jerk," she said out loud into the darkness.

He had propelled her into a meaningless one-night stand, and she had every reason to resent him. Or was she simply mad at herself? She'd never done anything quite like that before, and the very idea made her feel cheap and hollow. But the trouble was, none of it had seemed cheap or hollow at the time. She had felt such a sweet, profound oneness with him. If he hadn't tricked her that way . . . if it hadn't been for *The Snipe*, she would have thought it was . . .

Turning over on her side, she slammed her head into the pillow. But he *had* tricked her, and he *was* the man who'd walked off with her movie, and besides, she no longer had a weakness for dark, clever men. Hadn't she demonstrated the proof that very afternoon in Shankel's office?

George Nadel sat on the denim-covered couch in Joe's study and nodded. "Nice quiet place," he told

Joe. "You shouldn't have any trouble churning out the script here."

Joe looked remarkably fit, standing there stripped to the waist, in faded tan shorts and thong sandals. "You look acclimatized to the sun-and-sand country," George said, patting his own growing paunch.

"I never really get acclimatized," Joe said, handing George a glass of Coke. "This place is better than working in the studio, but I still haven't made a dent in the script."

"Well, you've only been here in the house for two days."

"Three," Joe muttered.

"You always piddle away the first two weeks, then crack out a complete draft in the third week. Don't you know your own M.O. yet?" George smiled reassuringly. He was flying back to New York today, having finally gotten agreement all round on the small print in Brad Alexander's contract. "Oh," he said, reaching into his briefcase. "I got you a present."

He handed Joe a small paper sack.

"Just what I needed." Joe grinned as he drew out a pack of Di-Gel, and to prove his point, he opened the pack and popped a tablet in his mouth.

"You've been living on those things since we left Kennedy Airport," George muttered. "I don't get it. You've got a cast-iron stomach back home."

"It refuses to travel West." Joe shrugged. "I guess it's smarter than I am. Listen, George, if Shirley should call your office looking for me, let her have this number, will you?"

George's chunky red face tightened with disapproval. "You don't need that."

Joe bristled. "Come on, George. What I *don't* need is another lecture."

"Isn't it about time you backed off?" George muttered. "Shirley's an incurable dingbat."

As if he didn't know. Joe closed his eyes. He knew everything he needed to know about his ex-wife. Her paranoia about her son. Her violation of visitation rights with Douggie's father. Her citations for contempt of court. Of course she was a dingbat. That was precisely why he felt so responsible for her. Someone had to be. But the lecture was coming, regardless.

"You were only married a year, and that was enough to clean you out. You've got your own problems now, and Shirley isn't one of them. Wasn't that the whole point of the divorce, Joe? Let them fight it out between them, her and the boy's father. Just be glad you didn't have a kid with her. She'd be pulling the same thing on you."

Joe stirred the ice in his glass with his finger. The point was, Shirley *was* his kid, ever since she stopped being his wife. "Just let her know where I am if she calls your office," Joe said wearily.

But George was still mutinous. "Shirley's a thirty-year-old adolescent—"

"You got it."

"And alimony or no alimony, you're not responsible for her cockamamie legal costs," George went on.

And she'd always be broke, and stubborn, and foolish, Joe added to himself. But you can't stop caring for someone out of expediency. She'd been on the move for months now, afraid that Douggie's father would kidnap him. The father was no monster, just a decent man who wanted to see his own child. Shirley was handling it all wrong. She was pathetic, but if she needed help from him . . . he could do as he damn well pleased with his own money.

"George, I don't want to involve you in my personal affairs," Joe said. "I'd tell her myself if I knew where to reach her, but I don't. All I'm asking is that you give her my number here if she calls your office. Okay?"

George made angry noises like a sputtering tea-kettle, then subsided. "Okay. I just hope to God she doesn't call."

Actually, Joe hoped so too, he realized suddenly. He went out for a run after George left. Jogging past the deserted blocks of the neighborhood, he felt a surge of anxiety about the screenplay. He really didn't need Shirley's problems right now. If he could stop cluttering up his mind with women, he might get this project completed. Jeez! For a hundred and fifty thousand, he'd better. He ran about three miles, then walked another two back to the house. But he still wasn't in the mood to work.

After a quick shower, he put on jeans and a short-sleeved shirt, just to make like he was at home on West Tenth Street, working on the book. Or on a new play. On anything but a still nonexistent screen-play called *The Snipe*.

But it did exist, he remembered, in that scrap heap of paper in Chalice York's living room. Over a year of her life down the tubes.

Dear God, how could he blame her for getting plastered? How could he blame her for letting fly at him? What was the matter with him anyway, that he hadn't told her until after they'd made love? She was the kind of woman who was very vulnerable to

passion. He'd sensed that. She hadn't just shared her
body with him, she had . . . *Damnittohellandback*!
He was at it again. Hadn't he just decided to clear
his head and get down to work?

He couldn't. The only way he was ever going to
get down to work was to clean the slate with Chalice
York. He wouldn't be able to think straight until
he'd got that squared away.

There were several C. Yorks in the phone book,
but he picked out the one that listed no address, and
hit pay dirt.

Her voice chilled into ice crystals as soon as he
said his name.

"I want to explain something," he began.

"Don't bother," she said, "I'm not in the mood to
listen, and I have nothing to say to you."

But *he* had something to say, and he'd choke on it
if he didn't get it out. He sensed she was about to
hang up on him, but she couldn't hang up on a letter.
"What's your address?" he asked quickly.

"Drop dead," she said, and hung up.

The Writers' Guild gave him the address, but he
found he could no more write a letter of apology
than he could concentrate on *The Snipe*. He wasn't
even sure what he was apologizing for. He tossed the
unfinished letter in the trash and called for a cab.

The ride seemed three days long, and by the time
he stood outside her door pressing the bell, his hands
were a bit clammy. He wiped them on his jeans.

"Come in, Luke," she called out. "It's not
locked."

He walked in, cursing the California climate. It
was against nature for the temperature to reach
ninety in March.

She was lying on her stomach with her nose buried

in a book. Scattered around her on the carpet were manuscripts, folders, a yellow legal pad, and an empty coffee mug.

"There's some money on the coffee table," she said without looking up. "Is it enough?" Then she turned and saw him.

He should have stopped at a florist and brought her some flowers, he thought. It might have softened the look she was giving him. "Hi there." He attempted a friendly smile.

"You've got some nerve," she said, and scrambled to her feet.

He'd forgotten how tiny she was. Small hands and feet, small heart-shaped face scarcely heavy enough to support those enormous eyes. Barefoot, she was no more than five foot one, he decided, and utterly irresistible with that natural flush on her cheeks. Her long yellow T-shirt ended midthigh, and it appeared to be all she had on. Lucky Luke, he thought, wondering what to say next. Why did he feel so crushed?

"You shouldn't leave your door open. There's a lot of crazy people out there. You just never know what murderous rapist might wander in." He winced at the words coming out of his mouth. Oh, inspired, Joe. Truly inspired.

She swept the coffee mug up in her hand and turned toward the kitchen. For a wild moment he thought she was going to offer him something to drink, when she turned.

"Well, you can just wander right out again," she said. "I'll keep it locked in future."

He stood in the center of the room, unable to decide. Should he follow her into the kitchen and say his piece or just leave before the going got really rough? The doorbell decided for him. The sound simply nailed his feet to the floor.

Chalice skirted around Joe as if he were a bronze monument that someone had just set down in the middle of her carpet, and opened the front door.

A teenager walked into the living room, an angelic overgrown child holding a sack of groceries. And she was calling him Luke. A delivery boy maybe? Whatever he was, Joe knew what he was not, and the sap flowed in his veins again. He held his ground and waited.

Chalice took a jar of iced tea mix from Luke and handed him some money. "Thanks. You saved my life."

Luke handed her back her car keys and grinned awkwardly at Joe.

"Luke, this is Joe Verdi," she said. "He was just leaving."

"How d'you do, sir," Luke said. Joe muttered something and shook the boy's hand. The silence was awesome.

Luke looked at Chalice, a little shy with the stranger in the room, and said, "Well, bye. Got to get going. My shift starts at five."

Joe didn't move until Luke had closed the door. Then he took a step toward Chalice, words forming on his lips.

She forestalled him in a crisp voice. "You were just leaving," she said.

"You said that," Joe pointed out, "I didn't. Oh, I'll leave all right, but not until I've had a fair hearing. I've been feeling like a jerk all week."

She was reading the iced tea label with minute care. "My heart bleeds."

"I didn't do anything to deserve this. Look,

writers have enough natural enemies without fighting among themselves. Hell, I'm not one of *them*. I'm one of the good guys."

"That's the message I got from you last time. I'm not renewing my subscription, thank you."

She skirted around him once more on her way to the kitchen, leaving a wide safety margin, as if he was radioactive.

"We could even help each other if you weren't so deter—"

"United we stand, divided we fall," she broke in, and gave him a withering half-smile. "What are you quoting? A tract from the Writers' Guild?"

He backed up against her desk, realizing he was babbling wildly. She wasn't making this easy. "I never raped you," he said slowly. It wasn't exactly brilliant, but it had the desired effect of stopping her progress to the kitchen.

She turned and pretended to think about it. "Not in the criminal sense."

"Not in any sense." Joe's voice became indignant. "You were no victim last week, you were a—consenting adult. And as for stealing your movie, Ryan offered me the job of working from a treatment. Common practice, you must admit. What was I supposed to do? Get suspicious and give him the third degree?"

His face looked so wretched, Chalice felt her sympathies touched. So far, it was a reasonable argument. There was nothing suspicious about working from someone else's treatment, she had to admit. But nothing in her stony expression suggested she was relenting, or even listening to him.

His hands curled around the edge of her desk in a fierce grip. "And what's more," he said, "the last thing I ever wanted was to write another movie. I just wanted to lay my hands on a lot of cash, that's all."

She offered him an incredulous icy stare. "I see! So you did it out of pure greed. Well, why didn't you say so in the first place? Of course! That makes it all right. You're all high principles and sterling values. Now that we're buddies, will you please leave?"

Patience and courtesy deserted him. In one furious leap, he pounced on her, grabbed her shoulders, and pressed her down on the couch, yelling, "Goddammit, there is nothing wrong with my principles! So stop with the sarcasm and listen to me."

She was so startled, she simply sat there with her mouth open, watching him back away.

"You couldn't possibly understand this, but I just have to get my parents out of the rat hole they live in. *I have to*." Joe reached her typing chair and straddled it, so that he was facing her, his words tumbling out in a sudden rush.

She must have pushed some button, she decided, because what poured forth seemed to emerge from some deep, emotional strongbox. For a few minutes, she forgot her hostility and listened, fascinated.

"Know what he calls me, my father? He calls me 'Joe College,'" he said. "Would you believe that? 'Joe College,' and to him, it isn't a joke. I'm the youngest of three brothers. Tony's a shoe salesman, Leo's a mechanic. I'm supposed to be the smart one, and that's a laugh if you look at the mishmash I make of my life. But I am stuck with the role, and for once I'm trying to do it right."

In out-of-sequence snatches, Chalice began to get the picture. His parents were retired now, and they owned their home. But the house was a piece of junk in a neighborhood so bad that it was a high risk every time they went out at night.

Last winter, Joe had taken his folks to visit relatives in Florida. In Key West, they'd fallen in love with a two-bedroom condo. It was the retirement house of their dreams, a new development with costly landscaped gardens and ocean views. On the spot he decided. He was going to buy it for them. He could comfortably qualify for the financing. But it was no go with his parents. His father wouldn't hear of it.

Papa Verdi was from the old country.

"No loans, Pepe. Cos, you don' pay, they breaka you legs."

They both knew it was a joke, but Joe had no choice but to play along each time.

"Papa, I'm not talking loan sharks. Just a regular financial institution. The same way you paid for this place. And I can handle the payments. You don't have to worry about that."

"Don' have to worry, he says. I grew old paying for dis place, but Joe College tells me I don' have to worry. What am I, a zucchini, I don' have to worry? No, my boy. If you ever got hundred eighty thousand dollars jess lying aroun, okay. But no son of mine going into a lifetime a debt, jess so his mama and papa can enjoy the sunshine in their ol' age."

Joe's divorce had cleaned him out. He had a house in Westport he couldn't seem to unload, and if it ever did sell, half the money would go to Shirley.

"The only way I had to swing a cash deal was one big fat movie contract," he wound up. "And as soon as I got the offer, I jumped at it."

"That," Chalice said, "is the most ridiculous thing I ever heard. Nothing stops you from buying the

property in your own name if you've got the down
payment, and just letting your parents live there."

Joe drummed impatiently on the vinyl back of her
typing chair. "Oh no? You still don't understand, do
you? Papa's not as dumb as he sounds. He'd check
out the property title as soon as the sale was
recorded. And if he ever found out I'd taken a
mortgage on the place . . ." A smile, slow and
fatally infectious, spread over Joe's face. "He'd
breaka ma legs."

Chalice smiled back in spite of herself. She had
steeled herself against his obvious appeal. But he
was more than dark and sexy. More than merely
clever. Joe Verdi, she realized, had an insidious kind
of charm that she'd been utterly unprepared for. She
could feel it creeping up and taking hold. She
wrestled against it tooth and nail.

Inch by inch, during his narrative, he had scooted
her typing chair over the carpet until he was just an
arm's length from the sofa. She planned to keep him
at arm's length. This absurd story was a ploy. Just an
outrageous bid for sympathy. And she was close to
falling for it. Why could she be had so easily?

"Bull," she said. "You think I'd swallow that?
That your father is expecting you to come up with
cold cash?"

"That's just the point, cupcake. He doesn't expect
it. He doesn't think it's possible. It's just his way of
saying, 'Forget it. It's only a dream. I don't want you
to take it seriously.' But it is serious. It's my obsession."

He looked abashed suddenly, as if he'd just been
caught in his underwear. "Anyway," he muttered,
"I didn't mean to dump on you. That's my problem.
And by the time I've finished this movie, it'll be

solved. I'll probably never venture west of Riverside Drive again . . . So the movie trade is all yours, and welcome."

"Do you really expect all this to make me feel any better about losing sixteen months of my life's blood?"

"No," he said softly.

"Then why tell—"

"I just wanted you to feel better about me. I'm not without scruples, and I'm not a jerk, out looking for quick tumbles. But you made me feel like one last week."

She drew breath to argue, but he cut her off.

"Hey, it wasn't a setup. I drove you home because I didn't want you to kill yourself. When you told me how much you'd put into the project, I felt bad for you. It made it much harder to tell you that I was the one who . . ." He stood up and pushed the chair away.

"It was just an impulse when I took you in my arms. It wasn't loaded with base motives."

He paused, searching her face for some sign of yielding, but she kept her eyes expressionless and said nothing.

He gulped. "When we made love, it wasn't your average one-nighter. Not for me, anyway. How about you?"

"I wouldn't know." Chalice rose from the sofa and folded her arms primly. "I don't indulge in one-nighters, so I have no way of averaging them out."

His hands passed over his jaw in a gesture of chagrin. "I may as well put the other foot in it . . . I feel an impulse to kiss you now." His voice became slow and tentative. "You're not in bed. You're not

just waking from a hangover. And you're not particularly vulnerable at the moment. You can't accuse
me of taking advantage of you—and anyway, I
wouldn't dream of trying to manipulate your feelings."

But she *was* vulnerable, she thought, particularly
to the way he was standing there, shifting his weight
from one foot to the other like a shy boy. And she
wasn't sure she hadn't been thoroughly manipulated
already.

He cleared his throat. "If I kissed you now," he
said, "would you scream rape?"

She smiled, wanting to touch him, then hesitated
very slightly before she spoke. "No, of course not,
but right now, I'd rather you just left."

"What kind of left? You mean never-darken-my-
doorstep-again left, or just—or just . . ."

"Just 'left' as in 'go away' because frankly I don't
know if I want you to kiss me or not."

He squatted down on the carpet, scratched out his
phone number on the corner of her notepad, then
tore it from the yellow sheet and thrust it in her
hand. "If you should make up your mind—about the
kiss, I mean—don't hesitate to call me."

He bussed her cheek lightly and grinned. "It's
only a twenty-dollar cab ride away."

"You probably got rooked," she said.

He shrugged. "So what's new? Good-bye."

"Joe," she called after him as he made for the
door, "you'll need to call a cab, won't you?"

Chapter 6

CHALICE SAT SOAKING IN THE TUB THAT NIGHT, RE-flecting on the two sweeping conclusions she'd arrived at so glibly in the last few days. She'd better straighten herself out right now, she decided, and throw them out with the bathwater.

One of these sweeping conclusions was that, just because Robert no longer gave her the flutters, her romantic susceptibility to dark, clever men was a thing of the past. Joe Verdi had neatly exploded the theory that very afternoon.

It had been impossible to stay angry with him, and it had taken a considerable struggle to tell him to go away—a struggle she had prolonged unnecessarily, first by letting him phone for a taxi, and second by letting him wait an excruciating ten minutes for the taxi to arrive.

She had ducked out of any undesirable conse-

quences by pleading a work deadline and returning
to her reading while he waited. She had been
preparing for her upcoming interviews, scribbling
down her thoughts on the restructuring of scenes in a
crime novel, when he walked in.

She had tried to pick up where she left off, but
with Joe standing behind her at the window, watching for his cab, concentration had become a mere
pretense. In fact it wasn't until he'd been gone for
two hours that she'd managed to resume any sem-
blance of a working rhythm.

Fishing around the tub with her foot, she found
the washcloth and hooked it on her big toe. She
lifted it above the water line, draped it idly over the
faucet, and dismissed Joe from her mind.

The other conclusion she'd arrived at so lightly
was that movies just didn't matter all that much.

Oh yes they did. If men like Shankel and Firestone
and her own father could devote their considerable
energies and gifts to the film industry, then movies
were indeed a serious business. More important,
they were her own special medium; they were in her
blood, and she was going to make her mark on the
big screen, no matter what.

There was no longer any excuse for her to be on
the fringe like this. She'd been at it for six years; she
had the technique; she had a sense of visual and
dramatic impact; she had the talent, and she had the
agent.

No more team writing on sitcoms, she decided.
There was enough money in the bank to coast for a
while and take true aim. From now on it was the big
screen or bust. And since every movie made these
days was a triumph over impossible odds, she certainly wasn't going to get sidetracked again. Not by

the frequent reversals that inevitably cropped up in this business, and not by amorous adventures. But it didn't have to mean a steady diet of all work and no play, did it?

Breathing the steamy fragrance of lavender bath cubes, her mind returned to Joe Verdi.

He was hardly the villain she'd tried to make of him. She was simply a victim of the system and using him as a scapegoat. She had overreacted as usual—to the *Snipe* business and also to the significance of Joe's lovemaking. The erotic interlude was neither fiendish abuse on his part, nor a prelude to eternal bliss. It just happened, that's all. And she still wasn't in the least sorry that it had, it occurred to her. In the future she would beware of blending fictive screen situations with the realities of life. And the realities were plain enough. Her life was here. His life was three thousand miles away. And whatever delightful prospects his visit conjured up, it was still just a visit.

"You just have to quit living at fever pitch all the time," she murmured. "It's a criminal waste of emotional energy."

And it was also why she'd instinctively avoided romantic attachments for so long; she could see that now. It was sheer self-defense—because she had absolutely no sense of moderation.

"Well it's time you developed some," she told the soggy washcloth, wringing it out fiercely. "At twenty-seven, enough is enough. Joe Verdi is kind and amusing and almost larcenously attractive. So why can't you just enjoy all those things without pledging your life away?"

She had his telephone number. He would only be around for a few weeks, so the possibilities were limited. But within those limitations the prospects were tempting. Companionship, laughter, affection, sharing. Exploration. Excitement. So many of the pleasures she'd forgone for a long time. It would be terrific . . . if she could just learn to keep the whole thing in proportion. But work came first. Until her third interview was over on Friday, she wasn't going to risk any distractions.

Chalice had been to the very best girls' school in Kent, where rigid self-discipline was an important part of the curriculum. She drew on those reserves now, and found it possible to throw herself whole-heartedly into her life's work, and to keep Joe Verdi on the back burner for three days.

On Friday, as she drove away from Malibu Beach, she congratulated herself. She would check in with Robert, tell him about her third and last interview. Then Joe Verdi could come off the back burner.

Carl Zanke was the last of the three producers she'd seen, and he had been noncommittal. To various degrees, so had the others. But they were all preliminary interviews. If any of them came through, she thought it would probably be Al Varney. He had optioned a two-act play, an eighties version of a drawing room comedy which had enjoyed moderate success in New York and London. There wouldn't be much to the adaptation, except broadening the scenes to suit the medium, but if she got it, she wouldn't complain. It was a vast improvement on *Return of the Killer Bees*, the only one of her efforts so far that had ever reached the big screen and actually been released for distribution.

She drove east on the Coast Highway, then pulled over at a gas station in Pacific Palisades to call Robert before he took off for the weekend.

"How'd it go?" he asked her.

"He was pleasant," she told him. "He asked me how I'd handle it and pretended to listen, but I don't think he really wanted to know. He did most of the talking, and it was mainly about distribution."

Robert didn't sound particularly disappointed. "Well, forget it. As I said, this was chiefly an exercise in exposure. I don't have high hopes of you clicking with any of them. Although Varney's the best bet. But if he came through right now and offered you a contract, I'd stall him for a few days. I've got other properties cooking at the moment."

"Like what?"

"Not yet. It's still blue sky. Maybe I'll be ready to talk Monday. Late morning. You gonna be home?"

"I'll be waiting to hear."

"Okay, Chalice. You did your homework and you made your appointments. There's nothing to do but wait now, so put it out of your mind for the weekend, and go get yourself a suntan."

She might just do that, she thought. For once she wasn't going to spend her weekend stewing about not working. She fished around in her purse for Joe's number. He was staying at the Westmont, she recalled. Only fifteen minutes away. She glanced at her watch. It was not quite four. He probably wasn't in his room, but she could leave a message.

When an impatient voice said hello, she was taken aback. "Oh! Er, um . . . I'd like to speak to Joe Verdi please."

"Speaking."

"Oh . . . . This is Chalice York."

"Well, *hello*," he said, his voice warming considerably. "And what exactly does 'oh, er, um' signify?"

She laughed. "You threw me for a moment. I thought I was calling a hotel switchboard," she said.

"Didn't I tell you? I've rented a house. Locking myself away from distractions is the only way I can work, I'm afraid."

"Well, I'm sorry if I disturbed you."

"No, no, of course you didn't. Are you kidding? I'm jazzed. I'm pretty much used up for the day, anyway."

"Me too," she said. "I've just finished a meeting —a job interview—and I stopped at a gas station to check in with my agent before he left for the weekend, and then I found I had another dime and—"

"Where are you?"

"Pacific Palisades."

"What's that? I'm in Brentwood," he said. "Are we within hailing distance?"

"Spitting distance."

"Oh, er, um," he said after a moment. "I'd rather you came in person. Feel like paying a mercy visit? The jail's not hard to find."

He was wearing a crisp white shirt with a tie when he came out to the driveway to greet her as she drove in. He must have been listening for the sound of her car, she thought, and his stride under the dark slacks was springy and welcoming. Before she was out of the car, she felt an involuntary reaction, slight, but unmistakably erotic. Moderation, she reminded herself, and greeted him casually.

His smile was warm as he led her into the house. "I'm glad you called," he said. "I mean, I'm really glad you called. How was your interview?"

She told him about it briefly as she looked around

his living room. It was a roomy house, plainly furnished and ivory-walled. He had found a nonde-script middle-class neighborhood tucked between the old established luxury of the Palisades and the flash of Bel Air.

It was a quiet place to work, he told her.

He had sounded busily at work when she called. "Do you always dress like that when you're work-ing?" she asked him.

"I changed after I spoke to you," he said. "If you don't mind being chauffeur, I'd like to buy you dinner. Some place where the steaks are prime and the lobster's fresh?"

She settled on a Westwood steak house that met those requirements and offered secluded booths where they could talk quietly.

He looked a little surprised when she asked for a tonic and lime to drink, and it made her think of the last time he'd seen her with a glass in her hand. She had been drinking vodka for the first time in her life. She had actually been to bed with this man. There was something disturbing about the superficial level of their acquaintance.

"We don't know each other at all, do we?" she said shyly.

"No?" He lifted his glass of Chianti, then changed his mind and set it down. His hands rested on the table, lightly clasped, and he looked down at them, as if he was about to say grace. "I've seen you drunk, I've seen you naked, and I've seen you very angry. I know you write well, make love passionately, freeze your bread, then eat it burned to a crisp. And I know your English accent isn't Hollywood-phony, because it only comes out when you're three sheets to the wind." He grinned. "Could there be more?"

There must have been at least a dozen brilliant retorts, but she couldn't think of one. Instead she turned scarlet and said, "I guess not." He had said 'Hollywood-phony,' she noticed, as if it were all one word. It wasn't a putdown directed at her, but something about it laid down a gauntlet.

"Well, I certainly don't know much about you," she said. "I assume all Italians have a strong sex drive and tell comic-opera stories about their papas. What else? Besides being a New York chauvinist, I mean."

He leaned back in the seat and narrowed his eyes at her. "Lady, how would you like to be picked up on a charge of racism?"

She raised her hands in mock surrender. "Excuse me. I suppose there are a few Italians who—"

"First of all," he said firmly, "if we're going to get down to ethnic origins, I'm only half Italian. Second: That comic-opera story happens to be the truth. And as for my sex drive, it hasn't been foremost in my mind for a long time. Not since my wife moved out of our bedroom and into her son's, as a matter of fact. She's my ex-wife now," he added after a tiny pause. "But divorce hasn't exactly turned me into an Italian stallion, if that's what you're getting at."

Chalice stared into her glass, feeling awkward. "My mistake . . . And your son?" she asked in a gentler voice.

"Not mine. There was a husband who preceded me, and—" He shook his head. "Let's drop it, shall we? It's just another comic opera and a costly one. I won't go into it."

Chalice wasn't sure whether he meant costly in money or in heartache, but a grimness passed briefly over his face, and she guessed at residual pain in him. She was touched to think of him as vulnerable, but the moment passed and neither of them mentioned it again.

After the meal, they strolled in Westwood village for an hour, taking in the local color of the evening. Fashionably dressed students from the University of Southern California dotted the prosperous streets and browsed in expensive specialty shops and bookstores. Art movie houses, wine bars, and boutiques were still open for business. They stopped and drank espressos and brandy at a sidewalk cafe near the campus.

Joe watched her with a bemused expression. "Is that all you're going to do? Just sniff it?" he said.

She handed him her balloon glass. "Could you drink it?" she asked. "I shouldn't have let you order it. Not after the Chianti."

"You had a teaspoon of Chianti," he said. "You really weren't kidding about being a nondrinker, were you?"

She shook her head. "Do you mind?"

"Of course not. I just have this feeling we're back to square one."

"That's exactly what I was trying to tell you earlier. You met me under atypical circumstances, to say the least." She took a deep breath to control the wave of unnecessary defensiveness she found sweeping over her. It didn't stop. "I never drink, like that," she found herself blurting out. "I never even knew what vodka tasted like before that night. And I never invite strangers into my bed, and—"

"Hey, it's okay," he said gently, and reached for her hand. "You don't have to work at it. I understand what you're trying to say." He gazed squarely into her eyes. "Look, I'd be lying through my teeth if I said I didn't want to make love to you again. But I'm not going to hustle you."

On the drive back to Brentwood, he rested his head sideways on the back of the seat and watched her.

She felt utterly at ease with him now; the defensiveness had melted. "What's the other half?" she asked him. "The part that's not Italian, I mean."

"Jewish," he said. "I was wrestling with an identity crisis before the shrinks gave it a name, I think. A Bar Mitzvahed altar boy, that's me."

"Now you really are teasing me." She grinned into the windshield.

He sat up straight and addressed her profile earnestly. "Okay, but the truth is just as nutty. My mom sneaks tiny matzoh balls into her minestrone. Honest to God. I was twelve before I learned they didn't belong there, bobbing around on top of the salt pork and vegetables."

She was still grinning to herself about that when she pulled into his driveway. He got out and opened her door.

"Thanks for being my driver," he said. "And my tour guide."

She sat behind the wheel listening to the hum of the motor running, and a wave of awkwardness engulfed her. She couldn't quite bring herself to turn off the ignition key. It seemed too loaded a gesture. "Thanks for dinner," she said. "It was a fun evening."

"It's not over yet, is it? It's only ten. Aren't you going to come in for a while?"

She didn't answer. Couldn't answer.

He held out his hand, and when she took it she felt

the slight tug of his arm, inviting her out of the car. She resisted it, shaking her head. He didn't press her, but leaned down and kissed her lightly on the lips.

Too lightly. The urge to pull him back was overwhelming. She gripped the steering wheel as if her life depended on it.

"Good night, then," he said.

"Good night, Joe."

He heard the small, reluctant quality of her voice and squatted down on his heels. His hand rested lightly on the open car door as he searched her face. She couldn't drive away until he drew back, she thought. She couldn't even close the door.

"Are you sure?" he said.

Her fingers reached out and slid under the lapel of his blazer. "No, I'm not."

He straightened up, and in a smooth movement, drew her out of the car and into his arms. For a moment he held her cheek hard against his.

"I didn't think so," he said, drawing his head back to look at her.

She felt the warm escape of his breath as he spoke, and she laughed, drawing confidence from the intimacy of his body. "Sometimes, I don't seem to know what I want," she confessed.

"I know what I want." Slowly, he closed the distance between their mouths and kissed her as if he meant it. She leaned into his embrace, tasting the deep bouquet of old brandy on his tongue, knowing that if she didn't pull back soon, she would be powerless to do so.

But it was Joe who drew back. He turned to the Honda, grinning broadly. The driver's door hung open, the headlights were on, and the motor was still humming in park. He reached in and took care of it, removing her purse and keys from the car.

"The symbolism's too heavy," he said, taking her by the hand and leading her into the house, "even for a B movie."

"They don't make B movies any more," she told him dreamily, trailing him into the hallway.

"Hah! That's what you think." He whipped her into a sudden stagey embrace that arched her into a backbend, and then he kicked the front door shut.

It was not a position from which she could easily recover, so she hung there, trusting the strength of his arms, while he leaned over her breathing, "Leave us now, all of you. I would take this woman to my tent."

"Joe," she said, giggling as the blood rushed to her head, "this is a marble floor. If you let go of me now, I'll crack my skull."

"Aah!" He swept her off her feet and began to carry her in a slow ritualistic stride up the stairs. "Nevah, nevah will I let you go, my exquisite passion flower."

He evidently wasn't taking this very seriously, but then there was no reason why he should, she reminded herself. The thought saddened her even while she laughed at his antics.

But when he set her down on her feet in his bedroom, he was no longer clowning. He reached out to remove her suit jacket, then let his hands rest on her shoulders. For a moment he looked contrite. "That was hammy," he said. "And devious. You're in my bedroom in three seconds flat because I'm in too much of a hurry to act civilized. I said I wouldn't hustle you and here I am, hustling you. I'm sorry. You—"

"I'm not," she broke in.

"You do have a choice, I was going to say."

There was a slight hump on the bridge of his nose. She passed the tip of her finger over it in a light caress. "Yes, I know I have a choice," she said. "I believe I just made it."

His sigh was a blend of relief and exultation, and his voice was shaded with boyish pleasure. "This is the first time I was ever happy to be on the West Coast," he said, and touched his head to hers. "I'm so very glad you're here."

It seemed more like the first time than a reunion, she thought, this naked play of their bodies. She had forgotten the dense pressure of his muscles and the feel of the crisp, dark curls on his chest. And she had never noticed the calluses on his hands that made his caresses as rough as they were tender.

He was a gentle lover, leisurely and affectionate with her until his control retreated before his own pent-up need, and he broke like a dam, storming her body and flooding them both with released pleasure.

I love you utterly, she thought, but said nothing. Moderation, she thought. But there was nothing moderate she could say as their hands clasped afterward, nothing moderate in the way she felt. As her pulse gentled, her heartbeat slowed, and the heat of passion ebbed from her body, there was only an insane, unjustifiable bliss.

Moderation, she kept reminding herself. Stop harboring such excessive feelings. He is just a good lover, that's all. It was surely enough.

Chalice woke to a feeling of unutterable luxury. She was a well-tended fledgling in a warm, enveloping nest. When she became aware that the warmth was human, she opened her eyes. A softly overcast morning filtered through the drawn drapes.

It was Joe's curled body she was nesting in. One of her breasts lay cradled in his sleeping hand, and she had no wish to move. She let her eyes roam over the dresser against the wall and the mushroom carpeting, without turning her head. Her green blouse lay over the arm of a brown upholstered chair. There was a travel clock on the nightstand, but its face was out of her line of sight. It didn't matter what time it was. It was Saturday, she remembered, and felt the light pressure on her breast as Joe's hand tightened.

"Good morning," he whispered into her hair.

His thumb stroked softly over her nipple, which rose in quick obedience to his touch.

Just the slightest movement of his thumb, she thought, and she quickened. Deliberately, she lay still, trying to quiet the swift clamoring of her body, but it would not be subdued.

"Mmm, you're awake, I see." Joe's voice was teasing and affectionate, but he remained quite still except for the light movements of his thumb.

Involuntarily she leaned into the firmness of his torso against her spine, and felt his hand slide over her belly and up to her other breast.

"Well . . . half awake," he said.

His caresses were unstudied, lazy almost, like a man idly petting a cat. The leaping response in her loins was out of all proportion; it made her feel enslaved. She could master her desire only when it was under lock and key, but once she uncaged it, she was no longer in control.

"Don't," she whispered.

But there was no uncertainty in him now. In reply, he merely shifted her to her back, clasped one of her breasts firmly and tilted it into his mouth. As he suckled, his hand coasted up and down her body with light, almost pressureless strokes that slowly deepened.

One open palm pressed into the small of her back, and she no longer knew whether it was his hand or her own eagerness that caused her body to arch.

Utterly subjugated by his touch, she offered herself up to him, as his hands and mouth sought out every secret of her body with an assertive authority he had not shown before. When at last he entered her, she urged him deeper, crazed with a desire to be filled with him. His slow thrusts goaded her, then waxed fierce as he pressed her from one crest to another until his own shuddering fulfillment flooded her, bringing nirvana in its wake.

He lingered inside her afterward, his body half resting on hers. "Don't tell me no when you mean yes," he said after a while.

She fancied she heard a slight smugness in his voice, like a man well pleased with his performance. "Part of me meant no," she told him.

He wove his fingers through hers and squeezed. "I was only addressing the other part, the part that left claw marks on my shoulders and squealed with joy."

"I don't claw," she told him, "neither do I squeal." But she knew that sounds she'd never made before had colored the air with her passion.

He chuckled, letting it pass. "Would your various assembled parts like a shower and some breakfast?" he asked, rolling off her and rising to his feet.

When she didn't answer, he looked down at her with a funny lopsided smile.

"There you go, pulling up the sheet again. Cupcake, we've just made abandoned love. I feasted on

your breasts. I touched and tasted your body inside
and out, and took thorough possession of it with
your very eager consent." His glance fell to the
sheet, where the sprawl of her limbs was clearly
defined. "And you're still warm and wet to prove it.
Do you resent me looking at you now?"

"Just go take your shower," she said.

"Damnit, not before you let go of the dumb
sheet," he said, ripping it from her hand in a flash of
anger.

Chalice froze, not knowing what to expect as he
uncovered her. But all he did was challenge her eyes
for a moment.

"I'll leave the shower running for you," he said,
and turned away, heading for the adjacent bathroom.

She had no idea what that was all about. Whatever
it was, she felt a need to make herself decent before
he returned, but she didn't want to dress before she
bathed. Rummaging around in his closet, she found
a faded blue T-shirt, slipped it on and sat on the bed
waiting, trying to figure out his anger.

When he came out, he was wearing a pair of navy
shorts, and she could hear the water still running.
She headed toward it, but he blocked the doorway
and she waited for him to step aside.

He glanced at the pale blue cotton covering her
from neck to knee, and smiled. "It looks better on
you than it does on me," he said, reaching for her
hand. He held it for a moment, then he kissed her
cheek. "I'm sorry." His voice had dropped to just
above a whisper. "I don't know why I did that."

"No big deal," she said. "It's okay." And somehow it was. Everything in the whole wide world was
okay.

"There's a clean towel in there and a bathrobe hanging on the door," he said. "See you downstairs."

A lemon tree blossomed outside the kitchen window, and its fragrance mingled with those of sausages and eggs and Sara Lee croissants, all waiting for her on the breakfast nook table.

A couple of times while they ate, he glanced at the terry cloth robe she wore, as if he were pleased she hadn't yet dressed, but he didn't mention it.

"Are you working this weekend?" she asked him.

"I'm afraid so. I've only got one more week to complete the first draft. How about you?"

"No work. No started projects that I'm committed to, that is. I could think about another original idea, I suppose, but I'm just not ready yet."

Joe pushed his plate away. "When you are, I'm sure it'll be good. *The Snipe*'s good, you know. Did I ever have a chance to tell you that? It's a terrific story. I just hope I can do it justice. I'll bet the draft you tore up was every bit as . . ." He laid down his coffee spoon with a clatter. "Oh, damn! All those wasted months. Do you hate me for it?"

How could he think that now, she wondered, when she had just risen from his bed? She glanced down at the robe she wore so casually.

"Are you serious?"

He didn't answer. He was obviously very serious indeed. And he'd never settle down to write feeling that way, she thought.

In her heart, she was able to change places with him. Under the cynical, wisecracking surface, Joe was painfully sensitive; she had weighed him down with guilt. She had thought it all resolved by now, but she could see him still struggling with it, empathizing with how she might feel at any given moment. That probably explained his flare of temper a little while ago, she thought. She had covered herself with the sheet, just an instinctive unthinking gesture, but he saw a reproach in it, a kind of distancing.

You can serve my pleasure when I'm in the mood, but that doesn't mean I like you or trust you as a human being. Is that what he was picking up from her? Could a man really be that sensitive? She thought of his plays. The rich subtleties of interaction between characters. Yes, of course he was sensitive. How could she doubt it?

She left her seat, went over to him, and kissed his bent neck. There really were fingernail scratches on his back.

"I never scratch and squeal with men I hate, Joe," she said in his ear. "Look, you didn't rip off my movie. I got mad at losing out, that's all, not because you did anything unethical. I had it coming, you know. I'm well versed in movie politics, and I persistently ignored my agent's advice. But I've put it behind me now. I'll come up with more ideas, so stop feeling sorry for me." Her voice brightened. "The jury finds you not guilty."

He reached back for her hands, pulled them forward, and kissed her palms. "Fair enough," he said. "Now sit down and finish your breakfast."

She returned to her seat and drank a second cup of black coffee. "That was delicious," she said. "Thank you."

"That's all you're having?" He glanced at her plate. "You eat like a bird. Are you trying to fade away?"

"Just a few pounds' worth," she said.

"You're speaking of the few pounds I love." His

eyes turned to the curve of her breast in the widening V of the robe. "You're just perfect the way you are."

"Well, thanks, but I've had quite enough to eat, and it's time I got out of your hair, anyway."

"You mean I can't talk you into staying the weekend?" he called after her as she left the kitchen. "We could burn up hundreds of calories together."

She started climbing the stairs, then turned to look at him when she was halfway up. He was standing at the bottom, gazing up at her, and she couldn't help responding to his rogue's grin.

"Don't be silly. You have a script to write, Joe. You're busy."

"But you're not," he said. "Wouldn't you like to stay and inspire me at appropriate intervals?" He stroked the spherical knob at the foot of the stair rail. "I work fast when I'm motivated."

"I've noticed."

"Seriously. Brief spurts of brilliance and protracted spells of—"

"Seriously, my foot! Joe, I do believe you're looking up my skirt."

"It's my skirt," he said, racing up the steps to her, "and I was doing nothing of the kind. I was just getting a crick in my neck from that supplicant position." He stopped one step below her, gripped the lapels of the robe, and muttered, "Please," into the warm cleft of her bosom. "I'm not planning to spend more than a couple of hours at the typewriter. Really. There are books, records, and tapes in the family room. You can sunbathe. Relax for a while."

"I'd have to go get a change of clothes at least," she said, weakening.

He walked her to the top of the stairs, assuming

victory, then kissed her with passionate triumph in the doorway of the bedroom. "Okay, go home for clothes if you must, but you may never get to wear them," he said.

While Joe spent the morning working, Chalice ran errands and played house, stocking his refrigerator, puttering around the quiet downstairs rooms, and preparing food. She didn't ask him how it was going, because it was never a question she welcomed herself when she was into a script, and he never referred to it.

The rest of Saturday slipped away in idle, companionable pursuits that later she was never quite able to recall, except for their frequent bouts of passion. Everything they embarked upon seemed to end in the desire to embrace. Meals were left half eaten, conversations gave way to caresses, and the movie they decided to see that evening in Westwood was preempted by a sudden, more pressing engagement.

On Sunday, Chalice awoke to a series of chinks and clatters. It was Joe, showered, dressed, and approaching the bed with an enormous brunch tray.

"It's noon," he said, placing the tray on the empty side of the bed. "And if you don't rouse yourself soon, there'll be no more Sunday left."

"You look as if you've been up for hours," she murmured drowsily.

"Since dawn," he said, handing her coffee. "At the typewriter. Then a quick trip to the deli for bagels and lox. I'm devoting the rest of this day to serious R and R."

"Serious R and R? Isn't that a contradiction in terms?" She was sitting up in the bed, naked except for the sheet drawn to her waist, and she laughed at the low growls he made as he brushed his lips across her shoulders.

"Not from this view . . . I was planning to start with a leisurely brunch. Looking at you right now, I'm not sure I can handle leisurely." He held out her robe. "Here, cover yourself, hussy. And I'll try to contain myself."

It was almost two before she slipped out of the tangled sheets. They had feasted on food and then on each other, and at the moment, Joe was dozing, his face buried in a pillow.

This is getting to be an orgy, she thought, trying to wash away under the shower the sinfully lazy effect of too much sleep and too much love. In his presence she felt as if they were two halves of one unit with a predisposition to interlock and become one. When they spoke, it was teasing inanities, the small change of besotted lovers. The one substantial factor they had in common was writing. Yet it was a subject they barely touched on.

Wasn't Joe in the least curious about how she'd approached *The Snipe*? she wondered. But they hadn't mentioned it since that first breakfast.

She at least was curious about what he was doing with it. He was deeply asleep when she tiptoed out of the bathroom. She left him to his well-earned rest and went downstairs.

As she passed the study, the door was temptingly ajar, and after a long moment's hesitation, she gave in to the temptation to peek at his work.

He was a much neater worker than she was, she noted, looking around the room. The typewriter was shrouded in its dustcover, the pencil holder held its proper contents to military attention, and two crisp stacks of typing lay squared and face down on the desk.

The shorter stack, she discovered, was merely a scene plan roughly following the sequence of her own treatment. The other, then, must be the script.

The top sheet was numbered page ninety-eight. So he was about two thirds through it. Unable to resist, she turned the stack face up and leafed through the opening pages. At the tenth page, she began to read carefully.

She recognized it as the first scene between Millie and Sal, almost exactly as she had set it up, except that it read quite differently now. It was tighter, with less dialogue and more action. The scene took place in a luncheonette. In a series of short takes, it built swiftly, inexorably, until the man and woman were screaming at each other out on the sidewalk.

Chalice stopped reading abruptly and indulged a moment of envy and writer's despair. It was good. Very good. With Joe's visual directions, the audience would be grabbed by the throat in a few seconds, and hopelessly hooked.

She came out of the study trying to shake a slight sense of pique. There were no sounds of Joe stirring yet, so she lit up a cigarette and took herself out to the back patio. Rocking in the swing chair, she tried to reason herself out of the feeling. It was absurd. Would she feel better if he'd ruined her story instead of improving it? Of course not. Her name would be on the title scroll, wouldn't it?

Her thoughts of rivalry were small and unworthy, she decided, picturing Joe asleep on his bed, this man who had become so immediately and so thoroughly her lover.

She heard his footsteps and determined that nothing was going to spoil this day.

"Sorry to conk out on you," Joe said, coming toward her, smiling. "Why didn't you wake me?"

"You didn't sleep that long. Just enough time for me to get showered and dressed . . ." She frowned, thinking of the cunning dynamics of the scene she had just read. "You're pretty hot stuff, Joe Verdi."

He touched the tip of her nose. "It's you. You make me insatiable. Are you complaining or is it a compliment?"

"I'm talking about your script, dummy. I peeked."

He didn't seem to mind. His head tilted and one eyebrow went slightly askew. "And?"

She frowned. "It plays so well it makes me sick."

"That's ridiculous, cupcake. It's your scenario. Ninety percent of it's yours. And nobody knows how it will play until the actors have at it."

"*I* know." Her voice was gloomy. "I can tell. It's got a quality it didn't have in my version, Joe. Let's face it, you've got something I don't have."

He ruffled her hair and bent to kiss her cheeks. "And vice versa," he said fervently, and made a comic face. "And vive la différence."

Chalice pushed him away, smiling broadly. "You have a one-track mind. You're incorrigible."

"That's what my—" He stopped abruptly, visited by a stab of resentment.

You're incorrigible. It was something Shirley used to say when they made love. He was suddenly aware that he hadn't given her a thought since Chalice's phone call on Friday. There was no point in deliberately revisiting pain. He dropped the thought instantly with a conscious act of will, something he had never quite managed before. Chalice's face was turned up to him in a smile of anticipation. The sun glanced off her hair, turning it into a reddish bronze halo that tightened his throat for a moment.

She leaned forward out of the sun, and the halo faded. "So finish the sentence, Joe."

"Huh?"

"What were you going to say?"

He reached out for her hands and pulled her out of the swing chair. "Nothing worth hearing. It's sweltering out here. Tell me, what do Californians do on a lazy Sunday afternoon when the temperature soars?"

"They head for the nearest beach, of course."

She didn't have a swimsuit with her, but the water was far too cold for all but the fanatics. The smooth sand, however, was hot to the touch. In a brief knit top and shorts, she sprawled on a towel beside him lazing away the afternoon. She had suggested they bring something to read, but her *Hollywood Reporter* and Joe's book still lay unopened in her tote bag. Curious, she reached in and examined the book jacket. It was the new David Oestermann novel.

"Pretty tony stuff for a guy from South Philly," she murmured, setting it down on the towel.

"I'm a faithful fan," he said. "I've read them all." Joe lay stretched out beside her. With his muscular chest furred with dark curls offered up to the late afternoon sun, he wasn't exactly what she imagined an Oestermann fan would be like.

"Do you read him?" he asked her.

"I'm afraid not."

He laughed. "Shame on you, Chalice York!"

"I know, I know. But he has a reputation for being overly wordy and erudite. Is he really that good?"

"For me, he's the best of all the contemporaries—only I guess he's not contemporary since last month."

"Strange, wasn't it?"

The grisliness of Oestermann's death had made headlines last month, and had turned his last book, *Many a Man,* into a bestseller. "A pretty sordid way to go," she said. "The obits said he was a scholarly, quiet sort of guy."

"Strange and awful." Joe moved closer until they lay touching, and pillowed his head on his hands. "Oestermann gave us at least four of the greatest novels in the English language. But he had to die mutilated outside a New Orleans brothel in order to be widely read. Now the movie moguls will be bidding for the rights. I doubt they'd ever heard of him before the New Orleans bit. It's amazing what a little publicity will do."

"Don't," she said, shuddering. Ugliness didn't belong in this island of time. "Would it make a good movie?" she asked him.

"If it's handled right, I suppose. I'll pass it on to you when I've finished. You can judge for yourself."

But he certainly wasn't going to finish it at the beach. They dozed for a while, and when the wind began to freshen, they sat up, wrapped the towel around them and watched the sun go down in apricot flames.

On the way back to Brentwood, she realized reluctantly that it was time to head home. There were a dozen weekend chores she had postponed. It was time to gear herself up for Monday morning.

"I'd better get my stuff together now," she told Joe after they dined lazily on leftovers and iced tea.

"If you must," he said, following her up the stairs.

Sand was trapped in her knit top, and she could feel it gritty against her breasts. She slipped off the top and looked around the room for her cotton shirt.

Joe looked at the tiny flecks silvering the tops of her breasts down to her nipples, and smiled broadly as she tried to brush them away. "Do you want to shower?"

She shook her head. "I'll wait until I get home."

"Then at least let me brush you off," he said, still grinning. He had a white sports sock in his hand and began to dust her breasts lightly, but her skin was moist and the flecks were stubborn.

"Hmm. They want to cling. Let's try this."

His arms went around her and his mouth lowered to her chest.

"Mmm," he murmured. "Sea salt. You taste like the Pacific Ocean."

"Joe!" Her voice quavered as his tongue flicked her nipple. "You'll get a mouthful of sand."

He breathed some unintelligible words onto her areola, and she felt the sound vibrate exquisitely through her nervous system.

"Joe," she moaned. "Stop that. You're turning me on."

"Me too."

Slowly he unhooked the waistband of her shorts and tugged them down over her hips, taking her panties with them.

He lifted her and laid her down naked on the bed,

then kissed her gently, feeling her tongue meet his, and her hips stir anxiously beneath him. His knee nudged gently between her own.

"I'm supposed to be going home," she said accusingly, "and you are definitely turning me on."

"The feeling is mutual," he whispered, pressing the evidence firmly against her thigh. "I've never made love to a mermaid. But if you have to leave immediately, don't let me detain you."

He lifted his body away from her and froze for a moment, as if to prove he spoke seriously.

"Detain me," she said, locking her arms around him to press him closer. "For God's sake, detain me."

"Mermaid," he whispered, brushing his lips over her skin, caressing her with slow, measured tenderness, until she forgot what time it was, what house this was, or that she had a home of her own to go to. When he was inside her, she was home, and Joe seemed to be the very air she breathed. Soon she was inhaling great gulps of air and crying out his name.

"Don't stop," she pleaded.

"You gasped—I thought I hurt you."

She pressed him deeper. "No—not that kind of gasp—I just—I . . . aah, Joe . . ."

"Sweetheart. Sweet cupcake. How I love loving you!" he sighed.

And I adore you, she thought, brimming with love for him. It was a vast, ineffable feeling that left the inner walls of her body with a sensation of fullness long after he withdrew, and mysteriously swelled her heart too. She lay there for the longest time savoring it. Wondering.

"Now I really must go home," she murmured at last, stroking his damp hair while his face lay across her chest. "Let me up." She glanced at the luminous clock dial on his night table and saw it was almost ten.

When she stirred, his hand tightened on her thigh, and he pressed his head between her breasts, reluctant to let her go.

"In a minute," he said in a muffled voice. His tongue lapped playfully at her nipple until it stiffened. She lay passive to his touch at first, so sated that it could not affect her. Then she felt nerves quicken, deep muscles constrict with yearning.

She was getting aroused again; this was ridiculous. She tugged at his hair, trying to pull his mouth away from her breast.

He was slow to respond, enjoying her pleasure. She was exquisitely sensitive to his touch, and he was delighting in his growing knowledge of her body. He had always been drawn to tall statuesque women before. Now he wondered why. Smallness only enhanced this woman. Like a naturalist must feel, stumbling on an entirely new species, he was endlessly fascinated by the delicate proportions of her body.

At last he raised his head unwillingly. "Did I pay you for the groceries?" he asked.

"You know you did, so stop stalling."

He sat up with a groan. "My back."

"Overexertion," she said, brushed his lips in a quick kiss, then scrambled out of bed before he could catch her again and turn her to putty.

Joe stretched lazily. "I wouldn't be a bit surprised —but we'll be fine after a hot tub." He looked at her invitingly as he rose.

"I'm sure you will—but not the kind of hot tub you have in mind."

He came toward her, his eyes gleaming with desire.

"Oh no you don't, my insatiable friend. After what you just did to me, this has to be pure bluff." She backed away, pleased, laughing, and reached for her clothes.

"Did you say something to me on Friday about having a tame sex drive?" she asked him, slipping a cotton sweater over her head. "A likely story!"

He watched her dress. "I said it hadn't been my most pressing problem for a while. It's the absolute truth, love. I just got stuck in high gear this weekend," he said, and stroked her silk-clad buttocks affectionately as she stepped into her jeans. "It's the effect you have on me. We really haven't done a damn thing except eat and smooch for two days, have we?"

"You did get some writing done," she reminded him.

"Some," he agreed. "But there's been a lot more lust than lit. I haven't been able to keep my hands off you. It's not really like me—I mean my appetites are not usually excessive."

He flashed a grin. " 'Fess up, cupcake. What have you been putting into my food? Twice you ordered me out of the kitchen."

Chalice wandered around the room, collecting her scattered belongings. "Oh," she said, "just a little ground rhinoceros horn and a pinch or two of powdered elves from the Black Forest."

"Well, it hasn't worn off yet, and you're deliberately provoking me now."

"Mellow out, Joe. I'm just getting dressed."

His eyes locked on her breasts as she tucked her sweater into her waistband. "You're not wearing a bra," he protested.

"I ran out of clean underwear."

"You lie. And your sweater's clinging to every inch."

"I told you I had a few pounds to lose."

"Don't give me that. It's deliberate provocation."

In reply, she turned to the dresser mirror and smoothed the loose cotton over her breasts until it did indeed cling, sharply defining the lift of the small, tight nipples he could still taste on his tongue. It was the act of a courtesan. "I'm perfectly decent," she told him with mock innocence.

Joe groaned and fell heavily into an armchair, bending double in mock agony. "The woman's trying to send me to an early grave."

Chapter 7

CHALICE BREATHED IN DEEPLY, SAVORING THE GHOST of Joe still redolent in the car. Leather and lime, musky and astringent . . . It swam through her senses, more fancy than fact, and made her think of damp, twisted sheets and glistening muscles. Olive skin and gravelly endearments. And strong, callused hands.

Her movements were desultory as she unpacked her bag and prepared for bed. She was besotted with the afterimage of his embraces, her body limp and submissive to his lingering imprint. Just remembering how she had arrived at that utter lassitude pricked her with a desire for more. The act of love, feeding upon itself. It was indecent, she thought. If he were in this room right now, they would probably be falling upon each other again.

Sweet cupcake, I love loving you.

That wasn't love, it was chemistry. But how could

mere chemistry engage every scrap of her essence like this? Even after her shower, she could feel the texture of his tongue lapping at specks of sand on her skin, his fingers exploring her mound. Floating toward sleep on the sultry residue of passionate excess, she smiled. Chemistry or love . . . Whatever it was, it had unquestionably been the most blatantly carnal weekend she had ever experienced in her life. It was like having climbed Everest, having reached the pole; it left her content, with no further ambition.

The following morning the languorous mood persisted, enveloping her like a heavy cloud, until it was dispelled by the express package that arrived just before noon. She opened the package, and Joe vanished from her mind as though he had never existed.

Inside the envelope was a slim, untitled manuscript, and it was accompanied by a shoe box filled with four-by-five-inch photographs. With the manuscript was a handwritten note on Robert Shankel's small letterhead.

"Call me after you've read this. The author is a news photographer who lived with a rebel family in Afghanistan for a year. He can't write, but the details are meticulous—everything he heard and saw and ate and felt. Is there a story line in it? If it strikes you as commercial film material, I can probably get it for you. It'll be much more challenging than Varney's farce, but less money."

Chalice put on a full pot of coffee, then sat down at her desk with the package. It wasn't a simple piece to figure out, she discovered, struggling through the numbered photographs and trying to match them with the text. The miscellany was a journal, written with more haste than method, and confusingly interspersed with rambling captions which only occasionally corresponded to the pictures. But the detail was overwhelming.

It was five o'clock before she was through. Dialing Robert's number, she felt the first stirring of creative excitement she'd known since her last lunch with Sam Firestone.

"What's the deal, Robert?" she asked him. "I'm interested."

"I thought you might be," he said. "But you'd better know the worst up front before you make up your mind."

"And that is?"

"It's a skinny budget—a director you've never heard of is producing it himself with what seems to be Mexican money."

"Can he pull it off?"

"He's done it before, but only in Canada. He's a Canuck by the name of Gerry Damboise. He's produced and directed two full-length features, actually. Not moneymakers, but one of them picked up several award nominations, and they both did well enough to break even. This time he's connected with Cosmos Studios."

"So there is a distribution deal?"

"Not really. There's no marketing money to speak of. They'll probably release two prints and pray for word of mouth."

Robert was playing the downside for all it was worth, she thought, but there was an enthusiasm in his voice that he couldn't disguise.

"And you still think he's got enough financing to get it made?" she said. But if he hadn't thought that, he wouldn't have asked her to read it.

He laughed. "When it's wrapped, he'll probably

have to borrow a few hundred for the prints. But yes, there's just enough to cover production costs, using a cast of unknowns."

The absence of stars didn't put her off. Some of the best talent available was virtually unknown to the public. It never hurt a film artistically; it merely increased the risk for the investors. The Mexicans were prepared to take that risk, apparently.

"Afghanistan is off-limits for shooting, of course," Robert went on, "both politically and financially, but the author says the High Sierras could double for the Afghani highlands, and he has pictures to prove it. Kabul would have to be reproduced in the studios, but I don't think that would be a problem." He paused for a moment to think.

"But the thing of it is, Chalice, your contract would only guarantee you fifty thousand. There's no room for negotiation. You might not ever see a nickel more than that, and you'll have a hell of a writing job to do. As you can see for yourself, there's no story line to work from, just extensive resource material."

A deep layer of her mind began to agitate. Unformed ideas laboring to be born. She recognized the signs, and with a leap of excitement, she knew the story was just days away.

A story of hope and suspense. Guerilla warfare, heroic struggle, sabotage, dangerous sorties, and an East-West love story pressed out of the ravages of a mountain winter.

As she listened to Robert outlining the logistics of the project, her eye roamed the photos laid out on her desk and her carpet. And while she looked, she remembered the essence of the captions.

Soviet soldiers with high school faces, briefed to

expect a trained army, and appalled to be facing eight-year-old urchins. Children armed with carbines they are barely big enough to hold and aim. Russian teenagers fresh from home facing their own shocking version of Vietnam. Toddlers with black hair and huge accepting eyes. Fierce, bearded tribesmen, and women aged with timeless suffering. An ignorant Western journalist, desperately in love, afraid, and trapped in a tragedy he can neither escape nor change.

Her hand tightened on the phone. "There may not be a story line yet," she said, "but all the elements are there. Get it for me, Robert. Please."

Damboise was a slender young man with light hair and a rather delicate face that looked overburdened with his heavy horn-rimmed glasses. Cosmos Studios hadn't yet cleared him a working space, so he was meeting with Chalice in the small conference room adjacent to Robert's office. They sat alone at one end of the long conference table, and they sized each other up over cups of powerful office coffee.

His Quebec origins were detectable more in his formal hauteur than in his diction. "You might as well know," he told her, "the only reason I'm considering you is because you seem willing to work for a pittance."

For an unknown director on a shoestring budget, he was a bit short on charm. Flattery will get you nowhere, she wanted to say. But she was too interested in the job to risk sarcasm at this point.

"You've written four screenplays," he went on, blinking behind the heavy lenses. "I know that only one of them was ever produced, but you must be used to more generous terms than this. Your willing-

ness to undersell your services suggests several possibilities, but I hope it means that the project truly
interests you as a writer."

"It does," she said.

There was only one other thing it could have
meant: that she was desperate—either for money or
for a screen credit. Chalice sipped her coffee, strik-
ing an attitude which she hoped was carefully poised
between creative interest and personal indifference.

He smiled at her, a little friendlier now. "Robert
is confident you'll do a fine job. In fact he talks most
impressively of your conceptual skills." His palms
lifted in a faintly Gallic shrug. "But then, he's your
agent. I've seen samples of your television work, and
it's not at all what I have in mind for my film."

"I should hope not," Chalice said evenly. "But
one rises to the challenge in this kind of work. Or
stoops to the level of others. Whatever is required."
That wasn't quite accurate. She had never felt a job
was beneath her while she was writing it; the man's
arrogance was catching, she thought.

But the pompous remark seemed to sit well with
Damboise. He nodded. "I'm from Montreal," he
said, "and I know little of Mr. Varney except what
Robert has told me. Is it true that you've just turned
down his offer of ninety-five thousand dollars for a
simple adaptation, so that you could work with me?"

Chalice gulped. "Yes."

His gentle laugh relaxed her. "A silly question,"
he said. "I could hardly expect you to deny it, but
let's get down to specifics. What can a young woman
of your background know of the realities of guerilla
war in the Hindu Kush?"

"About as much as George Lucas knows of inter-
galactic wars," she said.

"But we're talking fact, Miss York. Not fantasy."

He was right of course. It was a thoughtless retort, and it wouldn't wash. Chalice pushed her Styrofoam cup aside and sat up straight. It was time for a serious statement of her credo, and she spoke with care, weighing everything that Robert had told her about Damboise.

"I don't know as much about the subject as Fred Hallifax at the moment. I doubt anyone in Hollywood does. But Hallifax can't write a screenplay. He does have a talent for keeping records, though, and an extraordinary eye for literal detail. I have his photo journal, and Robert tells me the man will be available for consultation. By the time I've finished, I'll know exactly how it was and how it felt, down to the tastes and the smells and the fear."

His look suggested skepticism.

"That's my responsibility as an artist," she went on. "To take in knowledge—firsthand, secondhand, anyway I can get it—and then transform it with inner knowledge and skill."

He was listening more attentively now, and she continued with confidence.

"It's also the artist's job to know what to omit, how to bend the facts to serve the artistic truth, how to build a story line that works. In other words, to complete a script from which you can create a rich and textured emotional experience for the audience. I can do that. Hallifax can't."

Damboise removed his glasses and sat quiet for a while. Then he asked, "Have you formed any ideas yet?"

"I only received the material yesterday, but yes, I have."

In point of fact, Chalice had stayed up until four

that morning, roughing out the treatment. The entire story had jelled in her mind and poured itself out, faster than she could commit it to paper.

"I think it should be freer than a docudrama, but less contrived than pure fiction. Unlike the journal," she told him, "I would show the story from three points of view—the American's, the Afghani girl's, and the young Soviet soldier's."

"That would be difficult." Damboise looked troubled.

It wasn't the obvious approach, she knew that. It would maximize the technical problems with foreign dialogue and lay a heavier burden on the principal actors, the cinematographer, and the director. It would also require bold leaps of imagination from her, but she had already made most of them. She was convinced it was worth the effort, and she was eager to convince Damboise. Watching him, she decided he was open to persuasion.

The distance between them seemed to fall away as he leaned his elbows on the table, openly interested.

"Go on," he said.

Twenty minutes later, when Robert Shankel walked in on them, Damboise was gesticulating, and his French accent had thickened with excitement. Chalice leaned toward him, shaking her head and interrupting him. Or rather they were cutting in on each other, exchanging mysterious sentence fragments which were intelligible only to them.

"I take it you two see eye to eye," Robert said drily. "You're fighting already. Good sign."

Rapt in their exchange, Chalice and Damboise looked up at him with similarly blank expressions. Robert's presence had become totally irrelevant to both of them. He smiled.

"Don't give the store away yet, Chalice. I know it's crass of me, but I'd like a signed contract before you put out." He turned to the Canadian, whose boisterous laughter filled the room, and knew the man was already high on the idea of working with Chalice.

"What are you," Damboise quipped, "her pimp or something?"

"My, but we're elated," Robert mumbled, and joined them at the table. He cast Damboise a rueful look. "And so you should be. You just bought yourself the services of a top-flight screenwriter for a steal."

"Here's my hand on it," Damboise said, "before she changes her mind. I'll tell Cosmos to prepare the contract immediately."

In terms of the studio's legal department, immediately meant three days, and it was Friday before Chalice heard from Robert again.

"Four copies are sitting on my desk," he told her. "That was damn fast. And when you take a look at his production schedule, you'll know why. It'll curl your hair. You'd better get your fanny in here this minute and sign, so you can start on the prelims."

"I'm on my way," she told him.

She didn't tell him the treatment was already finished and that she was waiting right now to hear back from Damboise. In fact, if his hiring schedule hadn't been so grueling, she would have already met with the director again. She had tried to reach him twice. But he was doing a thousand things at once as he settled into his office at Cosmos. He was casting the principals single-handedly, combing the talent agencies for the right ethnic types, and hunting down

Russian and Pushtu interpreters to consult on dialogue. He didn't even have an assistant yet. The only way she could leave a message was through an executive's secretary at Cosmos.

Perhaps it was just as well, Chalice thought, as she dodged the late lunch traffic on Century City Boulevard. Robert would have strangled her if she'd shown any material to Damboise before the contract was signed.

It was past five by the time she got home from Robert's. She tried Damboise again, but the studio switchboard had closed for the evening. He was probably there right now, she thought, in one of those rabbit warrens they had over the soundstages, but she didn't have his direct-line number.

A recorded voice thanked her for calling Cosmos Studios. "Please call us again between—" Chalice hung up, swearing at the bankers' hours they kept, and checked her answering service. The service, at least, functioned around the clock, and they had heard from Damboise while she was out. Debra, the night operator, read out the message.

"He says he'd like a script session at seven on Tuesday morning," the operator told her. "And drop off a copy of your treatment at the Belmont Hotel as soon as you can. He wants to study it before you meet. He gave me two numbers where you can reach him."

Tuesday, she thought, jotting down the phone numbers. It seemed like a long time to wait, when she was raring to go.

"Did you get those numbers?" Debra asked. "The first one's his hotel. The other one's his office line."

"Got it," Chalice said.

"And please don't call him unless you have to, he

says. He's very busy. There's only one other—
Would you hold, please? Got to catch another call."

Chalice waited and thought about the frustration
of three wasted days. There was no sense in starting
on the script until they'd agreed on the narrative
approach. Even then, directors had a penchant for
throwing out scenes and demanding new ones all the
way down the line. She smiled to herself. Damboise
wouldn't, though. He'd be too damn busy spreading
himself thin. Perhaps she could spend the time
roughing out a few—

Debra's voice came back on the line. "Chalice,
are you still there? That was Joe Verdi again. He
hung up before I could connect him. He called
before and left his number. Do you have it?"

"Yes."

"Okay, then. That's all I have for you at the
moment."

After she hung up, she wrote Damboise's numbers in her card file, scratched in the Tuesday
appointment on her calendar, then looked at the
large white envelope on her desk. It was a clean copy
of her treatment, all ready to hand over to
Damboise. She'd wait until the traffic thinned out,
then run it over to his hotel, she thought. Knowing
how preproduction schedules went, she figured he'd
probably read it in bed that night if his eyes would
stay open.

She was a little reluctant to call Joe. Since the
package had arrived on Monday, the memory of her
weekend had shrunk considerably. When her mind
was engaged with a new project, there was little
space for anything else.

The week had been eventful and filled with challenge. She was in top form, and the work in hand

was nourishing. Creative work made her feel strong, fulfilled, and in control. Joe made her feel weak and doll-like, ruinously out of control. He had satisfied her sexually, and yet those satisfactions had led only to a renewed hunger for more of the same. A sensory circle, she thought. A vicious circle. But now she was halted on the job for three days . . .

When she dialed Joe's number, she was irritated with herself, knowing that the sound of his voice would promptly break down the delicate balance of mind and energy that were so perfectly tuned for work. She hung up the phone and laughed. He wasn't home. He'd called from outside. All that fussing over nothing. Hunger pangs reminded her that she hadn't eaten all day, and she headed for the refrigerator.

A frozen dinner was cooking in her oven when Joe called her again.

"Gotcha," he said. "I'm at Pacifica Studios, and I've just dropped off the completed first draft. It's done, and I feel like celebrating. I've got until Monday before Ryan starts tearing it apart. Do you feel like being wined and dined and so forth?"

He hadn't missed her either, she thought, unaccountably piqued by his airiness. "I just signed a movie contract," she told him.

"That's wonderful! We'll celebrate that instead. Let's see." He paused. "We could start out at the Polo Lounge, go on to Ma Maison . . . Or The Bistro maybe? Scandia? That's all I've ever heard of out here." He paused. "Look, you'll have to help me out. You know this town a lot better than I do." He waited for a response.

"Hey, York! Are you still there? Cupcake, you're

not saying very much. You're not working right now, are you? Did I break in on it?"

"No, not exactly. Actually I can't work now. I'm waiting approval, so I can't do a thing before next week. I was thinking about it, that's all. I'm just not in the mood to get all dressed up, and . . ."

"Well," he cut in eagerly, "you'll get no argument from me. If you're in a mood to strip down, that's okay too. More than okay. Don't move. I'll be right over."

That wasn't what she meant at all, and a flash of anger seized her at his lewd flippancy. But it drained away before she could express it. Instead, she seemed to be explaining herself, half apologetic. "What I mean is, I'm pretty compulsive when I'm working, Joe. I generally don't stop till I drop."

"Wait a minute. You just said you can't work until . . ." He broke off, then came back warily. "I guess . . . Are you sore at me or something? I know. I'm a selfish crumb, not calling you all week, then expecting you to drop everything and—"

"I'm not sore, Joe. It's not that. It's just . . . well . . . don't you ever get so hooked into your work that you just can't change gears?"

He sighed. "Of course . . . I'm sorry. I'm a prize idiot. You want to talk about it? The new contract, I mean?"

She had an errand to run at the Belmont Hotel, and she agreed to meet him there. He took a cab from the studio and arrived long before her. By the time he'd hung around the red and gold lobby for twenty minutes dwelling on his flaws, Joe had come to the conclusion that he was a hopeless klutz. He had no finesse at all. No sensitivity. A loser with women. When had he lost his touch?

Chalice was clutching a large white envelope when she hurried into the lobby, and without looking around for him, she dropped it off at the desk. In clinging blue jeans and an old windbreaker that was the same color as her eyes, she looked remote and classy. He could have sworn she was even several inches taller than he remembered, striding purposefully across the gold carpet in her sneakers. She looked like high society slumming at the faded old hotel.

But she insisted she was "far too scummy" to dine out, so they stopped for some Chinese takeout on the way back to her apartment. It was a slow drive in the thick of the Friday dinner traffic, and he spent the time trying to make amends for being a grade-A boor, drawing her out about her new job.

It wasn't hard. She was totally wrapped up in it. The aristocratic remoteness dropped away, and waves of frank enthusiasm lit up her words as she talked. In the dimness of the car, she glowed like a candle, igniting him with desire. She was in some high cerebral gear, and he tried to follow her there, when all he really wanted to do was unwind. He longed to release the coiled tightness inside him, to cover her with kisses, and find her breasts under the loose windbreaker. But he behaved impeccably throughout the ride. He'd been warned. "I don't stop till I drop," she'd told him.

They could both smell it as she unlocked her front door.

"The oven!" she screamed, and fled for the kitchen.

What had once been frozen chicken and oriental vegetables had baked into a passable prehistoric fossil. When she threw it into the kitchen trash, it disintegrated into fine black carbon. She drew her hand out of the oven mitt and laughed. "Did I mention that I get absentminded when I work? I get oblivious of everything around me."

Joe drew white boxes out of the sack from Lu-Wong's and set them on the kitchen counter. "Then maybe I should remind you that the egg Foo-Yong is cooling rapidly."

"Not to worry, love. I can heat it up in the microwave."

She was next to him, reaching for dishes on a high shelf above the counter. She had removed her windbreaker, and her breasts pressed against the pale cotton of her shirt as she stretched up.

And she had called him love.

"Can I get those for you?" he asked. His voice sounded pleading to him, desperate with the need to hold her against him, but she was drawing out the dishes as he spoke.

"Thanks. I've got them." She set down the china and kissed his cheek.

When she tried to draw away, he caught her up again and yielded for a few moments to the temptations he'd resisted in the car. He couldn't even disguise the urgent tempo of his breathing. "I've been wanting to do that ever since you picked me up," he said.

Their lips met, their tongues touched, her breast flowed into the hollow of his hand, filling his palm with undulating warmth. She kissed him back, murmuring sounds of encouragement from deep in her throat. So frankly responsive now, that his heart began to thud.

"I should warn you," he said, pulling back and laughing at the sudden thickness in his voice. "I don't stop till I drop. We'd better eat. I wouldn't want to ruin two meals in one night for you."

"I have a microwave," she said, and drew his head down again to find his mouth. "It'll keep."

She tugged the hem of his knit top and led him to her bed. But he was watchful, hesitant, as if he feared to break the ground rules she'd laid down for the evening. With desire squeezing his lungs and shortening his breath, he still cared more about harmonizing with her mood than gratifying his need. The knowledge touched her, curling around her heart like wisps of gray smoke as she undressed him, peeled off her clothes, and held out her arms to him.

This was different, she thought, covering him with her kisses, her hands, her body. Quite different from the stormy ravages of last weekend. This time it was she who was making love, anxious to please and satisfy, and deriving more sensual pleasure from his responses than from her own. He was gentle, tentative, almost subdued, as if they were strangers and her body was quite new to him. It filled her with a desire to give and with the sudden knowledge that never before tonight had she been much more than a passive partner in the act of love.

There was a moment of culmination beyond words, beyond mere chemistry, when he shuddered at the crest, and she felt the hot spurt of his sap pass from his core to the innermost depths of hers. Fulfillment, she thought, was unrelated to the flesh. It was a function of the soul. Then she smiled at her fancy, like a mad prophet whose blinding flashes of clarity were imponderable to the sane, and held him tightly in her arms and let him rest.

When his breathing slowed, she slipped out of bed and put on a tunic sweater, then searched through her closet for her father's old cashmere dressing gown. She couldn't wear it herself without tripping over the hem, but there had been times when she'd wrapped herself in it for comfort.

She brought it to the bed. Joe lay on his back with his eyes closed. His hand was idly feeling the sheet, searching for her.

"I'm here," she said. "I'm going to heat up the food. You don't have to get up yet. I'll call you when it's ready, and you can wear this. It was Dad's." She laid the soft, camel-colored garment on the bed. It had never occurred to her to lend it to a lover, but somehow it was important that Joe should wear it. For the first time in ten years, a man would fill it.

It was startling the way thoughts of the screenplay rose up to greet her as she heated the food. It was as if she had set them down in the kitchen, and they had developed like Polaroid photos while she was gone. She could see the shots clearly now—the pans, wipes, close-ups, long shots.

The group huddled into a snowbank, hidden from the road; armored jeeps laboring up the road, nearing a wire that trips a crude mine. In the second jeep rides a soldier who is little more than a schoolboy in his ill-fitting uniform.

The vision faded as Chalice put a kettle of water on to boil. They were about to eat Chinese food. Somewhere in the pantry she had some China tea to go with the food. She found the package, then stood, waiting for the water to boil . . .

The Russian kid is familiar by now, and so is the

*picture of his girl back home, another blond Ukraini-
an in her midteens. He always labors over his letters
to her. How can he tell her they're killing civilians?
That he shot a little boy? We can guess he's still
thinking about that. One quick flash of the Afghani
child's face, superimposed as the jeeps approach the
hidden tripwire.*

Chalice dragged her mind back to Santa Monica
and set plates on the table. Cups. Forks . . .

*Dark faces, motionless against the snow. The
American full-bearded now, under a hat made of
black lamb's fur. He is indistinguishable from the
others, except for the eyes. The pale blue eyes narrow
as the sound of motors rises. Flat crunch of tires on
snow as the lead jeep passes right by them . . . the
explosion only seconds away—*

She jumped and let out a stifled scream as a hand
touched her shoulder. Then she sagged against the
refrigerator, clutching her throat and laughing.

"Sorry I startled you," Joe said.

"You sure did. Bare feet. I didn't hear you come
in."

He grinned, folding his arms over the wrapped V
of the dressing gown. "And you were about six
thousand miles away with a bunch of bearded mountain men in tall fur hats."

She nodded, looking a little sheepish. "How did
you guess?"

"Look, it's okay if you want me to shut up while
you think. As long as we can eat at the same time."

But she had no desire to close him out. On the
contrary, thoughts of work evaporated as soon as
she laid eyes on him.

"How did *The Snipe* turn out?" she asked him as
they dug into the Manadarin feast.

He shrugged. "It went smoothly enough once I got down to it. I don't doubt Ryan will discover serious flaws, though. But you must have had enough of *The Snipe* to last a lifetime. Tell me about your new director. What's he like?"

She told him, describing her first meeting with Gerry Damboise.

"You're putting me on, aren't you?" Joe said, over a mound of shredded beef and snow peas.

"What do you mean?"

"Well, you didn't actually say that."

"Of course I did."

He put down his fork and rested his elbows on the table. "I mean all that stuff about the artist's responsibility and inner knowledge?"

Chalice tilted her head at him, narrowing her eyes for a moment. Then she gave a slow smile. "If you think that was a bit pretentious for an interview, well, I guess you had to be there. The guy was holding court."

Joe shook his head, puzzled. "I wasn't thinking pretentious so much as, well—entirely irrelevant. How did art get into this?"

She went on chewing, staring at Joe blankly, and then she swallowed. "The subject was a movie script," she reminded him.

He nodded. "My point exactly."

"Okay, Joe, okay." She rolled her eyes with a mocking lift of her head. "So it's *not* legitimate theatre. So the industry's rife with exploitation movies and most of what's out there is pure junk, just like most music and most television and most printed fiction and most paintings. So *what*? It doesn't mean that, at its best, the motion picture can't qualify as an art form."

Joe spluttered, then rested his head on his hand, shaking with laughter. "Bullshit! You think using tony words like 'academy' and 'cinematography' can turn this ball of wax into an art form?"

Chalice sat tall in her chair. "No. But the right blend of artistic skills under good direction can. Just because it's an illusion and multidisciplined doesn't mean it can't be classified as a performing art."

"Oh yeah? Name me another performing art where the audience eats popcorn all the way through the performance." He flashed a bright grin. "Cupcake, it's art like a baseball game is art. Like a three-ring circus is art."

Heat crept up her throat and touched her neck. "Don't cupcake me. You know what you are? You're an intellectual snob."

"Me? I'm just a guy from a blue-collar neighborhood of South Philly . . . I give up. What do I know, anyway?" He touched the tip of her nose in a conciliatory gesture. "Are you going to finish that?" he asked, looking at the remainder of food on her plate.

"No. Do you want it?"

He shook his head and rose, taking their plates and scraping them off into the sink.

She was sitting at the table, her mind still on their argument, when he came back and stood behind her, rubbing the nape of his neck. "All I want right now is to make nice."

A pleasant ease suffused her as his fingers slid up the short sleeves of her tunic, caressing her shoulders.

"Know something?" he murmured, breathing into her hair. "Arguing with you has a potent effect on me. All that charged talk about the performing arts," he murmured. "Watching you sitting there in that abbreviated shift, getting so heated. It turns me on. I don't suppose you're in the mood . . ."

She wasn't sure what mood she was in. It was hard to determine anything when he was stroking her this way. But the argument was fading from her mind. It was pleasing just to sit there and have her slightly ruffled feathers smoothed.

He massaged her neck and shoulders. "I'm a Philistine, I suppose. An animal. You probably would rather kick me out and settle down to listen to Mahler's fifth," he said ruefully, "instead of having me breathe hot lust on your neck . . . your shoulders . . . your ears . . ."

The soft touch of a cashmere sleeve brushed her arm. His hands crested her shoulders and smoothed along the curve of her collarbone. "You have a tiny heart-shaped freckle tucked in the hollow of your left collarbone," he said softly.

"It's a birthmark," she breathed, shivering as he kissed it.

"It's beautiful."

His palms slid down over the tunic, and his fingers spread, stopping just short of the tips of her breasts. She caught the warm fragrance of plum sauce and tea as his lips rounded her cheek, and gasped at the surge of heat that rose in her.

Twisting around in her chair, she smiled up at him and slid her hand over the soft cashmere, pressing it against the hard muscles of his stomach.

"The natives are restless," he said, capturing her hand and pushing it lower, against the hard swell of his desire.

"Insurgencies in the lowlands," she murmured, curling her fingers around him. "What shall we do, Your Excellency?"

He scooped her from the chair and carried her out of the kitchen. "Call in the brigade," he muttered, "and take strong, active measures."

Chalice thought no more of work until she parted from Joe on Monday morning, coasting through the weekend with him in a profusion of delight and wonder.

Chapter 8

Joe felt a strange detachment from his work throughout the following week. The rewrites in the script were not extensive, no more than a day's work. He took a week over them, though, partly because there was no hurry, but mostly because he couldn't seem to stay at the typewriter for more than an hour at a time. He broke up his work sessions with long bouts of jogging and reflection on the phenomenon of Chalice York.

Always the same route; he would point himself east outside the house, then turn north at the second intersection. By the time he passed the white picket fence of the Hickory Dickory Preschool, he was running on second wind, no longer conscious of physical effort. He would climb the steep grade of the hill at an easy pace, his mind coasting free, until he saw himself in her kitchen again, eating egg Foo-Yong on white porcelain plates and arguing . . .

Putting down the film industry to Chalice York of all people, while he lounged around in her kitchen wearing Jeffrey York's dressing gown. How could he be such a tactless idiot?

She was giving him a severe case of two left feet, that girl with her finishing school diction and her movieland parents.

Chalice. He couldn't even bring himself to address her by her given name. It was funny how he had no trouble at all badmouthing the York family trade.

Cresting the hill, he would plunge steeply downward, weaving across the pavement to slow himself down.

Late Friday night, she had spoken of her childhood. Even her mother turned out to be royalty. Kyla Storm, the star who had reigned for a few memorable years as the epitome of Hollywood chic; at least for Joe she had. He must have been about sixteen at the time, he figured. He had seen all Kyla Storm's movies and he still remembered her quite clearly, a dark-haired, seriously beautiful woman on the order of Ali McGraw and Audrey Hepburn.

Chalice York. This girl who lived in an ordinary apartment, dressed in gray sweats while she worked, and wore her hair in unruly bangs, this girl was flesh-and-blood daughter to Kyla Storm. Jeez! He'd been making it with a genuine princess. And shooting off his mouth like a fool. She had no right to come on like such a real person; it made him forget her awesome pedigree.

She seemed to make him forget a lot of things, he realized, not least among them, Shirley.

Not even George had guessed the extent of his desolation this past year. George assumed that a divorce couldn't do much damage when the marriage had only lasted a year. As if the same arithmetic applied to human relationships as applied to savings plans or treasury bills. That's not the way it works, George.

Sure, Shirley was only wife-for-a-year, but it was a year when he'd forgotten any other way to live. He had been flush with money at the time, tired of flip relationships. Ripe for marriage. His days had slipped quickly and irrevocably into a new pattern: A mortgage in Westport. A sweet, lovely, scatter-brained wife, and a solemn toddler who had started to call him Daddy-Joe. Then the jarring back to a single life he was no longer equipped to cope with because, although Shirley had left him, a part of her stayed, some part that had become as intrinsic to his feelings as the grain on wood.

But that was no longer true, it dawned on him. Shirley had actually stopped haunting him, and he could thank Chalice for that. He'd also quit living on Di-Gel's, and he supposed he could thank her for that too. She had made Hollywood palatable.

Joe tried to figure out what it meant, his first romantic preoccupation since Shirley. He hadn't been looking for it; it was the wrong time for him, and the wrong place. He seemed to have slipped into this away-from-home affair by pure happenstance—with a princess of celluloid, no less. It was comforting and dizzying by turns, and often downright infuriating. But it was filling the voids, salving wounds. Perhaps it was no more than a Band-Aid, this sudden attachment. He refused to believe he was falling in love again when he still wasn't over the last attack. Still, it was more than just getting laid.

Frighteningly more. By Monday evening, when he called her and she wasn't home, he started missing her as if she were a million light-years away.

All week he thought about it, talking to her on the telephone a couple of times, but not seeing her.

Once his rewrite was finished, Ryan put Joe on hold for a few days. Preproduction was in full swing and he wasn't needed. Preproduction, that Hollywood euphemism for the widespread chaos raging at Pacifica Studios as Walter Ryan and his battery of assistants raced toward zero hour on *The Snipe*, the first day of film production. Once they were into it, he'd have to be on the set for grueling twelve-hour days of shooting—mostly just hanging around in case they needed him. It seemed like a terrible waste of time, but thus it was written in his contract; and they were paying enough for it.

"Rest up, Joe," Ryan told him. "Conserve your energy. You'll need it." But time hung heavy on his hands.

Chalice was submerged in her own script. He had called her one morning and woken her from a sound sleep. She'd been working just about round the clock and had just gone to bed. He promised not to disturb her again, suggesting she call him when she wanted to take a break. But she hadn't called. He was frantic to hear from her, pining like a teenager, but he wouldn't acknowledge it. He wasn't going to climb out of one dark pit just to fall into another. Oh no.

He passed the time reading and working out at a Brentwood health club, where they offered him a guest membership. The club was four miles from the house, and if he jogged there and walked back, it took up whole chunks of the day. Afternoons, he would laze around reading in the backyard and sunning himself if the weather was right. March could be capricious, he discovered, even in Lotus Land.

On his third and last free day, he was returning from the market with a sack of groceries when he heard the phone ringing inside. By the time he'd got into the house, it had stopped.

It was ten in the morning and already hot enough to make the four-mile run to the health club seem like a drag. With no hope of seeing Chalice, the idle day stretched out before him like a wasteland. It couldn't have been her phoning, he thought; she was deep into *The Hindu Kush*. She didn't know he existed. It had probably been the studio reminding him to show up tomorrow.

After he put away the groceries, he couldn't stand the wondering, and dialed her number.

"I just missed a call," he said. "I was hoping it was you. If it wasn't, I'll let you go. I know you're busy."

"Yes, I called. I just finished the script, after a fashion. A hundred and thirty-five pages." She sounded punchy.

"That's fantastic," he said, "but won't that be over two hours' running time?"

"Not really. A whole bunch is crossed out. I worked so fast, half of it doesn't make sense, but it does to me. It's just editing and polishing now, about ten hours' worth. Only I can't do any more, my eyes are crossing. I've worked myself to a standstill. I can't even sleep. I've been trying for an hour, but my brain's overstimulated. Are you still at loose ends? If so, could I come over for a while?"

"I'll come to you," Joe said. "You shouldn't be driving in that state. You're liable to hallucinate."

"But Joe, it's such a long cab ride, I—"

"No arguments. I'm on my way."

When he arrived, she wanted to drive them down to the beach. He insisted on taking the wheel, muttering about Californians who would get in their cars just to visit a next-door neighbor.

"But it's almost four miles," she told him.

He squeezed her shoulder and beamed. "In that case, maybe we should charter a plane."

As they crossed the road that fronted the beach, they were brushed by a whispering breeze that lifted their hair and set the palm fronds swaying high above the boulevard. A scattering of old folks sat on park benches enjoying the weather, but the beach itself was empty. It was a spring day of pure gold, except for the silver iridescence on the water.

In cropped pants, string shirt, and headband, she looked like a flower child from the sixties, he thought. She strolled beside him along the water's edge, kicking idly at stranded clumps of seaweed. Hyper from too much coffee and brainstorming, she wound herself down by talking nonstop about *The Hindu Kush,* then drifting to the subject of audiovisual entertainment in general. His heart was light, and he was happy just to listen and nod for a while.

Joe scooped up some small shells, and began to play jacks with them as they walked. "I'll go along with that," he was saying, "but not when it comes to commercial TV. That doesn't even qualify as mass entertainment, much as it pretends to. It's an advertising medium first and foremost, just like a billboard."

Chalice stopped to slip off her sandals. "I suppose

'so, but nobody sponsors theatrical movies to sell soap and breakfast food. At least you can't call them an advertising medium."

"I didn't."

"So you admit at least that movies are entertainment."

"Not primarily."

"Come on!"

"These days they're more often loss leaders. Come-on ads to promote the sale of popcorn, soda, and overpriced candy."

She poked him in the ribs and ran off down the beach, calling, "Popcorn to you too, buddy!"

"The industry doesn't make one red cent on the concessions," she told him when he caught up with her. "Only the theatre owners profit from that. If what you said were true, the whole movie business would collapse."

The color that had been briefly whipped up in her face from the sea breeze was beginning to fade, and he could tell how fatigued she was under the brittle nervous energy. A wave of protective tenderness seized him, and he put an arm around her shoulder. "For your sake, I hope that doesn't happen."

"Of course it won't," she said. "In the fifties, television was going to kill it. In the seventies, it was inflated production costs, home video recorders, and wall-size TV screens. You name it and it's always supposed to be the kiss of death to the movies. But they still build hundreds of new theatres each year, with bigger and better equipment. And now, pay-TV and home videos are providing a new secondary market for movies. It's about forty percent of the revenues and climbing every year."

"You're right," he whispered.

"Aren't you going to argue with me?" she asked, a shade disappointed.

"Nope."

"Aw shucks." She sat down on the smooth sand and stretched out, exhaustion suddenly washing over her like a warm wave.

"Hey, this is damp," he said, hunkering down beside her. "It'll soak through your clothes."

"Who cares?" She curled up on her side and pillowed her hands under her cheek. "I want to take a nap."

"Come on, babe," he said. He hauled her to her feet, brushed off her clothes, and steered her back across the boulevard. "I'm going to take you home and put you to bed."

And that was quite literally what he'd done, she remembered, waking at seven the next morning. He had put her to bed like a child and even scraped out the sand from between her toes because she was too sleepy to take a shower.

Groggy from sixteen hours of sleep, Chalice soaked in a warm tub and thought about the note Joe had left on her pillow. She felt slightly cheated by her long sleep.

"Cupcake," he had written, "In the refrig is a frozen dinner I cooked for you earlier. But I didn't have the heart to wake you when it was ready. I suppose you could revive it in the microwave? I waited until 11 p.m. and you didn't stir, so I've gone home. Have to be in the studio at the crack of dawn.

"The key on the kitchen table is to my place. Feel free to use it whenever you feel like it. I'll be getting home around seven tonight and every night until we go off on location. Sleep tight. Judging by the state of your desk, you've earned it. I'll give you a call around noon."

She was touched and wanted to tell him so. But it would have to keep until he called.

The morning was chilly, and after her bath, she drew on sweatpants and a fleecy top, then turned to her work. One good session, and it would be ready to clean-type, she decided.

The rough version lay on her desk, the numbered pages still scattered as she had left them when she'd stopped abruptly in the middle of reading it through. She turned back to page one, pen in hand, borne on a fresh wave of energy.

Luke was down-in-the-mouth. She knew he'd done a lot of auditioning recently and had been passed over for several parts, but it turned out to be more than that. She invited him in for a chat the next evening when he came off his shift at the Chickeeburger.

"Sharon just got engaged to an engineer," he told her. "She said she was tired of waiting. We've been going steady since eleventh grade. Know what she said? 'It'd be different if you were ever going to make anything of yourself, but obviously you're not.'" Luke hung his head, staring into his tall glass of milk as he bent over her kitchen counter. "Do you think she's right, Chalice?"

"Of course not. I'm sorry about Sharon, but another girl will come along. You'll have no problem there. As for making something of yourself, you have to give it a bit more time, Luke. You've only been at it a few months. It just doesn't happen overnight."

He sighed. "It does for some people."

Her heart went out to him. In his yellow and orange striped dungarees with the ridiculous Chickeeburger logo on the bib, he looked like a tragic clown. "It happens to one in a hundred thousand, maybe," she said. "The rest of us just do it the hard way, if we do it at all."

"Well, will I ever do it? Or do you think I might just as well go home now?" he asked mournfully.

"I don't have a crystal ball, honey, but don't go home yet. Not just because of Sharon, anyway," she said gently. "You owe yourself at least a year, don't you think?"

She watched him nod solemnly, feeling apprehensive about the influence she had over him. No matter how she protested, he seemed to think her advice was infallible. But perhaps it was the wrong advice. She knew his parents had agreed to a year of partial support while he explored his dream. Once he quit, he'd never have another chance.

"I'll leave you to your work," he said. "Sorry to barge in like this. I know how busy you are."

After he left, she wondered how he would handle the part of one of the Soviet draftees in *The Hindu Kush*. He was the right age, and he would look convincing enough in a Red Army uniform. He was quite capable of learning a few Russian words . . . Perhaps a nonspeaking role? There were several of those.

She discarded the idea, glad she hadn't mentioned it to him when she'd been making comforting noises. She really didn't know Damboise well enough to make that kind of suggestion, and anyway, he was already down to final decisions. Auditions and screen tests had just closed. She grinned. She'd been thinking like a stage mother. She was getting awfully maternal toward Luke.

There were unexpected advantages to a low-budget movie. Chalice discovered them as she worked with Damboise. Usually, the production of a full-length feature film was an unwieldly and wasteful extravaganza. But Damboise's production was trimmed lean and hard.

Actors had less rehearsal time, but not a second was wasted on imperious whims and narcissistic demands, because there were no big-name prima donnas who expected to be pampered. The principals were deep into their character study before their lines were ready.

The special effects man was severely limited in time and funds, but Damboise had chosen a newcomer to Hollywood who was determined to make his mark, and necessity sparked the man to astonishing invention. Damboise was something of a magician, she decided, because a similar alchemy seemed to be at work for the set and costume designers. In fact, just about everyone involved in *The Hindu Kush* was imbued with a sense of dedication.

Chalice could feel the extraordinary magic at work in herself. She didn't have the luxury of toying endlessly with second thoughts and leisurely polishing. Haste should have resulted in awkward transitions and stilted dialogue. Instead, sequences flowed naturally, and the spoken lines were urgent, sparse, and utterly spontaneous.

The mix of extreme time pressure and a difficult theme had brought out the best in her. Thrown back on the resources of a challenged imagination, she had risen to the occasion with an outpouring that surprised even her.

It also delighted Damboise, and he spent little time nitpicking on the script.

The narrative of *The Hindu Kush* spanned an entire year, requiring snow scenery for the winter and a matching topography of rocky red mountains for the summer. It sent Damboise and his designer scurrying to New Mexico, Utah, Colorado, and Nevada during preproduction, to find two locations that could pass for the same place, one for the winter scenes and one for the summer. As soon as they found what they wanted, production began.

Then he was plagued by the endless logistical and artistic problems raised by three hundred employees all plying their diverse trades and skills to one ambitious end. Given his schedule and his severe lack of staff, it was a backbreaking, mind-bending project.

Damboise had little time to question Chalice's choices, so he forced himself to trust her. She enjoyed such unprecedented freedom that the final shooting script was actually threatening to bear a recognizable resemblance to the first draft she had written from the treatment—a situation that was practically unheard of in Hollywood.

She worked a total of four weeks on the writing, but the intensive creative work was all done in the first ten days. The rest was easy: a minor change of action here and there to fit the limitations of the locations, a cut or two in the foreign dialogue to minimize the subtitles. It was all painless, effortless work. And it didn't cramp the blossoming of her friendship with Joe Verdi.

And it was blossoming.

Joe was confined to the Pacifica compound daily, but his evenings and weekends were free. She began to make more and more use of Joe's spare key, sometimes even surprising him with a home-cooked meal when he returned.

She was getting the hang of moderation in all things, she decided. A love life, an absorbing job, and a satisfying balance between the two. There was an even tenor to her rhythm of work and play.

There was an intense glow about the hours she spent with Joe. She had never felt so intensely alive with anyone, and yet afterward she could plunge into her work and submerge the thought of him for hours. And each time she came back to him, it was with renewed enthusiasm. It was as if their relationship was always fresh and couldn't go stale. It was ideal, she thought. Perfect. And she accepted that, like all perfect things, it would end.

She wouldn't be able to erase him completely when it was over, but she would handle it somehow. She was simply making the most of the temporary touching of two inevitably separate lives. She rarely allowed herself to give the relationship deeper significance, except at certain moments in their lovemaking, when the rules of the game seemed to crumble and her furthest horizons were filled only with Joe.

Joe was affectionate, but never sentimental. However, there were a few dangerous moments when he acted with such implicit tenderness that she began to wonder if either of them could ever draw back again and find themselves the way they used to be. But she would bury the fear as soon as she became aware of it.

One lazy Sunday, Joe even told her a little about his brief marriage to Shirley. A neurotic, Chalice decided, who had made a full-time profession of being a helpless little Southern woman. Perhaps that was only prejudice or an irrational dart of jealousy, she thought. Because Joe spoke of the woman with a fond indulgence that suggested he still cared for her.

"She still keeps in touch," he told Chalice vaguely.

He never said it, but somehow Chalice got the impression she only kept in touch when she needed bailing out of some folly. But that was only a momentary impression she couldn't pin down, and she didn't press him for details. Something told her the ice was a little thin there . . .

It seemed like no time at all before the last day of work on her contract rolled around, the Saturday when she would be tying up loose ends. The night before, she sat at her desk preparing herself for various last-hour meetings.

"We should mark the occasion," Joe said, "since there's no wrap party. Would you like to see a play or do something festive?"

Joe had been reading all evening, leaving her to work at her desk.

"Don't get tickets for anything," she said. "From the look of this clipboard, I'll be at the studio till all hours. I'd never make it by curtain time."

"But it's Saturday," he protested mildly.

"And the cutoff day on my contract, Joe. Damboise can't afford to be overbudget. This could go on till midnight."

Behind her, Joe made a rustling sound on the sofa. "Let's hope not. Maybe we can have a late supper when you're through. Somewhere different and special."

"Maybe. I sure hope so."

She had told him she had to stay home that evening and prepare for the meetings, but he had arrived at her apartment at six, armed with a barbecued chicken and a bottle of wine. "I'll behave," he'd promised. "But at least we can break bread together."

He had kept his word, insisting on cleaning up after they ate so that she could get back to her desk, then retiring to the sofa to read, quiet as a mouse. Three hours and she still wasn't through, and somehow she felt guilty about Joe sitting there all evening, waiting patiently for her to finish. Don't, she thought. You warned him. But she still felt bad about ignoring him all evening.

Behind her she heard him close the heavy book. "I have to touch bases with Fred Hallifax again tomorrow," she explained. "He wrote the journal. It's my last chance to go through the script with him. Checking out the facts. That's good for two hours. Maybe more. I'm making out a checklist for Fred right now."

She heard him rustling around on the sofa, trying not to be impatient.

"Then I'm due for a long session with the language interpreters."

"Is the foreign dialogue that big a deal?" he said.

Chalice swiveled her chair around and looked across the room at him. "Did you know there are twenty languages spoken in Afghanistan? Pushtu is the commonest, and that's the one Hallifax acquired to a degree. But Persian is the official language of government and the cities. There's a pivotal scene in Kabul, so we couldn't eliminate Persian entirely."

Joe chuckled. "Is anyone in America going to understand this movie?"

"We're talking about just a few lines, Joe. I've already cut foreign dialogue down to the bone, but what remains is crucial. The interpreters are complaining that the phonetic transliterations aren't coming out right in the mouths of American-born actors."

"Who'll know? Unless Pushtu or Persian is their native language of course."

Chalice sighed. "That happens to be the case for the translators. Damboise wants me to hear them out and give them the last word on the subject. He's a stickler for authenticity." She turned back to the desk, for once wishing Joe wasn't here. He was making her nervous. "And when all the itty-bitty problems are cleaned up, we come to the main purpose of the day, my sign-off meeting with Damboise."

Joe got up and stood behind her chair, rubbing her shoulders. "Do what you have to do, cupcake. I can take a hint." He kissed her cheek, then reached for his jacket. "See you tomorrow night. I'll be waiting for you no matter what time it is. I'm not going anywhere."

In bed that night, Joe was far too aware of being alone. It was scary how addicted he'd become to having her in this bed with him. It had only been four weeks.

He spent the next morning running errands and laying in some goodies, in case Chalice arrived that night too drained to go anywhere. He was straightening up the house late that afternoon when the phone rang.

It was typical of Shirley, he thought with a flash of irritation as soon as she told him where she was. One hundred percent typical. She had put off a simple telephone call until she was at the Greyhound bus terminal in Los Angeles.

"I need to see you, Joe. Right now. Now hush up baby, you gonna see Daddy-Joe any minute now."

She was doing her shoo-fly-honey-chile bit. Had she always talked that way? Was it just more syrupy over the phone? If it had ever enchanted him, it didn't any more. He could hear Douggie whining above the noise of a revving diesel.

"Good God, Shirley, why didn't you phone me before dragging the kid across America on a bus?" he said. "I'll be back in New York in a week."

"Well, we are heah now," she said, in the tiny voice of a Southern belle in distress. "Does that mean we are just not welcome to come on over?"

"Of course it doesn't. Get yourself a cab. Did George give you the address?"

"Besides," she cooed, "we weren't in New York. We came from Baton Rouge. How long of a cab ride is this, darlin'?"

"A long one."

"Well I really don't—"

"Don't worry," he said. "I'll pay for it at this end."

Didn't he always? he thought, slamming down the phone.

It was past six o'clock before Chalice got around to her final session with Damboise. She'd been in back-to-back meetings since breakfast in the commissary, and she hadn't had a chance to call Joe.

She hoped this wouldn't take long, but Damboise was nervous as a cat. If he needed Chalice after today, it was going to cost him a thousand dollars a day.

He walked around the southeast lot with her, inspecting the sets for Monday morning as they conferred. From a height of twelve feet, glaring halogen light fixtures turned night into day. A covered market street rose from the hard-packed dirt, displaying an exotic variety of wares on its jostling stalls. But there were no extras around making like customers, just three grips standing by waiting for Damboise to dismiss them. Before he did, he paced through the alley between the stalls, counting steps, then consulted the shooting schedule on his clipboard.

"You can put it to bed at this angle," he told the grips. "Don't jostle anything. Don't change it one millimeter."

The men began to unroll sheets of waterproof plastic.

Damboise moved on, Chalice beside him, wandering through a deserted town square with an imposing facade of government buildings. It had been erected since her last visit to the set on Wednesday, and it was eerily familiar from Hallifax's photographs. Under the fierce white lights, it looked breathtakingly authentic from anywhere inside the square.

"Fantastic," she said, her voice resounding oddly against the hard facades and the cobblestones. "But isn't it a bit clean? Fred says there's usually refuse in the gutters."

Damboise nodded. "It's in the property notes,

and it'll be there by seven on Monday morning." He examined a series of chalk marks, nodded, then headed across the dirt lot and into the hangarlike soundstage.

The oriental splendor of a rich villa stood in one corner, and in another were various simpler interiors, including a crude, one-room mountain shack. The fly walls were at a wide angle to allow camera access in the close shots, but she recognized the room like a flash of déjà vu.

It was where Fred Hallifax, a small-town news photographer from Florida, had lived for most of that year, where he had convalesced from his wounds, and where he had fallen in love with a Kirghiz girl.

The fly walls, or flies, would have to be hauled to the mountain locations for exterior shots. They looked substantial, like the walls of a real house with concrete foundations, she thought, and was glad the transportation of this enormous caravan wasn't her problem.

All through their stroll, they talked, each referring to a carefully prepared checklist.

Then, when she thought they had covered every last detail, he insisted on leaving the studio with her for a drink.

They sat at a low table at the bar of his hotel. Damboise was tired and beginning to show the strain. "Robert Shankel was right," he said, smiling. "You've given me a hundred-thousand-dollar screenplay for half the price. How can I thank you?"

Chalice grinned. "By making it a winner."

"I plan to." He rolled a glass of Irish coffee around in his palms. "We haven't discussed the credit titles," he said. "Story and screenplay by

Chalice York, based on the journal of Frederick Hallifax." He glanced up at her. "What do you think?"

She thought it was fine, and she thought of how few days were left to her with Joe. How their evening together was being squandered by Damboise's relentless attention to detail.

Damboise struck his forehead. "How terrible! It's after nine and you've been working nonstop since seven. I insist you have dinner with me now. The Grill Room here serves until ten."

Please no, she thought. But on this day, there was no way she could gracefully refuse. Silently, she said good-bye to her evening with Joe.

Shirley stepped out of the taxi, pretty and cool as always. Life never made a dent on her, Joe thought, but Douggie, half asleep on her shoulder, was ashy-faced with fatigue. Joe took the child from her and carried him straight upstairs. Douggie was nei-ther hungry nor thirsty, just dead on his feet.

"That old devil's havin' me tailed, Joe," Shirley whispered, as he laid the child down on one of the twin beds in the second bedroom.

"He's not a devil, Shirley."

The man was desperate, that's all. "Why must you torment him? You know how he feels about Douggie."

"Yes? Then why, pray tell, does my baby scream at the very thought of seein' his father?"

Joe saw that Douggie was dead to the world and edged Shirley out of the room. "Because you've turned Douglas Shaeffer into a boogeyman," he said. "Douggie's picking it up from you, this paranoia. And don't bat your lashes at me, Shirley. You know damn well what you're doing.".

Sometimes it startled him to remember that Shirley had once been a registered nurse. She could act like an eighth-grade dropout.

She sat on the sofa, sipping a Coke and smoothing her apple green skirt as she looked around the living room. "I'm not paranoid, Joe, honest. Why, I feel we're perfectly safe heah with you."

Sure you do, he thought. Until tomorrow, maybe. It was useless, but he found himself sucked into the old arguments. Weariness seemed to turn his limbs to lead.

"You can't run from the law forever, Shirley. Look what it's doing to Douggie! The boy's a wreck. I'll pay your airfare to Atlanta. Just go stay with your parents until you get yourself sorted out."

"I would, Joe honey, I really would, if I didn't owe fifteen thousand to that silly ole attorney."

Joe listened stoically while she went through her inevitable tale of woe. Shirley was a professional victim. When he'd had enough, he closed his eyes. "Just give me the bottom line, will you? I mean, to settle all the debts, square yourself with the judge in Atlanta, and make peace with Douglas."

"Fifty thousand would do it."

He didn't groan. "It's the last time. I'll do it if you swear you'll straighten yourself out."

"Cross ma heart an' hope to die," she said. "Oh Joe, you're so good to me. All I evah wanted was my independence, so I can git a real handle on this situation."

God knows what she meant by that. He looked at her suspiciously, through narrowed eyes.

Shirley had waist-length dark hair and the softest moss-green eyes. They were fastening on him now, flirtatiously. "Would you-all consider harborin' two fugitives from the law tonight?"

"Sure, you can stay here," he said. "Until Monday, when you and Douggie will be on a plane to Atlanta." What did she think he was going to say? *I'm turning you out into the street*?

But this would be the last time, he decided. The very last time.

"But listen, Shirley, I've got a late date tonight, so you'll have to fend for yourself. There's food in the refrigerator."

"You datin' at last? Why, sugar puff, I'm real pleased for ya. I surely hope she's good to ya. Now you just pay me no never-mind. I can take care of myself."

Joe went into the study and put a call through to Cosmos. Chalice couldn't be found. It was past seven. Perhaps she'd already left and was on her way. He wished he could give her some warning. Shirley was coming on pretty strong.

She stood in the kitchen, sipping a bourbon and Coke while she fixed herself soup and a sandwich, her eye glancing pointedly toward the kitchen clock every few minutes.

"What about your date, hon?"

"She's meeting me here. I don't know when," he muttered. *It's none of your damn business.*

He sat in the family room trying to read, but he couldn't concentrate. After two days on a bus, he'd expected Shirley to go to bed early, preferably before Chalice arrived. It would give him a chance to explain. But Shirley settled down to watch *Love Boat*. He wandered into the study, where he would be able to hear a car pull into the driveway. He took his book with him, but spent all evening with his ears pricked for the sound of the Honda.

After the eleven o'clock news, Shirley turned off the television and poked her head around the study door. "Your date's not going to make it tonight, is she, Joe?"

"It doesn't matter."

"But you must be disappointed. It bein' Saturday night and all? What a shame."

"It doesn't matter," he repeated. "She just got hung up, that's all. I'm going to bed. There's linen in the closet outside Douggie's room. Good night."

But she followed him to his room, closed the door and leaned against it sinuously, showing off her graceful figure.

She had long, tapered legs, a slender waist, and large handsome breasts which had fed Douggie for three and a half years, just to foil his father's visitation rights.

Her voice was soft as thistledown. "Don't fret, sugar. I kin make it up to ya." Her eyes turned to the king-size bed. "We could have a high ole time. Just the two of us."

"There's a second bed you can use alongside Douggie's. That's where you preferred to sleep anyway, isn't it, for the last four months of our marriage?"

"Not tonight, now he's safely tucked in and sleepin' like an angel." She draped herself around his neck, rubbing her cheek against his. "Why, after what you just did for me, I'd be happy to . . . you know . . . just for ole time's sake." She laughed. "Besides, Joe honey. When could you evah say no to me?"

He gripped her upper arms and pushed her away.
"I'm saying it now," he said.

Her green eyes grew round with genuine astonishment, as if she could hardly believe her ears.

Joe held the door open for her. "You still have a pretty face, Shirley. And your body's as lush as ever. But if you think I just paid fifty grand for a night in bed with you," he broke off, his anger rising. "Now please get out of my bedroom."

It was after midnight by the time Chalice got home. She had tried to call Joe, but there was a run on the phones in the lobby, and it was rude to keep excusing herself from the dinner table. Joe must have given up on tonight hours ago, she thought as she fell exhaustedly into bed. There was no point in waking him now. Tomorrow she'd pack a few things before she drove over to Brentwood, she decided. He'd be leaving for location work in a few days. There wasn't much time left for them.

A brilliant sun woke her at six-thirty. She left Joe's number with her service and put on a dusty-pink sundress. She hung some ultrafeminine outfits in a garment bag and packed a weekend case with the rest. A little before eight, she headed out for Brentwood. On a Sunday morning, it took less than fifteen minutes. Perhaps he'd still be asleep, and she'd be able to wake him with coffee and kisses. They would laugh about last night, and she would spend the next few days making up for that stupid wasted evening.

There was a sharp bend in the road just before his house came into view. She took it slowly, rounding the corner just as his front door swung wide. Chalice blinked, then slowed the Honda to a crawl.

A tall, slender woman had emerged from Joe's

house. She had very long hair and a very short nightgown. Chalice watched as the woman glanced around the porch, walked in long graceful strides over the front lawn and tilted her head up to Joe's open bedroom window.

Chalice hovered at the driveway, then let the car glide right past it. She came to a halt in front of the house next door and let the motor idle. Without turning, she could still see the woman in the side view mirror.

"Joe, honey?" The Southern voice poured over the quiet suburban morning with insidious sweetness. "Joe, don't you have yo' milk de*livah'd*?"

A small boy in a yellow pajama top ran out of the house, and she shooed him back in. "It's all right, sugar. Mama's gonna fix French toast, and Daddy-Joe'll go for milk, soon as he's out the shower."

Chapter 9

CHALICE LAID THE GARMENT BAG FLAT ON HER BED AND unzipped it. She began to unpack with meticulous care, restoring each garment to its drawer or dress hanger and smoothing out folds so that nothing got wrinkled in the process. She opened her toilet case and emptied brush and comb, toothpaste and make-up, and laid them all out on the bathroom counter. Then she shrugged at the mirror.

"So she keeps in touch," she said softly. Moderation in all things . . . "Okay, kid. Let's see it. A little cool, calm moderation."

Whistling the *Godfather* theme, she hung up the empty garment bag and replaced the weekend case on the top shelf of her closet.

In the living room, she tackled the litter of discarded notes and typed sheets that covered her desk, sweeping them off into the wastebasket. Then she called the answering service. Debra had just come on duty.

"Change of plans," she told Debra. "I left a number with Connie this morning, where I could be reached for the next day or so? Scratch it. I'll be home."

Having run out of mechanical little chores, Chalice sat and swiveled back and forth in her desk chair, her fingers drumming on the telephone. It was barely nine o'clock. The round-trip to Brentwood and back could have taken no more than half an hour.

It was going to take longer than that to decide how she felt about tripping over an ex-wife on Joe's front lawn. But she didn't really feel like mulling it over right now. In fact she didn't feel like staying cooped up in the apartment. Alone. It was a pretty day, and it wasn't as if Joe was her only friend in the world. Rachel and Glen, for instance. Except for one phone call, she hadn't spoken to either of them in weeks.

Right now, they would be sipping their first cup of coffee as they shared the Sunday *Times* in bed. She smiled inwardly when it struck her how well she knew them.

Rachel would be into the Calendar section, scanning the stage and television reviews. Glen was reading Business, or Opinion. You could tell a lot by the way a person worked through the Sunday papers. Obversely, if you knew them well, you automatically knew what they'd read first . . .

She found herself dialing Rachel's number.

"You awake yet?"

"Hi, stranger. Let me guess . . . you finished your screenplay." Rachel sounded wide awake and very perky. "How'd it go?"

"Just great. They're in full production now. The sets look terrific, and I signed off the project yesterday."

"Good. So you're back among the living?"

"Yes. I thought that, before you started feeding your faces this morning, I'd invite you two out for a champagne brunch. Marina del Rey, maybe. It's a lovely morning for it. Do you have any plans?"

"Not until later on. I'd love to, Chalice. Only Glen isn't here this morning. It'll be just me."

"Well, call him," Chalice said. "I want to treat him. For the past six months I've been enjoying his cuisine. It's high time."

Rachel paused before she answered. "It'll be just me. He's, er . . ."

"He's not cowering under your bed, is he? Scared to face the man hater?"

Rachel's laugh sounded sheepish. "No, of course not. What time do you want to eat?"

"Could you work up an appetite by one?"

"Earlier. I've got to be in Beverly Hills by three, and I want my money's worth. I presume you're talking buffet. All you can eat? We can talk and eat nonstop for two and a half hours. Sheer heaven."

"Maybe you can," Chalice told her, wondering once again how Rachel kept so wafer-thin.

"Could you make it noon?" Rachel said. "Then we can catch up on everything, and I can hear all about Joe Verdi."

"Consuela's at noon," Chalice said.

She wasn't sure she had much to say about Joe Verdi, not after this morning, but she was at Consuela's by ten of twelve and was lucky enough to capture the last terrace table, right by the water.

Every eye turned as Rachel appeared a few minutes later and walked down the narrow terrace to their table. She wore a white sleeveless jumpsuit that plunged down to the waist in a deep V between her breasts and clung to her narrow hips like skin. Only a tall wand of a woman like Rachel could have worn it with such nonchalance.

"You look stunning and positively sinful," Chalice said, as Rachel seated herself. "Are you testing for *Dynasty* this afternoon, or *Dallas*?"

Rachel laughed. "When you're a beanpole, you get to wear fun rags. There has to be some consolation for being flat-chested."

Chalice rolled her eyes. "You bear your terrible affliction very bravely, my dear."

They sipped mimosas, then circled the buffet, Rachel piling her plate with everything in sight, Chalice mostly looking.

"So how is your handsome chef these days? she asked. "I'm sorry he couldn't join us. Is he away on a business trip?"

Rachel scooped up a mound of pâté from the graceful arrangement that swirled around the base of an ice sculpture of polar bears. "He's a bit miffed at me at the moment," she said. "It'll keep. First, I want to find out what you've been up to."

They wandered back to the table and began to eat. Chalice had settled for a small piece of smoked whitefish and two green olives. "There isn't much to hear. I told you about Damboise and *The Hindu Kush* last time we talked."

"Did you ever!" Rachel smiled. "You took up my whole coffee break bending my ear."

"Sorry about calling you on the set," Chalice said. "I got tired of trying to reach you at home. You're never there these days."

Rachel broke off a piece of her croissant and lavished butter all over it, and for a while they exchanged shop talk and caught up on mutual friends.

"Enough of this," Rachel said, after she'd demolished the last morsel of smoked salmon on her plate. "Tell me about the dark and sexy Verdi. You took up twenty minutes yakking about work last time we talked, then threw in that teaser, just when I had to run. What did you mean, he's quite nice after all? Have you been seeing him?"

"No big deal." Chalice turned all her attention to picking minute bones from the whitefish. "He'll be gone pretty soon anyway. He really can't handle Hollywood. I don't think he'll ever be back."

"Something tells me . . ." Rachel stabbed a thin slice of marinated cucumber.

"Tells you what?"

"That it's more of a big deal than you say it is."

Chalice pushed her plate aside and stared out morosely at the sailboats in the marina. The sunlight was harsh, and she fished out her sunglasses.

"For a start," Rachel pointed out, "you never see anyone socially when you're on a job, so if you've been seeing Joe Verdi in the past month, that in itself is a big deal." Rachel's plate was empty and she was ready to go back to the buffet for more goodies, but she obviously wasn't going to budge until she got some kind of answer.

Chalice's voice was offhand. "We just spent some time together, that's all."

"Uh-huh."

"So what? It can't go anywhere, so I've quit. As of this morning."

"You've quit? You make it sound like a habit.

Look, Chalice, you said he won't be around much longer. Can't you just relax and enjoy—"

"That's the whole problem," Chalice said. "It was getting to be a habit, so I've decided to quit while it's easy. The last thing I need is to get hung up on a man who lives three thousand miles away." She pushed her chair back. "I'm going to try the cucumber salad," she said. "Coming?"

Rachel returned from a second foraging trip with enough hot food to keep her mouth occupied for a while, and Chalice was grateful for the respite. She needed time to think this through.

She had never thought of Joe as a habit before. Seeing Shirley in his house had just caught her unprepared. It had thrown her for a loop, in fact. But if the woman had just descended on him, as she suspected, it was hardly Joe's fault. If she had come to him for help, traveling across the country with a small child, it was only natural that she would stay the night. So why was the thought of it so prickly? Why was it beginning to feel like a splinter working its way deeper and deeper into the tender sole of a foot?

"Anyway," Chalice muttered, "sexually based attractions wear off pretty fast. As for anything else, we're terribly polarized in our thinking. We're always arguing. We don't see eye to eye on anything. He's an intellectual snob, an East Coast chauvinist, and—"

"Okay, okay. I get the message." Rachel took the last sip of mimosa from her champagne glass and grinned. "It's just that seeing you with him, I got the feeling something very special was happening. Something rare."

Chalice laughed. "The only time you ever saw me

with him was at Mort Shaffer's party. It was rare all right; I was rip-roaring drunk for the first time in my life."

"I suppose so." Rachel chewed thoughtfully for a while, then reached across the table and squeezed Chalice's hand. "It's just that I do love you, Chalice, and I'd like to see you truly contented before I die."

"Rachel, you're not sick, are you?"

"No, of course not, but I am getting on in years."

Chalice leaned back and exhaled, aware that she'd been holding her breath. "Oh, cut it out, will you? You're such a good actress, I never know when you're kidding me. You really had me wondering for a moment."

"Well, I'm not kidding right now. Out here an actress can never admit her age when she's over thirty—not if she doesn't want to be relegated to minor character roles for half her career. But I think you're a good enough friend to trust with a trade secret."

She's thirty-one, Chalice thought. She couldn't possibly be a day over that.

Rachel rose from the table and bent to Chalice's ear. "I'll be forty-three in June," she whispered, then swept down the terrace and inside, to inspect the dessert table.

Chalice was suitably impressed. Her mother of course was another example of everlasting youth, but Kyla devoted most of her waking hours to her body and complexion. Rachel was no lady of leisure married to a Brazilian millionaire.

She glanced at the sturdy wedge of chocolate mousse cake that Rachel returned with. "What's your secret?" she asked. "It obviously isn't diet."

"Sleep, liquids, meditation, and exercise," Rachel told her. "I don't diet, but I do fast twice a week. And a new resolution—no food passes my lips after six p.m."

"That must be terribly frustrating for Glen," Chalice said. "He loves leisurely dining. Is that why he's miffed at you right now?"

Rachel's face was a deep peach color when she blushed. "He's mad because my ex is in town, and I've been seeing him."

She'd been more than just seeing him. It was written all over her face. "Brad Alexander?" Chalice said, not knowing how else to respond.

"Who else? There's only one ex. I never make the same mistake twice."

"Are you quite sure?" Chalice examined her friend's expression. It lay somewhere between guilt and defiance, with something else she couldn't quite name thrown in.

"He's still gorgeous. And charming when he wants to be."

Chalice didn't doubt it. But it was hardly the point. Rachel never talked much about Brad, but Chalice had once heard the whole story from Sam.

Brad Alexander had many gifts—physical beauty, camera presence, acting ability, wit, and a spurious kind of charm. But kindness, loyalty, and scruples were noticeably missing, she gathered. Rachel had blown the chance of a lifetime for that bastard. And he'd walked out on her just as soon as his name was established.

For Chalice, Rachel was a role model—self-sufficient, capable of rising above any setback and picking up her life without a backward look. But this was a backward look with a vengeance. Was she going to be Brad Alexander's bedfellow and handmaiden again? His doormat? It was outrageous and horribly disappointing.

"His current marriage is a disaster," Rachel was saying. "He called me the morning after he arrived in Los Angeles, and pleaded to see me."

Chalice stirred her coffee. "So of course," she said drily, "you could hardly wait."

Rachel fixed her with a steady gaze, then looked past her into the bay. Under the black mascara, her eyes chased back and forth across the water, anxiously scanning the weekend sailors—each motor launch and pleasure boat, and each brightly colored sailboard ridden by a golden-boy skipper clinging with bare toes and young muscled arms as he surf sailed over bright water. For a few moments, her eyes searched the water, almost as if she were searching for a missing child.

A look of panic passed over her features, then quickly disappeared. "I just told you my age, Chalice. It's the truth. Television cameras have no mercy, you know, and I'm hopelessly typecast now. If my glamor goes, my career goes too. Have you any idea what it does for my ego to know that Alexander the Great still finds me desirable?"

"Rachel, this is ridiculous. I've never known anyone more strikingly beautiful than you. You can hardly need that kind of ego boost. Not from the complete egomaniac himself."

"He's always made a much more considerate lover than he has a husband."

"Should I be happy for you?" Chalice shook her head incredulously. "And what about Glen? He's crazy about you. And all these months I thought you really cared for him."

Rachel's broad shoulders lifted in a helpless shrug. "I do, very much. But he doesn't own me."

But apparently Brad Alexander did. All he had to do was crook his little finger. "I'm sorry," Chalice said. "I just don't get it."

"Nobody owns me," Rachel said. "Look, I'd never wish divorce on you, Chalice, but if you'd ever been through one, well maybe you'd understand."

"Understand what, for crying out loud?"

Rachel's voice dropped to a provocative stage whisper. "You've no idea how exciting it can be to find yourself in bed with an ex-spouse."

Shirley had promised Douggie a visit to Disneyland. By ten-thirty the next morning, they were gone for the day, together with Joe's MasterCard and most of his cash. He breathed a sigh of relief, poured the last of the coffee, and took it with him into the study to collect his thoughts. Somehow he couldn't think straight anywhere else. The whole house now seemed saturated with Shirley and the sweet, light scents she drenched herself in.

Chalice didn't answer her phone. She didn't answer when he called a half hour later, and she still wasn't answering at two-thirty. By that time he was covered in a light sweat and trying to erase the persistent vision of a car crash. She hadn't even called to say she couldn't make it yesterday. It wasn't like her. Or maybe it was. When her mind was on work, nothing else existed.

Only one human voice broke up his afternoon, but it wasn't Chalice. It was the man Shirley had been

living with for the past two months, calling from
Baton Rouge. He wondered when she was coming
back. She owed him a couple of thousand dollars.

Joe was coolly polite and noncommittal. Good
luck, fella, he thought when he hung up. No wonder
Shirley had lain low for a while.

His shirt felt sticky and he needed another shower. But he might miss the phone if Chalice called
while the water was running. He tried her number
again and let it ring eight times until her answering
service picked it up.

Chalice had checked in that morning, the girl said.
"I guess she's gone out. We don't hear from her too
much on weekends."

It reassured him to know that she'd been alive and
well that morning. But where the hell was she?
Maybe at Cosmos. Some last-minute business on the
movie.

I will never swear again. I will never belittle the
movie business again. I will never speak ill of Los
Angeles. He made a dozen promises he would never
keep, if she would only call. Or pull up in the
driveway. Or at least be home to pick up the phone
on his next try.

On his next try, she picked up the phone.

*You've no idea how exciting it can be to find
yourself in bed with an ex-spouse.* If she'd said it at
the beginning of brunch, Chalice thought, instead of
right at the end, then maybe the words wouldn't be
still buzzing around her like pesky mosquitos. Anyway, she was sure it wasn't true. Not universally
true. Of course it wasn't. It was just one of Rachel's
hyperboles, thrown out to camouflage the fact that

she was doing something definitely shabby. Shabby to her self-esteem and shabby to Glen.

Chalice had let it pass because it was getting late for Rachel to make her three o'clock date. They went their separate ways, Rachel no doubt towards Brad Alexander's five-room suite at the Beverly Wilshire Hotel, and Chalice towards Santa Monica.

She was in no particular hurry to go home, so she browsed around the little specialty shops off Second Street, trying to deflect her thoughts from the subject of ex-spouses. She had that slightly disoriented feeling which always followed upon the completion of a writing job. She stopped outside the Methven Grant bookstore. Writers, she thought. They lived most of their lives in the world, but not of it.

The center of the window was devoted to a display of *Many a Man*, the book Joe had been reading on the beach. She wondered if he'd ever finished it. She'd been taking up most of his leisure time since that day. This was not the time to think of Joe, she decided, and concentrated instead on the red and gold pyramid of books arranged in the window. The hardcover edition was priced at $19.95. She wouldn't be borrowing Joe's books anymore . . .

She went into the store and bought her own copy, browsed a little longer, then went home.

Without realizing it, she had spent most of the day trying not to react in an extravagant way and distancing herself from a relationship which had suddenly become too complicated to cope with. She was beginning to feel a little blah, and resigned to feeling that way until Monday. There was usually an anticlimax at the end of a project, she told herself. Tomorrow would be different. She'd start thinking

about another original screenplay. And she'd call
Robert Shankel and remind him that she was free to
work again. Maybe there was some interesting property floating around.

When the phone rang, a few minutes after she got
home, she was calm, almost to the point of being
wooden, although she guessed it would be Joe.

"*Chalice!*" It was the first time she could remember him using her name, and somehow it sounded
faintly ludicrous, like the last gasp of a dying king.
She almost giggled.

Instead she said, "This is she," as if she were
fielding a call from a stranger.

She could tell how much it bothered him. There
was fluster and a touch of outrage in his voice. And
he was talking in italics. "Where have you *been*?"

"Out," she said airily. "I had brunch with a
friend, then shopped for a bit. Why?"

He paused for long seconds as if he were struggling for breath.

"Joe? Are you still there?"

He came back sounding strangely subdued. "Shirley blew in unannounced yesterday. She's been
driving me—"

"Yes I know," Chalice cut in. "I came by the
house this morning."

That seemed to stun him, and he began to bluster.
"You *did*? You came by the *house*? You *didn't*. What
do you *mean*, you came by? Why didn't you come
in?"

While he blustered, the words were forming in her
throat. Her voice dripped fake magnolia blossoms.
"*Joe honey, don't you have yo' milk delivah'd?*"

He groaned. "Oh darling, I'm sorry. I wish I

could've warned you. Did she snarl at you or something? Did she say anything bitchy?"

"No, nothing like that. As a matter of fact, she didn't even see me. I cruised right by the driveway and kept going."

That was exactly what she'd done, and as she said the words, she realized there had been something furtive about the way she acted. Damnit, why the instant discretion? She wasn't the other woman. She wasn't!

Joe was hesitant. "I wish you had come in, instead of sliding off like that. She'll be gone tomorrow. She's gone right now, as a matter of fact. She's taken Douggie to Disneyland. I don't expect them back until ten or later. Are you—Would you—"

"I don't feel like going out again, Joe. Yesterday was a marathon of back-to-back meetings. I didn't get home until way after midnight. This evening I need to unwind. Quietly."

"What does that mean? You don't even want me to come over?"

She paused, struggling for just the right tone. "Not really."

She heard him exhale noisily, as if the conversation wasn't going at all the way he intended. "This weekend will have been a total loss without seeing you," he said.

"Not really."

"For God's sake, will you stop saying 'Not really' in that languid tone," he snapped. "What's the matter?"

"Nothing's the matter. I just think we've been getting a bit too exclusive for my taste. I think we should cool it."

"You think we should cool it," he said woodenly. "It's Shirley, isn't it? Look, I had no idea she'd just arrive like that. She called from the bus station, for crying out loud. They'd been on the road for three days. I had to . . . Chalice, there are four beds in this house. You don't for one minute think that I—"

"Of course I don't, Joe. And even if you did, that's hardly any business of mine. As I told you, I don't believe in exclusive relationships."

His voice cracked with exasperation. "What d'you mean, *as I told you*? You *didn't*. You *never* told me that." He paused, and his tone became more controlled. "Look, I'll call you tomorrow when you've . . . unwound." There was a touch of sarcasm as he drew out the last word.

"There's no need," she said in the same languid, singsong tone.

"*Not really*," he said in the best British Public School accent he could manage, and hung up.

There was nothing more punishingly tedious, Joe decided, than hanging around a movie set in case you were needed. The filming of *The Snipe* proceeded in takes that were roughly forty seconds long, and after each take, everything ground to a halt. The flies would be moved and the set broken up. Dozens of technicians would swarm over cables, lights, acoustical equipment, cameras and props. And then, as often as not, the identical scene would be shot again, with the focus on a different actor, or a different angle.

In a dim corner of the huge soundstage was a trestle table, lit by a single seventy-five-watt bulb hanging from an electrical cord looped over an overhead girder. Joe divided his time between sitting at the table and pacing up and down just outside the doors of the building, on a kind of concrete stoop. He didn't go outside too often, not after he discovered it made Ryan very nervous when Joe wasn't visible, even though he was within earshot.

He was invited to watch the rushes each day with Ryan. He didn't. It would have been too depressing. As it was, he knew that each grueling day was producing a little over two minutes of finished film. The order of shooting was decided by technical expediency, so it bore no resemblance to the narrative sequence of the story. It was therefore almost impossible to detect any forward progress. Life seemed to offer little encouragement for him on any front at this point.

There wasn't even anything to look forward to in the evenings. Chalice had mailed back his key with a very terse note: *Won't have much time to use this. Thought you'd better have it back before I lose it.*

Her response on the phone was terse too. "Look, I can't talk now—I'm just on the way out the door." Or, "Hi, Joe. I'd really love to chat but I'm on a deadline. Some other time, okay? I'll give you a call when things settle down around here."

He couldn't pin her down to admitting anything was wrong between them. She didn't sound angry or even upset, just the eternally pleasant princess. Noblesse oblige, he thought. It was just always the wrong time to talk. After a few attempts, the message came through loud and clear anyway. He was being unceremoniously dumped.

What was wrong with him anyway? He was deteriorating rapidly, that's what it was. Shirley had tired of him in a year. Chalice had taken only four weeks—ironically, the same four weeks it had taken him to discover that she was a good deal more than a playmate.

Shirley's coming had made it very clear what Chalice had become to him. Or could become to him. But he was damned if he was going to put himself through the wringer over a woman all over again. Life was complicated enough.

As you were, he told himself. The last four weeks never happened. You're just out here gritting your teeth through an evil necessity, so that mom and papa can live in Florida while they're still young enough to enjoy it. Then back to New York when it's over.

But it wouldn't be over when *The Snipe* was wrapped now. He'd made a commitment to Shirley. Dumb. Dumb. Dumb. He was fifty thousand dollars short of his goal. He'd already called George about following up this project with another quickie contract.

"Joe," George had growled at him over three thousand miles of telephone cable, "do you think offers grow on trees in Central Park? What's the matter with you?"

There was nothing the matter with him that fifty thousand couldn't fix. Maybe the real estate market would change, and someone would buy the house in Connecticut. Failing that, George would just have to come through. Fifty thou could pop a lot easier on the West Coast. He would grit his teeth and stick around.

Chapter 10

NOTHING ABOUT PLATO KALAMANDRIS SUGGESTED formidable strength or giant proportions. He was small-boned and brown-eyed, and very soft-spoken. But in the trades he was often referred to as an industry giant, the power behind many a studio merger.

At this moment he was seated at his desk, watching his secretary set down the glass of iced Perrier he had requested. He admired the grace of her movements. She had the face of an angel and a body almost as spectacular as Sylvan, his current mistress, had.

"Thank you, Lacy," he said softly.

If she'd had any ambition at all, he thought, he would have made her a great star. She wouldn't need any talent, just careful direction. Her looks were eloquent enough.

But Lacy was quite content to serve the undisputed head of Pacifica Studios, to keep his desk calendar uncrowded so that he never missed a tennis date, and to take minutes in the boardroom.

"Lou Hosner's on the line again," she told him. "He wants to see you as soon as possible."

"He can see me right now," Kalamandris said.

Lacy hesitated. "You don't have long. I'll tell him now, but only if he can get over here before eleven-thirty, and make it brief. You have to leave around then for the ASCAP awards luncheon," she reminded him. "You're addressing them in behalf of The Motion Picture—"

"Ah yes," he said, nodding. "Did you type up my notes?"

"I'm just finishing them now," Lacy said, and turned to leave. "I'll tell Lou to come right away."

Plato swiveled his chair to the window after she left, and stared out at the rolling brown hills of the Los Angeles basin. His penthouse suite sat atop the tallest building in Century City. It wasn't tall by the standards of other cities. Only fourteen floors. But Los Angeles was not comparable to other cities, and this particular location suited him perfectly.

Pacifica was only ten minutes away by freeway. The Kalamandris Tower was close enough to feel the daily pulse of the studios, but far enough away so that Kalamandris was in no danger of being sucked into the tedious business of carpenters, electric cables, chalk marks, and star tantrums. He had no interest in the nuts and bolts of the industry, and he couldn't afford to be sidetracked by it. He was concerned only with the beginning and the end.

The beginning was always a question of money and talent, vision and courage. The end was su-

preme satisfaction—and more money, provided you
made no mistakes. Plato Kalamandris had vision and
a gift for money. He made very few mistakes, but he
had never lacked the courage to make them. Occasionally he had been disastrously wrong. But it was
all part of the wonderful game, the most glorious
crap game ever devised.

Lou Hosner knew talent, but he had no boldness
when the stakes were high. Kalamandris knew very
well what Lou wanted to discuss this morning. Lou
had acquired an option just three days ago, and
already his courage was failing. Like everyone else,
Lou was overwhelmed, finding the property too hot
to hold. The sheer stature of it was burning his
cautious little fingers.

Kalamandris had finished reading *Many a Man*.
His heart was still expanded from it. Of course the
stakes would be higher than most. But when talent
scaled such heights, fortitude must rise to meet it.
He smiled out at the distant mountains.

Lou Hosner was a little man, for all his lumbering
two hundred pounds of brawn. He could make crisp
executive decisions, but there was a degree of magni-
tude beyond which his nerve failed. It was precisely
why Lou ran Pacifica Studios, while Plato Kalamandris owned it.

The towering plate-glass edifice where Plato sat
reflected his Olympian attitude. He trusted Lou in
most ways, and he rarely interfered with Lou's
decisions at the studio. But there were rare occa-
sions when he felt impelled to step down from
Olympus. This was one of them.

"Plato," Lou said, hurrying through the door at
precisely eleven twenty-nine, "Columbia's offering
twenty-five thousand for our option on *Many a Man*.

I know you expressed an interest in this one, but I told them they could probably have it for thirty. Let's face it. It's a mighty novel, but we've had some mighty losses this year. We don't need another highflier."

"We won't sell," Plato said.

Lou looked at him curiously. "I only paid fifteen for it."

Plato's gentle laughter filled the room. "Since when are we in the business of making ten thousand dollars on an option trade, Lou? No. We're going to exercise the option, and soon. While Oestermann's name is still in the news."

"We could take a bath on it," Lou said. "I know it's tempting, but I think you're making a big mistake."

"Some mistakes are worth making," Plato said, as Lacy walked into the room, holding out his sports jacket.

"Eleven-thirty, Mr. Kalamandris," Lacy whispered. "Time to leave for the Beverly Wilshire."

Plato stood up, shrugged apologetically to Lou, and slipped into his jacket. "Lacy," he said, "arrange a time when Lou and I can spend a couple of hours together. As soon as possible. We have some figuring to do."

Lou followed his boss down the curved flight of stairs and into the private elevator. "I'll ride to the hotel with you, if I may. Perhaps I can talk you out of this."

Plato's smile showed small white teeth, capped to perfection. "I doubt it. But you're welcome to try."

Lou smoothed back his sparse, sandy hair and smiled back as the elevator doors slid closed. "Plato," he said reasonably, "it's like a virus, that's all. Every studio executive goes through it. Something big comes along, and because it's just a question of option money, they can't resist owning the rights to it for a crazy day or so. Then they take a serious look at the logistics and come to their senses."

Plato leaned against the wall of the elevator with his arms folded. "David Oestermann is one of the immortals," he said. "Now we must find his screenwriting equivalent for the adaptation. I want to move fast."

"There is no screenwriting equivalent," Hosner muttered.

"A team then. Come, Lou. You know them all. Put on your thinking cap."

"Plato, you're not serious. You'd have to be a madman to go through with it."

Plato put his arm around Lou's broad shoulders and shepherded him out into the lobby. "Of course you have to be a madman," he said mildly. "What other kind of man is there in this business?"

Observing the way Robert Shankel was dressed, Chalice realized that his clothes were always an infallible indicator of his calendar for the day. When he wore one of his fine broadcloth shirts, a conservative tie and an expensively tailored suit, he was meeting with Big Money. When he was dealing only with talent, he favored open-necked knits in vibrant colors, casually tailored slacks and loafers.

Today he either had come from Big Money or was headed for it after lunch. Chalice noticed that his silk tie was pierced by a small pearl pin.

She had recently become expert at noticing small things that were neither here nor there. Lately it was becoming an art form with her, she reflected, this focusing on the banal, the trivial, the inconsequential. She'd always had an eye for detail, of course. Screenwriters were meticulous observers. But this was getting ridiculous. She was beginning to hypnotize herself on that tiny pinpoint of opalescence on his tie . . .

Chalice had waited ten days to see him, and for ten days she had given herself over to a frenzied regime of physical fitness interspersed with moody periods of inactivity when she devoted herself to such idle, numbing details as the hairline crack in the plaster of her bathroom ceiling, the perfect roundness of a pearl in a tiepin. She had been trying hard to be productive, to come up with a story idea. But nothing seemed to come except the threat of hysterical panic. She was still striving for moderation. At least a certain calm could be derived from concentrating on insignificant details.

She was making progress, she assured herself. She had managed to end an affair without melodrama; she could congratulate herself on that. But true inner tranquility was eluding her. She could discipline herself not to think of Joe, but without a work project to occupy her thoughts, she was struggling with a sense that her whole life had suddenly ground to a halt. Rachel had said she needed therapy. Nonsense! A contract, a deadline, a firm work commitment, that's all she needed. Something to anchor her mind to, before it became irrevocably enmeshed in an endless, meaningless circle of aerobics and health foods, tiepins and cracks in the ceiling. She needed work. She craved work. And she was trying to get the message across to Robert now that he had finally surfaced and was taking her to lunch.

But she wasn't going to give him the impression that she was hysterical about it. She wasn't. Chalice had shown up at Hoffsanger's Deli in a natural linen safari dress, all shoulder tabs and utility pockets, and reeking of no-nonsense efficiency.

"Is there a stain on my tie?" he asked.

Chalice shook her head. "I was just admiring the pin."

"So what d'you say to kicking back for a few weeks," he resumed, munching on a dill pickle. "You're not hurting for money right now. Damboise might call you back to Cosmos for rewrites. I think it would be a good idea for you to hang loose when you can afford a break."

Chalice shook her head. "Damboise will do nothing of the sort and you know it. He can't afford one extra day from me. You fixed it that way on my contract."

Robert shrugged. "So much the better. Take your time, and work up an original idea. The pickings are lean right now anyway. I'd be able to find a buyer if you came up with another *Snipe* idea. There's nothing floating around the industry you'd want. Get yourself caught up in something original."

It was all very well for him to say that. The only thing she'd managed to get caught up in, aside from ceiling cracks, was David Oestermann's novel. For two days she had steeped herself in it. As soon as she'd finished it, she had felt freed up to think creatively. Only nothing seemed to jell. She was seized by emotional aftershocks, and she didn't know whether it was simply the impact of an extraor-

dinary reading experience, or the same warm, tugging waves of regret she found herself coping with
every time she heard Joe's voice.

He had called several times, and although she had
fielded each call with a deft little sidestep, the
exchanges had left her wrestling with a tangle of
unresolved feelings that she forced herself to ignore.
Atrophy. The slow dying off from improper nourish-
ment. That was the way to break it off with Joe. No
big confrontations. Just let it wither away from
neglect. It had worked, she supposed. He had
stopped calling since last Friday. And from Rachel
she learned that the *Snipe* production was going on
location at the end of the coming week. Joe would be
gone. Even if he returned for a few days until *The
Snipe* was wrapped, they would be hectic days for
him. She was unlikely to hear from him again. She'd
brushed off his calls too many times. That was that.
It was over, without any big, icky scenes. Meanwhile
she needed a job to sink her teeth into.

Chalice poked reflectively at her crab salad. Robert didn't seem to understand her present need. She
wanted some structure, some practical commitment.
A short-term goal. Not endless idle hours in which
to dream up new ideas. She'd only be spinning her
wheels.

"What I'd really like," she told him, "is to work
up a treatment on *Many a Man*. The David
Oestermann novel."

He smiled. "Who wouldn't? Look, Chalice, the
option on that property is moving around faster than
the eye can follow it right now. It's changed hands
five times at the last count. You read the trades,
don't you? Every studio's panting for it, then chick-
ening out when they get their hands on it."

"Why?"

Robert laughed. "Oestermann was never what you'd call a fast read. It'd be a very ambitious project for any producer. If you want a shot at it, you'll have to wait until the dust settles. Sooner or later, some producer will summon the guts to exercise the option. But no one's even looking for a writer yet. If you coast for a while, we'll wait and see who ends up with the property."

But that could mean months and months of waiting. An edge of impatience crept into her voice. "Robert, get me something. Anything. I just can't stand doing nothing at the moment."

Robert glanced at her hands, and she became aware that they were busy shredding and pilling a soft dinner roll. He raised his head and gave her a shrewd, penetrating look. "What are you so antsy about, Chalice?"

"I'm not antsy," she exploded. "I'm a writer. I want to write. What's so bloody unusual about that?"

"So write. What's stopping you?"

"I can't. Not original material. I'm blocked. But if you got me a treatment, a play, anything under option, that'd be different."

He reached for his tall lager glass and smiled into it before he drank. "Okay. If you're going through a rough patch, let's take a look at the television scene . . ."

"Let's not. I'm not going back to the tube."

Robert examined his brisket sandwich with a neutral expression, chewing unhurriedly. "Chalice, I know how you feel, but the time for looking down your nose at the boob tube is over and out. The spectrum's so much broader these days, and there's some excellent material being developed. The budgets are getting to be comparatively—"

"No, Robert. I said no!" She thumped the table with her fist, then took up her napkin to mop up the water that spilled from her glass onto her knuckles.

He frowned, ignoring her outburst. "I told you already. Outside of TV, what's up for grabs right now is nothing but sleaze, Chalice. You wouldn't touch it with a ten-foot pole."

Chalice threw down her fork and leaned across the table. "Try me. I'm agreeable to anything you can find, so long as it's aimed at the theatre market. Just get it through your head. I will not write TV."

Robert pushed his plate away and gave a lazy shrug. "If you want to be a masochist, I'll see if I can find you a bed of nails to lie on," he said, rubbing his chin. "I should worry. It's all money to me."

By the end of the week, she had her bed of nails. Eighteen pages of contract signed by Amos Bane, and a synopsis that ran to four pages of typing, but could have been summed up in one word. Trash. The working title was *Hubcaps*.

She had signed the contract in Robert's office earlier that day. Now, looking at the material again as she sat at her desk, she dropped her head in her hands and shuddered. Then she turned back to page one of the synopsis, and tried to be completely impartial. Surely this wasn't quite as bad as she was making it out to be. It was work, wasn't it? It hadn't looked so awful when she'd read it in Robert's presence that morning.

Rising from the desk, she took her coffee and the four sheets of typed bond to the sofa, closed her eyes for a few moments, and blanked out. When she opened them again, she decided she was going to read this as if it were the very first time. No unfavorable preconceptions.

"Hubcaps Johnson is a nineteen-year-old hunk with just three things on his mind," she read. *"Girls, stock cars, and punk rock."*

She groaned and read on. It got progressively worse with every reading. No way could she write this screenplay. Why on earth had she bulldozed Robert into putting her name forward for it? Well, at least she didn't have to start on it yet. In fact Robert had told her to just sit on it for a few days, because the whole project was beginning to look flaky to him. If it was flaky enough, she thought hopefully, maybe it would fall through completely and invalidate the contract. The odds on that happening might even be in her favor.

No, she decided, dialing Robert's number. Counting on the odds just wasn't good enough. She was beginning to get catatonic just from reading these four pages of idiocy. She wanted out. Emphatically and unequivocally.

"Robert," she told him in a penitent voice, "you were absolutely right of course. *Hubcaps* really isn't my bag."

"Oh no you don't, baby," he said. "You're not backing out now. You signed a firm contract this morning. Remember?"

Of course she remembered, along with the fact that he'd advised against it. She took a deep breath. "I didn't realize how . . . ill-equipped I was for this kind of stuff. Look, I'm a pro, right? I figured they want garbage, I give 'em garbage. I'm used to that. But after Damboise, I just can't seem to switch gears to this extent."

Robert Shankel was not inclined to sympathize.

His voice became thin. "I'm your agent, Chalice, not your fairy godmother. I can field the offers. I can make recommendations. But I can't crawl inside your head and remodel it. Now don't play yo-yo with me, kid. I don't have the time."

Tears of frustration sprang to her eyes. "You're a hard man," she muttered. "Are you telling me I have no choice?"

"Sure you have a choice. Stand by your contract, or flake off and find yourself another agent," he said cheerfully. "Look on the bright side, Chalice. The whole thing may just fold up on us anyway. Just put it away and don't think about it until I call you. Is there anything else? I've got another call waiting."

She came back docile. "Not a thing, Robert. Sorry to bother you."

She'd really outsmarted herself this time. She had been so cool about phasing Joe out of her life with no big scenes. This was going to be the turning point of her career, she'd decided. Starting with *The Hindu Kush*, there would be no looking back, no time-consuming interruptions, no close encounters of the romantic kind. For a while, she would throw her heart into work and nothing but work.

Chalice sighed and put the four sheets inside an unmarked folder on her desk, so she wouldn't have to look at them. How could she throw her heart into that? She couldn't blame Robert for being hard-nosed with her. What an idiot she'd been. Perhaps he was right. Perhaps she was becoming a masochist.

She put on the Lalo Schiffrin tape that Joe had bought her, after they had danced to it one night in a funny little bar in Venice. That night crowded around her again, every last detail hemming her in. It was the first time they had ever danced together, had discovered the wonderful seamless feel of their bodies moving together to music. A magical drifting Saturday evening when his arms around her had felt like a natural adjunct to her body.

Warm, tugging regret invaded her, poignant sensations borne on waves of rhythmical melody . . . Yes, she probably did have masochistic tendencies.

Joe had just under a week in New York. He stayed at his apartment on West Tenth, but didn't see much of it. He was part of *The Snipe's* traveling circus. Eighteen actors, forty-two technicians, fourteen hair and makeup artists, thirty-five prop and wardrobe guardians, a dozen miscellaneous gofers and grips and carpenters and continuity girls. And over nine hundred pounds of personal luggage, props, and production equipment.

He spent whatever free time he could snatch trying to set his affairs in order. His play was still limping along at the Schubert. His house was still listed for sale with no takers.

His folks' retirement dreams seemed to hinge exclusively on what George or his West Coast associate could unearth in the way of quick, lucrative writing assignments.

On his third night in town, he took George to a late dinner at Sardi's, and threw four recent issues of *Variety* and the *Hollywood Reporter* under George's nose.

Joe pointed out the items ringed in heavy black ink. He'd combed the issues for likely writing projects.

"Shirley hit me up for fifty grand, George. Don't say anything. I know. But if I stay on in Hollywood for a few weeks, surely you can find me something to recoup. It's not that much. Look at these trade columns, for crying out loud. On the Coast, they drop fifty thousand like they discard used toothpicks."

George eyed him sourly. "So do you these days, it seems to me. Come on, Joe. *The Snipe* was a pure fluke. You know I can't pull a rabbit like that out of the hat every time you go off the deep end. And I think you'll be more than ready to leave Hollywood when this project is over. Stop being so quixotic about your parents and get back to what your life is all about. You're beginning to look pretty damn grim. D'you know that? If you'd listened to me about Shirley—"

"I'm cured of Shirley. But it was a damned expensive cure, and that's what this conversation is all about. A fifty-thousand-dollar job to pay for the cure. Don't change the subject, just read those trade items. Three issues in a row they've been puffing this thing called *Hubcaps*. And the second issue mentioned that Amos Bane fired the screenwriter. Couldn't I step in?"

"*Hubcaps* doesn't need a writer," George said, flipping through the business items. "It's a vehicle for Les Foley."

"Les who?"

"A teen idol. It's not your bag. It looks like another audiovisual orgy for the teen market. Stock car racing and demolition derby played out against a background of cheesecake and hard rock. What do they need with a real writer?"

"Stop being lofty with me, George. You're my agent, not my literary guru. I'm serious."

"So am I. Anyway, according to this, they've been playing kick the can with that property from one studio to another for a year or more. No one in his right mind would fall for that. Be sensible."

"I'll be sensible," Joe said. "I'll give 'em a scenario of grunts, squeals, and the crunch of metal. A thrill a minute. The point is, they'll hire another writer whether they need one or not."

George held the paper out to Joe. "They already did, according to this."

Joe snatched up the paper and read the tiny two-line item he had missed before. "Amos Banes signs Chalice York to replace . . ." He threw the paper down with a distinct flash of disgust.

So Miss Art-of-the Cinema was going to write grunt-squeal-crunch to the backing of steel guitars. He scowled at his sole meunière and pushed the plate away furiously. From *The Hindu Kush* to *Hubcaps*. For this, she was too damn busy to talk to him?

"Things must be bad all over," he muttered behind clenched teeth.

Walter Ryan would not have agreed with Joe. For the movie, things were going very well. In Manhattan, the weather smiled on them, and port and borough authorities cooperated. In a rare spell of smooth sailing, the traveling circus managed to complete ten minutes of finished film in as many days.

On a showery April morning, they packed up their unwieldly make-believe world again and trundled it home to California.

Joe left New York with a reluctant promise from George.

"I'll find you something to work on as soon as I can. But these things take time."

Some things took no time at all, Joe thought on his

second day back on the Coast. He drew in a sharp breath, then let it out with a string of expletives. He was standing by the news vendor's stall on the corner of Palm and Sunset, where he'd picked up the latest issue of *Variety*. He was not taking kindly to the story on page two.

SCREENWRITER SIGNS AND COLLECTS
The decision to cancel *Hubcaps*, the much discussed current project of producer Amos Bane, has resulted in a rare windfall for screenwriter Chalice York. Signed to write the screenplay just days ago, York has now been officially released from the terms of her contract, and under a unique clause of Western-Global's insurance policy, will stand to collect the entire fee of eighty thousand dollars, without having delivered one word of script.

York's last screenplay, THE HINDU KUSH, is now being readied at Cosmos Studios for release sometime next year. Reached in Santa Monica this morning, York had little to say on the subject; "The money's neither here nor there. This was never my favorite project, and it's a relief to be free of it."

Agent Robert Shankel, who negotiated York's contract, was unavailable for questioning today.

His stomach coiled into a tight ball of frustration. *The money's neither here nor there.* Damn that woman and her princess remarks. *Hubcaps* would have been the perfect job for him. The dream job. All the money he needed for the price of a signature. Still burning, he called George that night.

"I know about it," George told him. "I got a call from Norman just now. It was just a glitch in the insurance policy. What do you want from Freak City?"

"I should have such freak windfalls happen to me. How come when I'm in town, George, you're forever jetting out to the Coast?" Joe snarled. "Now I'm stuck out here and I need you, where are you?"

"I told you I'd be out there next week, Joe. Norman wants me there for meetings. Stay cool. Something will turn up."

Norman French was George's Hollywood side-kick. Joe knew that when George flew out for meetings, something unusually big was afoot. He was neither encouraged nor curious. He wasn't looking for anything big, just quick redemption from Freak City.

Meanwhile, he was still in bondage to *The Snipe*. Joe plunged back into the regime of cabs to Pacifica studios and endless cups of black coffee that tasted of Styrofoam.

The money was nice, Chalice decided. And getting out of that atrocity for Amos Bane was even nicer. But she was left with a void. Mercifully, it only lasted a couple of days. Robert called with the news late on Thursday.

"When was the last time you collaborated?" he asked her.

"When I worked on the *Night Watch* team," she told him. "Why?"

Night Watch was a network series. If he was pushing television again, she was way beyond being choosy. "I'll take TV if that's what you're asking Robert."

"I'm not. I'm talking big movie," he said. "So big that the producer is convinced he needs two writers.

Are you ready for this? The option on the Oestermann book has found a permanent home at Pacifica. Lou Hosner's going to exercise it before it runs out. I never thought he'd have the guts. Maybe the Greek's got something to do with it. Anyway, you've got a chance to cowrite. How does that grab you?"

She wanted to whoop for joy, but it was several moments before she could utter a sound.

"Hey, out there," Robert said. "Can you hear me?"

"Oh, Robert, you're a miracle man. For an opportunity like that I'd collaborate with Mickey Mouse."

He laughed. "That might be a little easier than the collaborator Hosner has in mind. The two of you are chalk and cheese when it comes to style. But he's good, and Hosner thinks maybe this is one property where those opposing styles could be synergistic." He sighed. "It could also be a tug-of-war."

"I'll bend, no matter who it is. I've done a lot of team work in the past. Who would I be working with anyway?"

"Joe Verdi. He's just finishing up on *The Snipe*. So he'll be available. Are you familiar with his work?"

"Yes. I know him." It was no more than a voiceless whisper. *Double whammy*. The bucking movements of her heart were making it very difficult to breathe, but Robert didn't seem to notice.

"Verdi hasn't given an answer yet. Not that I can imagine any writer turning this one down. But his agent says he's never collaborated before, and basically he's a stage playwright . . . never stays in Hollywood longer than he absolutely has to. So I don't know."

The receiver was becoming warm and slippery in her hands, and Robert's words were beginning to run together in her mind, like one long string of scenery glimpsed from the window of a speeding train. This wasn't exactly nonchalance, she thought, grasping for it as if it could be plucked from the air. Pay attention. Never mind Joe Verdi. This is Robert talking about a plum job.

"He's got some heavy credits," Robert was saying, "but he's a tough, two-fisted, gut-level writer, and unless you can blend with him seamlessly, I can't see it working out. Anyway, I've set up a meeting for tomorrow afternoon. The Polo Lounge. Verdi and his agent will be there, and Lou Hosner wants to give you a pitch. Verdi only takes screen jobs when he's hurting, and he just picked up a nice bundle on *The Snipe.*" He paused and cleared his throat discreetly. "Should've been yours, of course. But that wasn't his fault. No hard feelings there, I hope . . . Chalice?"

She forced her mind back to his voice. "No, of course not, Robert. No hard feelings."

"Good. So wear something sexy, will you? We'll need all the help we can get."

Chapter 11

CHALICE HAD TAKEN ROBERT'S ADMONITION TO HEART. She sat at the cocktail table wearing misty gray-green: modified harem pants that tapered down her calves to a slender hugging of her ankles. The loose matching blouse had a softly draped neck, and slim-heeled sandals gave her height and presence. It wasn't blatantly sexy, but it was a soft and graceful outfit. It would give her a feminine edge, she had decided, in the otherwise male congregation of button-down shirts and square-shouldered jackets.

But once she was seated with the men, Joe's presence made the bare skin below her short sleeves feel moist and vulnerable.

In dove gray pants and dark blazer, Joe looked centered, undistracted by her presence. He had shaken her hand in greeting, as though she were the most casual of acquaintances. His eyes, usually so

expressive, were as opaque as olives, earnestly attentive to Lou Hosner's opening remarks.

Hosner had joined them, it seemed, like a lay
minister, to solemnize the meeting with a corporate
blessing from the studio.

Chalice sat politely straight in her chair, trying to
pay attention to the man who ran Pacifica. He was
rolling out long, sonorous statements about doing
justice to the memory of a great writer, and handing
out compliments about the sharp edge of Joe's
writing and the soft subtleties of Chalice's. And
there were several weighty sentences which began:
*Once in a great while, it behooves the Motion Picture
Industry* . . .

But when the studio boss rose to go, leaving the
four of them to get down to business, Chalice
realized she had missed great chunks of what he'd
said. The very nearness of Joe, she discovered, was
beginning to cook her brains.

She struggled against distraction and felt the edge
of panic advance. Even while the two agents covered
the important points of Hosner's offer—the time
frame and the payments involved—she dimmed out,
aware of little but Joe's lean brown hand resting on
the arm of his chair to her left, the solemn set of his
clean profile hovering at the edge of her range of
vision. She longed to turn and face him but dared
not. She fought with herself to listen, her muscles
constricting with effort. But her concentration was
fine sand falling through a sieve.

This wasn't going to work, she thought. She was
coming unglued, and sooner or later someone would
notice. *But it had to work.*

With a monumental act of will, she turned back

into the discussion just as Robert was saying, "a third up front, a third at the start of production, and the balance when it's wrapped."

For the first time, she realized that the script contract would run until the entire film had been shot.

"Joe? Chalice? It's up to the two of you now. You have to decide if you can work as a team," Robert finished.

George Nadel's pale blue eyes turned to Robert. "They've only got four days to get acquainted and explore this thing. Let's give them all the time available to come up with their answer. Why don't we split right now and let the talent confer?"

Robert rose as if on cue, and it occurred to her that leaving her and Joe alone together had been prearranged between the two agents. George held out his hand to Chalice and said, "Nice meeting you, Miss York." Then he gripped Joe's shoulder. "You know where to reach me."

"Order whatever you want, you two," Robert said. "The tab's taken care of." He turned to Chalice. "I'll be hearing from you by Wednesday, then?"

Chalice shook hands, smiled, nodded like a wind-up toy, and watched the two men leave, Robert all slender agility under his light tan suit, George Nadel thick-shouldered and heavily important.

Left alone with Joe, her muscles ached with the tension of the previous hour, which now intensified. She could think of nothing to say, she realized. Panic feathered her throat, furred her lungs. All her presence of mind was involved in breathing normally. She ought to be contributing to this, she thought wildly. But all she could do was give docile little nods.

It wasn't as if she'd come totally unprepared. She had expected an awkwardness at seeing Joe again, a sexual tugging which she would carefully subdue. But this total wrecking of her nervous system had taken her by surprise; she had no defense against it.

How utterly relaxed he was, she thought despairingly, sipping his Dry Sack on the rocks and apparently more amused than disturbed by her presence. Did it do nothing to him at all? Had he so completely forgotten what it was like with them only four weeks ago?

After cradling his drink for the longest time, he set it down, then slumped back in his chair with a theatrical sigh.

"Ah, Amanda," he drawled, "alone at last." He passed a distracted hand over his hairline, reminiscent of Noel Coward, and managed to make her smile. But she still couldn't find any words.

He became polite and distant, as he said, "How have you been?"

How have I been? I've been watching cracks in the ceiling until my brain is muscle-bound. I've been fooling myself that you don't matter to me, and the effort is incapacitating. I'm turning into a vegetable. I'm a nervous wreck.

She squeezed something appropriate from her throat. "Just fine, Joe. And you?"

He nodded, making a grudging sound behind lips that were thin with compression.

Thin, she thought. The sleek, hard body with its sculpted flesh packed so firmly under the skin was different now. The bumpy bridge of his nose seemed more pronounced, and it occurred to her that his face was starker, craggier than before. He had lost some weight.

He gave her a wintry smile, then looked down, examining his square-cut fingernails. "You look nice," he said.

"Thank you," she murmured helplessly.

He looked up again, and his eyes were flintlike above the tight smile. "I was wondering what would win out: the offer or your aversion to me. But you're here, so I guess that answers it."

"Aversion?" she said, shaken out of her numbness. "I have no aversion to you, Joe. I've just been struggling with—"

"Spare me the details, York," he cut in. "The point is, you're willing to consider a working arrangement or you wouldn't be here. Right?"

"Right," she whispered, trying to rise above the withering effect his words were having on her.

"Okay. So let's get down to it."

She glanced around the room, jittery. Happy hour was gathering momentum. All the tables in the lounge had filled, and the noise level had risen. In her painful oversensitivity, the chatter all around her seemed deafening. A hopeless distraction.

"Perhaps we could discuss this in a more private place? Somewhere quieter at least." She brought her hand to her temples and found them moist. "I just can't stand—I can't think in here. It's so rowdy."

Joe shrugged good-naturedly. "Whatever. Are you hungry? We could talk over dinner, I suppose."

There was a sickening emptiness where her stomach used to be, but she could hardly mistake it for hunger. "It's a bit early for dinner," she said. "But I have the car outside. We could go to your place, or mine."

Your place or mine. She folded inside as she heard herself say the words. That's just what she needed— to lay herself open to some snide retort.

But there wasn't a trace of amusement in his face as he rose to his feet. "My place is closer," he said neutrally, "but it's all the same to me."

She sat stiffly behind the wheel and pointed the Honda into the sluggish progression of six o'clock cars on Wilshire Boulevard. The air was stifling. She closed the windows and turned the air conditioner on full blast.

But his dogged silence was suffocating too, as they inched toward Brentwood. She could sense him beside her, challenging her to say something.

"Of course I want the job, Joe," she said, scowling through the windshield. "What screenwriter wouldn't?"

"None I can think of." There was flint in his voice too.

He was determined to keep this thick sheet of indifference between them. If she didn't break through, they'd never be able to talk properly. Her voice was watery. "I really don't have anything against you, Joe. Far from it."

"My mistake," he said drily.

"It's just that I really have been awfully . . . tied up."

"Sure. *Hubcaps.* I read about it."

Why was she lying to him? Panic began to tighten in her chest. Ignore it. Think of the project. They were prospective collaborators. It was just a writing assignment.

"I suppose the major problem with adapting the book would be the sprawl in time and settings," she said.

"So you *have* read it."

Such lashing scorn in his voice. Not the same man. *Cupcake. Sweetheart, I love loving you.*

"Of course I've read it."

"Then you must realize that the sprawl is part of its charm."

Sprawl. Limbs sprawled to receive him. His toes on her instep. His lips on her thigh.

"Yes, but there'll have to be drastic cuts and telescoping. I've been trying to decide in my head what's expendable. If we could agree on that . . ."

In a desultory fashion, they began to discuss ways and means of adapting the great masterpiece to the stringent limitation of sight and sound. But they were just making sounds. There was no bounce, no give-and-take of ideas. She was cut loose from the subject and vaporous, as if the lining of her body had turned to steam. The book, Hosner's offer, the words they spoke, none of it seemed real.

Only the devastating fact of Joe beside her was real, the deep vibrations of his voice, the polished gleam of his closely shaven jaw glimpsed out of the corner of her eye as the late sunlight penetrated the car window and stung her eyes. She asked him to reach back to the rear seat and get her sunglasses out of her purse.

Behind the smoked lenses, she pressed on with it. She tried to break out of this stupefying box that had closed around her, hearing his words, hearing her own coming from some detached and automated zone of her mind. It was so futile, like trying to get enthusiastic about discussing the weather when someone dear to you lay bleeding to death. Did he feel it too? she wondered. This hopeless futility? It was impossible to tell.

Her hands grew sticky on the hot rim of the steering wheel.

When she followed him into the Brentwood house, the full weight of nostalgic despair descended on her. The house roared out to her with happy echoes, past acts of tenderness, laughter, and completeness. All in the past. All irretrievably lost. But every shared moment still imprinted its tormenting afterimage on the enclosed space of the living room.

Left alone for a moment, she abandoned all thought of the screenplay and leaned against the window, staring out at the silvery leaves of the olive tree on the front lawn.

Her strategy with Joe had been stupid, she thought. This wasn't like an attack of flu, where you could predictably recover after a few days of rest and isolation. She had gotten away with her bland, self-protective lies on the telephone, but his physical presence stripped her of artifice. It mocked her feeble attempts to declare herself independent of him. She had let herself love him, and, like a virus, it still raged in her system.

He came toward her from the kitchen, bearing a glass of soda, but she declined the drink and he set it down.

"Joe," she said softly, "we're not getting anywhere with this, are we? There's something personal between us we have to resolve first."

"I thought you already had. Several weeks ago."

She plunged in before she lost her nerve. "It was

seeing Shirley," she blurted out. "I was simply startled at first, then I realized I was jealous, and hurt, and angry."

In the fragile silence that followed, she turned her back to him. "Oh God, this sounds so lame. I was suddenly teeming with feelings I had no right to."

She heard a movement behind her, felt the pressure of his fingers on her shoulders. Slowly he turned her around to face him. She expected him to protest his innocence, cut her off somehow, and refute every word she'd said. But he was silent. The flint had faded from his eyes, and the hurt she saw there made her voice falter.

"It was all so irrational," she whispered. "I knew that. And when I have irrational feelings, I tend to run for cover as fast as I can."

Pinpoints of flame played somewhere in the depths of his eyes, then disappeared. His voice was astringent. "Certain situations tend to foster irrational feelings," he said. "Why should you be immune? Nobody else is."

"That's the point; I'm not immune. It was such a powerless feeling," she murmured. "It scared me out of my wits."

She yearned for some kindness, a prop, a cigarette, something to hold in her hands. But she had left her purse on the sofa, on the other side of the room. He stood blocking her way. Instead of going around him, she stood there, the fingers of both hands entwined and twisting wildly. He noticed the movement, caught up her hands, and locked them in his own, squeezing them until she could feel her knuckles grind together.

His voice was gruff. "Powerless? That's a strange

word to use. When two people get as close as we did, where the hell does power come into it? I don't get it. Didn't you trust me?"

Trust him how? she wondered. Trust him to handle her with tender loving care? Trust him to be there always when it was a foregone conclusion that he wouldn't be? She stared at the faded rust carpet. "You'll be going back to New York when this is over."

"That's not a crime," he said.

This affectionate man, whose honeyed attentions had bound her to him, was addressing her with such a taut, deadpan face. Such harsh clarity. "New York is where my life is. But right now I'm here. We've been offered a project to work on together. Are we accepting it or not?"

His harshness seemed to strengthen her spine. She withdrew her hands from his punishing grip. "Could we work together without romantic involvement?" she asked him, surprised at the blandness of her voice.

He seemed to give it some thought, thrusting his hands deep into his pockets, and lifting one corner of his tightened lips. "I honestly don't know," he said after a moment. "Could we?"

I couldn't, she thought. I have no sense of propriety when I'm with you. My defenses are tissue paper. Silently she willed him to say something further.

"I can only speak for myself," he said. "Could I be with you day after day without wanting you? No. I'd be a liar to say anything different. But I want this job, and Hosner only wants me as half of this duo, so we're stuck with each other. But I'm not going to attack you. If you feel the need to set up conditions, feel free." A rising edge crept into his voice. "Write them into a side agreement and we'll have it notarized. I'll abide by whatever you . . ."

His voice trailed off in a descending scale. Something infinitesimal shifted in the desolate landscape of his face, and she knew. She could never have explained the source of that knowledge, but it was suddenly plain that he loved her. His deepest feelings were at stake. And if they worked together, he would be prying himself open to the pain of loss as much as she was. The thought buoyed her with courage.

She tried to imagine their collaboration. There would be weeks and weeks of working together, enmeshing their separate visions and skills, their minds and hearts. She could set up conditions, but they'd never work, not after all the embraces they'd shared. Their intimate needs would become mutually transparent again. They would touch, merge, ignite. They would be lovers again. And then the project would come to an end. They would go their separate ways, and for all her attempts at lightness, the parting would hurt as nothing had ever hurt before.

Was it really worth the final amputation? There would be other projects, other opportunities. It was wisdom to walk away from this one. But a mean and paltry kind of wisdom, she thought, to turn her face away from the richest experience life had ever offered.

"Let's go for it." Her voice was crisp. "A side agreement would be absurd. Let's just try to make like a writing team."

His arms opened as if he would embrace her, and she longed to slip into them. She hesitated just a moment too long and saw his mood change in the slight stiffening of his shoulders. "Partners, then?" He was holding out his right hand.

"Partners," she said, and they shook on it.

It was Chalice's choice to work in the Writers' Building at the studios, and she hadn't minced words.

Your place has too many distracting memories; so has mine. If we're going to work together, we need a neutral place that doesn't remind me of sex.

You couldn't put it more succinctly than that, he thought. So they were to use an office at the studio because he couldn't seduce her there. No conditions, she'd told him.

This wasn't going to be quite the way he'd pictured it, he thought as they walked away from the executive building, carrying their newly signed contracts. A disgruntled mood settled on him like heavy fog.

"I've developed a rough treatment since I last saw you," she said. "I'm sure you've done some preliminary thinking too."

Yes, he'd had plenty of time for thinking these past five days. He had thought they would spend those days together. They would take off down the coast, maybe to Mexico. Smooth out the wrinkles between them that had made them such sudden strangers. They would lie in the sun, discussing the book and making notes, then return to some cool adobe hotel for tender afternoons of lovemaking. It hadn't been like that, and apparently it wasn't going to be.

They had simply shaken hands on a partnership. She had refused to have dinner with him that night.

And when he called her the following day . . . *Let's not start working in tandem until the contract comes through. I need to read the book again. Make some notes. I'm not ready for any brainstorming at the moment.*

"At the moment, it's not your brains I'm thinking of storming," he'd told her, and knew immediately it was a mistake.

Now, walking beside her to the car, he balled up his hands inside his leather jacket and wondered if the whole arrangement was a mistake. He reminded himself of the condo. That's what this was all about. Was it? he wondered. Was it really?

"Well, today's shot," she said, bending her arm with military precision to check her wristwatch. "It's almost six. I guess we should get cracking first thing tomorrow. They said room 703 in the Writers' Building is ready for us. It's got two desks and a small conference—"

"Yes, I know what they said."

She slowed as they approached her car, and looked up at him with a bland smile. "Shall we start bright and early in the morning then?"

They should start tonight by celebrating, he thought. This was a big signing, for God's sake. She was brushing him off again, oh so politely. Screw her.

He nodded agreeably, returning her bland smile. "Is nine bright and early enough for you?"

She stood by the car, holding the door handle. In spite of his smile, there were tension lines between his brows. She was being stupidly officious and she couldn't stop. *I'm trembling inside, Joe,* she wanted to tell him. *For pity's sake, touch me. Be like you were.* He was on the other side of a thick wall.

"Do you want a ride home?" she asked in that clipped voice.

"I'm perfectly capable of getting back to Brentwood," he snapped, and turned on his heel. "I'll see you here at nine tomorrow."

Chalice threw herself down on the battered leather couch and shook her head. "I think the ending stinks," she told Joe.

They had been working in harness for three weeks now, and were finishing up the second draft. Chalice held a batch of manuscript in her hand; it was a pivotal scene they had just read through together. "Walter's about to destroy himself," she pointed out, "but that last line of his won't cut it. It's thrown away."

Joe perched on the edge of the desk and exhaled noisily. "Not thrown away, just handled subtly. Oestermann structured all his tragic scenes subtly. You may have noticed. He tended to favor the pen over the trowel."

She was not going to get drawn into a battle of sarcasm. Joe always won. "Look, there's a big difference between belaboring the point and simple clarity," she said slowly. She was tired, almost too tired to argue. Almost too tired to stop herself from smoothing the dark hair back from his ears. He needed a trim, she thought, and dragged her protesting mind back to the script. "Our medium's the screen, not the printed page. We've cut out all the internalizing. I'm not sure that Walter's intentions are going to come across to the audience."

"What do you suggest? We hit the audience over the head with a two-by-four? Come on, York. Think of the scene on the train. It's obvious what's happening to him. His life is coming apart at the seams."

So is mine, she thought suddenly. Chalice sighed and let her head fall back on the sofa. "Perhaps you're right." Her very bones seemed bruised from exhaustion.

It had been the hardest three weeks of her life. They never touched; they spoke of nothing but the script. They were writing partners and nothing more, meeting in this studio office every morning at nine and parting at six or seven, to go their separate ways.

The studio thought they were coming through beautifully. Ahead of schedule even. Hosner had acquired Cantrel as director on the strength of their first draft, and Tim Sacco had signed to play the male lead. Preproduction was almost complete. There would be much rewriting to come, but it would all be done on demand when they were on location in England, the setting for the bulk of the shooting. They were all taking Pan Am next week.

Yes, anyone would say they'd done well, she thought. But the unspoken tension between them was making her distraught. They didn't even need to be working today. But here they were, by tacit consent, boxed up in this room and arguing over a scene that would probably be reworded yet again in England. They should be off on some beach with their arms wrapped around each other. Did he really not find her desirable anymore?

Each day she would drive home bruised with exhaustion. Outside of script discussion, Joe was meticulously polite, civil and considerate about mealtimes and coffee breaks, but he was so utterly closed. Unreachable. This implacable detachment of his was becoming unbearable.

"All right," she said, too drained to pursue it. "No two-by-fours. Let's leave it the way it is."

Joe came across the room and stood looking down at her. Cool, polite concern etched the corners of his mouth. "Are you okay?" he asked her.

Chalice stared at the plaster ceiling. "Sure."

"You don't usually retreat that fast."

"I'm tired."

"Me too," Joe said. "Drained." He took the script out of her hands and pulled her off the sofa. "It's been a tough three weeks. Let's pack it in. We've got enough for Oliver to work on until Cornwall."

He was still holding her wrists.

In all the hours they'd spent alone together, this was the first time their skin had touched. The tactile sensation went screaming through her nervous system, and she leaned against him, feeling herself rapidly weakening.

Suddenly his mouth was opening hers with a fierce, demanding need. She felt a moment's astonishment at the instant reversal of his mood, then abandoned herself to the kiss. His hand moved down the small of her back, pressing her closer to him until she could feel the fierce awakening in his loins.

"All the time we've wasted," he breathed into her mouth, then pushed her away hurriedly. She spilled back onto the sofa behind her, eyes still closed. His footsteps retreated behind her, then came back.

When she opened her eyes, he was standing over her naked, reaching for the buttons of her blouse. "I locked the door."

He intended to make love to her here? She

watched his hands peel off her blouse and pass feverishly over her face, her shoulders, her breasts. Hot urgency wrestled in her with an ingrained sense of decency. They were in the studio. In the Writers' Building. Just a few steps away was a clerk. Outside in the corridor she could hear the *glug glug* of the water cooler. This was no place for intimacy. "Not here, Joe," she breathed.

"Yes here," he said, unhooking her bra and claiming her breasts with cupped hands. "Here, and now."

"There are people outside. We could go to your place. It's not far."

"It's too far. You're the one who insisted we work at the studio. 'A neutral place that doesn't remind us of sex,' you insisted. What an idiot you were. What an idiot I was to agree."

"Joe," she said, unresisting, "we could be in your bed in twenty minutes."

"You should have said that earlier." He took her hand and held it against the rigid spur between his thighs, whispering, "I can't go anywhere like this."

Her fingers curled tightly around his blood-swollen flesh. "What was I supposed to say?" she asked him. "I've come to the end of my restraint? In a few minutes I will want you so badly that we'd better leave now before it's too late?"

He was struggling with her tricky waistband. "For God's sake, take off your jeans and let me in," he said, tugging at the denim that guarded her.

She obeyed, suddenly helpless to do otherwise. "Supposing Cantrel drops in to see us?"

"Shut up," he moaned, and lowered his body to hers.

Weeks of spurious detachment slipped away as they burrowed blindly into each other. They were together, they were entwined, and they were one, spilling over the edge of pleasure too fast.

It was more like an exorcism than an act of love, she thought. There had been no question of holding back. His pent-up need had exploded as unstoppably as her own. She lay in a glistening tangle of limbs, while their essences mingled, skin on hot slippery skin, her sweat-darkened hair half pasted to his shoulder.

The leather couch felt clammy to her moist back, but she lay there, not caring. It didn't matter. And it didn't matter that he hadn't wooed her with the sweetly seductive foreplay she remembered of him, and had always savored as much as the act of love itself. My God, what had these three torturous weeks been but foreplay? *How did I ever develop such a terrible dependency on another human being?*

"Sorry," Joe said as they began to dress with a sheepish haste. "You've gotten me so damn horny I couldn't wait. Not when I knew you wanted me again."

Wanted him again, she thought. As if she'd ever stopped wanting him.

"If it's okay with you, let's scram. Take me home?" he pleaded. "I'd like to run through that again with a little more finesse," he said, the lopsided tilt of his mouth etching an embarrassed grin.

"It's okay with me," she said.

Lou Hosner swept by in a white limousine and waved to Chalice and Joe as they crossed the parking lot, hands tightly clasped.

It was midafternoon, and she felt strange stealing

away from the office. That was stupid. They were
ahead of schedule, and they weren't supposed to be
punching clocks, but still . . .

"He makes me feel guilty," she told Joe.

"Why?"

Her eyes brimmed with love as she looked up into
his face. "You know why."

Joe put an arm around her waist and laid his cheek
on her hair. "I know," he said tenderly. "Your
WASP propriety. You're incurably decent. But don't
worry. I won't do that to you again, cupcake."

"Let's not overreact," she said, fearing he might
retreat again behind that awful wall of civility.

"Not a chance." His hand spread over her waist,
then lightly touched the underside of her breast. "I
just meant in future, I won't attack you in the
Writers' Building."

"Ah. You quite sure?"

"Absolutely." He gestured over his shoulder with
a gay tilt of the head, as they left the building
behind. "We're not spending another minute in
there."

Chapter 12

PENRITH CASTLE STOOD HIGH ABOVE THE ATLANTIC ON a dramatic red cliff. The south face, built Norman style of massive gray stone slabs, had stood intact for six centuries, cloaking the crumbling interior. But the "new wing"—a mere three centuries old—had been cunningly restored and refurbished to house twentieth-century guests who could later claim to have slept in the home of a Norman baron. With its adjacent village, supported by fishing and tourism, Penrith Castle satisfied all the demanding visual requirements for the filming of *Many a Man*.

For most of May, Penrith would be occupied by Pacifica Studios, with Oliver Cantrel as king of the castle. The occupation had begun three days ago, but the principals had arrived only last night.

In the cool morning haze of early summer, the colors were breathtaking. Chalice had not seen the

West Country before. She leaned out of her window
in the guest wing that first morning and gasped with
pleasure. Cornwall in May was densely green, and
the moist air was redolent with the scent of flowering
privet and hawthorn. On the downs beyond the
castle walls she could see the cluster of trailers that
housed the production crew and the camera equipment, a sharp reminder of why she was here. But
beyond the production encampment, ousted sheep
grazed in a patch of bright green meadow gilded with
buttercups.

She glanced back at the bed where Joe lay in a
sleeping ball under the sheet. Movie or no movie, it
felt like a honeymoon.

They were still constantly at odds over the script,
but the verbal abuse between them was now suffused
with intimacy. They had been lovers again for almost
a week. There would be another twenty days for
them to be together, perhaps twenty-two if they
lagged behind schedule. And then . . .

A premonitory chill made her shiver. It was just as
well they found so much to argue about, she
thought. It warded off the cold. It kept her from
dwelling on how hopelessly she loved him, and how
much pain was in store when it was over. Because it
would be over. She needed Hollywood. Joe was an
incurable East Coaster, and Hollywood grated on
him. It was an insoluble problem, so they ignored it.
They never even discussed a time beyond this contract. At the moment, such a time didn't exist.

She thought of the weeks she'd wasted so stupidly
because of Shirley. She ought to have been grateful
to the woman. If it hadn't been for Shirley cutting
into his financial calculations, Joe would be back in
New York right now.

The chill of the flagstone floor began to seep through the soles of her bare feet, and she padded back to the sheepskin rug by the bed.

"Joe," she called out softly. "Time to wake up."

He stirred, rolled over on his stomach, and sank into the pillow. One brown leg protruded from the sheet.

"Hey, big-time playwright, what do you think this is, a vacation?" she said, sitting on the bed and placing an icy foot in the warm bend of his knee. "We have work to do."

"Some women," he muttered, "are given to good morning kisses." He flopped on his back, his eyes still closed. "I had to find the cold-feet type."

The sheet was wound around him from the navel up, exposing the warm brown chest with its dark curls.

"I'm not averse to a morning kiss." She lowered her mouth to his.

His arms came up to hold her, then pushed her away. "What's this? Dressed already?"

"I can kiss you with my clothes on."

"Yes, but—"

"But nothing," she said crisply. "It's almost nine o'clock and we have work to do. I'm going to make a start while you get dressed."

She drew on some socks and moccasins, then finished unpacking, placing underwear and tops into the second drawer of the fruitwood dresser.

Joe lingered on the high four-poster bed, watching her bustle about the room, and making soft groaning protests in his early-morning voice.

"Stop complaining," Chalice said cheerfully. "We really lucked out with this arrangement. Adjoining rooms! We could have wound up with me here, and you in one of those bed-and-breakfast places on the other side of the village."

"That wasn't luck, dum-dum. I told Dilly we wanted to sleep together."

Chalice froze, clutching a small makeup kit. "You told her?" Dilly, the production secretary, had taken care of all their travel arrangements, and it had never occurred to Chalice that . . . "You *told* her?" she repeated, shocked.

He was beside her instantly, cupping her face with hands still warm from sleep. "Yes, I told her, sweetie. Do you mind that much? I'm not ashamed of being your lover."

"I thought it was a private thing," she said. "Just between the two of us. You might as well have posted it on the call board."

"My face posts it, cupcake. Anyone could tell I'm crazy about you. They're not blind and they're not idiots. Don't you think they all know anyway?"

"I'm sure they know now." She could feel herself blushing.

"And now we have this haven to ourselves and the next-door room for working. As you say, we could have been at opposite ends of the village. Oh, cupcake, I love it when you blush. Have I offended you?"

She shook her head.

"I just wanted this time to be something we'd always remember. No glitches. It's such a little time."

He was nudging the tip of his nose into her hair, placing warm, soft kisses pleadingly behind her ear.

She smoothed her palms over his neck and felt the warm down below his cut hair. Yes, there was so little time and she was a fool to waste a moment. "I think I dressed prematurely," she whispered, and kicked off her shoes. "Let's snuggle up under the covers."

He took her to bed fully clothed, and for the space of a few heartbeats, simply held her in the secure vise of his arms and legs, flooding her with warmth. Then his arms relaxed, and his fingers slipped under her blouse, unhooking her bra and tracing the bones in her spine. His head disappeared under the soft quilt. His hand explored under her loosened bra. Then he began to kiss wherever he touched. He felt for the zipper of her jeans and slid it down from the waist.

"Ah love, not now. We should get to work," she said without conviction.

His lips moved against one of her nipples, and his words floated up to her, lazy and muffled. "You said you wanted to snuggle . . ."

Slowly, in the warm darkness beneath the covers, he slid wool and silk down over the curve of her buttocks, binding her thighs together. His fingertips edged into the tightness between her legs.

"Hey down there, come up here!"

His tousled head emerged, smiling as his fingers below parted her confined flesh. "You called?"

"I said snuggle," she whispered, knowing it was pointless. "Now you're turning me on."

"Can I help it if I'm irresistible to you?" he said, grinning.

She leaned away from him, trying not to smile. "It's scandalous. It's not . . . not British."

He hovered with his parted lips above hers. "Neither am I," he breathed fervently. "Neither am I."

It was another hour before she was in the adjoining room, reading through the notes of their last story conference with Cantrel. The notes had been taken during the flight.

"It boils down to this," she told Joe, when he emerged from the bathroom. "Tim Sacco's not happy with his lines in the last scene with Mary. And he thinks the first love scene should be more erotic."

Joe glowered. He hadn't met the star in person yet, but Tim Sacco had had five days with the script, and the feedback kept coming in. It didn't bode well. "Why is Oliver letting him get away with the changes?" he asked.

Chalice twisted round in the desk chair. "Because he has to, like it or not. It's the way Sacco's contract is written."

Joe remained standing in the bathroom doorway. He wore dark brown cords and a crewneck sweater she'd never seen before. "So who do we please?"

"Whom," Chalice said, straight-faced.

"Right." He grinned and pushed himself away from the doorframe. "Since you have all the answers, why don't you do the rewrite to please *whom*, while I scout around a bit. Sacco won't even arrive until tonight, and from what I've heard, he'll be more interested in prospecting the broads than discussing his script."

"Thanks a lot. Actually, we'll wind up having to please both of them."

Joe chewed his lower lip. "Both of them," he repeated. "And Oliver likes it the way it is at this point. Seems to me there's only one solution. Let's go find some breakfast."

"You go if you want," she said. "But if feels like the wrong time of day for breakfast, and I'm not hungry."

"Well it's not and you will be," he said, glancing at his watch. "They've stopped serving it in the dining hall, but we could go off into the village and find something. I'm ravenous."

She grinned and turned back to her notes. "You have a right to be. Go ahead, make like a tourist today. I don't mind going it alone for a while."

He had taken her at her word, she realized, when she went to the vast dining hall for lunch. Joe had walked down to the village, a cameraman told her, to do some exploring. After a meal of poached plaice and asparagus, she returned to work, already beginning to miss him.

The pressure was off them at the moment, and the work went faster alone than with Joe. They were both too strong in their ideas. It wasn't synergy, when they tried to write together. It was overkill. But still, after three hours without him, she had a sense already of being off center. She had slipped so quickly into this habit of having him around. How long would it take her, she wondered, to like being alone again?

She was just typing a clean copy of the rewrites when Joe walked back in the room. It was past five. "Still here?" he said.

"No, she left. You're looking at the ghost of Guinevere." Chalice rolled a fresh sheet into the machine to type the last page. She kept her back to him, although God knew, she was glad he was back. Too glad. She was unwilling to turn and show the utter joy she felt sure was betrayed in her face.

"You're a workaholic," he complained, sliding his hands over her shoulders.

"That's what we're here for. Pierce and Magnum are setting up tomorrow's shots. Cantrel and

Schmidt are out recruiting extras. The actors are rehearsing their lines or resting up for the siege. Where the hell have you been?"

He leaned over her, smelling of Harris tweed, cut grass, and country ale, and kissed her cheek. "Aarrr," he murmured, affecting a Cornish lilt, "the dulcet tones of me own true love." He pinched her earlobe, waggling it playfully. "You're beginning to sound like a wife."

Butterflies skittered through her stomach, and she was very glad her face was turned away. "I'm beginning to feel like one—left here slaving over a hot typewriter all day while you go gallivanting."

He lifted her out of the chair and into an exuberant bear hug, then swept her through the door. "I'm about to make it up to you."

Three stone flights down, the small black car in the middle of the cobbled courtyard looked squat and shiny and anachronistic.

"It was no mean feat," Joe said proudly. "The nearest car rental is Falmouth. I hitched a ride, hopped a bus, got off at the wrong stop. But I found one in the end. It's a Vauxhall," he added. "I'm taking you on all kinds of excursions."

She looked at him questioningly. One of the sad things about this business was, you got all hyped up about going to an exciting location, then never got to see anything but the film set and the trailers. This day was probably the only leisurely one they'd have. Cantrel was allowing for travel fatigue. "Excursions?" she echoed drily.

"Damn right." Joe's eyes were exultant, and there was a touch of rebellion in his voice. "We're in the West Country and we're together. It's a first and probably a last too. So work or no work, we're going to get the most out of it."

"Darling, we're rooming together. That's the most we can expect on location."

"There are union rules. Cantrel can't work us sixteen hours a day," he pointed out. "We'll take walks on the Cornish Coast Path, explore the pubs, eat pasties and clotted cream in thatched cottages. We'll drive across the peninsula to St. Ives and find the man with seven wives; we'll pay our respects to the ghost of King Arthur at Tintagel; and we'll drink wine and pick daisies amid the ruins of some crumbled monastery. The works. All the things tourists are supposed to do in these parts."

And lovers are supposed to do, she thought. If only they could. "And when are we supposed to work on the neverending rewrites?" she said plaintively.

"Hey, we can't do another thing before we meet with Sacco. First things first. Do you realize we haven't even looked at the ocean yet?"

Chalice smiled. "We saw it from the train."

"I want to see it from the castle turrets, where William of Penrith plighted his troth to the Lady Katherine and repelled the archers of the Genoese with flaming arrows."

"Are you making it up or have you been reading the brochure?" she asked.

"Both." He took her hand, and she was seized by the fleetingness of things. Tonight Tim Sacco would arrive. Tomorrow would be an endless round of fragmented meetings, fitted around the shooting schedule. Then Cantrel would discover those scenes that didn't play well, no matter how good they had looked on paper. From tomorrow on they would be run ragged. And they'd barely caught their breaths yet. There was hardly time for anything, she thought. Just twenty-some days to live a lifetime.

As the precious days slipped by, time pressed down on his chest like a leaden weight. Joe found himself resenting the endless hours they spent cutting scenes out, writing new transitions, putting scenes back after they'd been deleted. Interminable nit-picking script conferences. And worst of all, Sacco, with an absurd contract that gave him more say over his scenes than any mere actor ought to have.

Tim Sacco was a muscled version of Clint Eastwood, with a sickening charm that was fatal with the ladies, and an ego far wider than his shoulders.

There was a forty-five-second sequence that had been shot at least a dozen times, and still Sacco was dissatisfied. During the second week, Joe became detached from the script. It wasn't David Oestermann any more; it wasn't York and Dante; it wasn't even Oliver Cantrel's vision. It was just a bunch of meaningless words on a page, most of them minced up beyond recognition at the whim of a grossly overpaid actor. Only his leisure with Chalice made sense to him, and there was precious little of that.

By the end of the second week, Joe had surrendered all writing decisions to Chalice. It took a special temperament to handle the idiocies of the movie industry. She had it; he didn't. He had become nervous and snappy and excessively argumentative. His threshold of tolerance for the film world had been crossed and double-crossed.

"Why did they have to hire El Sicko for Walter?" he complained one morning, while Chalice read through the notes on their last script conference.

It had stopped raining. They shouldn't be cooped up in here working, he thought. They should be out exploring the coves. Or exploring each other in that four-poster bed. He had never made love to her in the rain. Maybe he never would now.

He grabbed a chewed pencil from the desk and snapped it viciously. "With anyone else playing Walter, almost any other actor on God's green earth, we'd have been through by now. The whole enchilada would be in the can, and we'd be coasting blissfully through the last days of the contract."

"You saw the dailies," Chalice mumbled, trying to read her own writing. "He can act. And he's loaded with charisma."

Joe ground his teeth. "I can think of another name for it," he said, then turned to reread Chalice's latest version of the sex scene that would be taking place in a shooting brake. In desperation, she'd written a tour de force of acrobatics. Too acrobatic.

"That is a bloody physical impossibility," he declared.

"What is?"

"That," he said shoving the paper under her nose.

She took the sheet from him and reread it carefully before handing it back. "It's perfectly possible in terms of the camera," she said. "You'll see."

"No, *you'll* see. If you can't do it, you can't shoot it. Here, let me show you." He tried to tug her out of the chair, but she shook off his arm angrily. "Stop it, you maniac. It's eleven o'clock in the morning and I'm trying to write this scene."

"Well what do you think I'm doing? Fishing for herring?" Joe dropped the scene onto the pile that was still under question. His eye fell on the top sheet of the stack that was final. Chalice had penciled in some margin notes.

"I thought we got this okayed," he said. "'*It's an achingly beautiful morning*'? How is a mere cameraman supposed to capture the ache in the morning?"

Chalice sighed, and gave up all attempts to finish what she was doing. Maybe it would never get finished. And at this moment, she didn't care much.

"All I'm trying to do is spark a mood. What he'll capture hopefully is the pulsing movement of leaves in the breeze, the play of light and shadow. Achingly beautiful means so briefly perfect it could break the heart."

Like these days we have together, he thought. And I'm willfully destroying them—with a little help from Sacco and Cantrel. "Hollywood schmaltz," he mumbled, squatting down and putting his lips to her wrist. "Teach me all about Hollywood schmaltz."

Her voice went as soft as silk. "First, we lock the door."

"I already did," he said.

She stood up and slipped into his arms. "You're pretty damn sure of yourself," she murmured between kisses.

His face was solemn as he drew a finger back and forth across her lower lip. "Cupcake, except for the fact that we've got to talk to Oliver at lunch, and the fact that right now I'm going to make passionate love to you . . . I'm not sure of a damn thing anymore."

"We've got the bulk of the shooting script licked now," Oliver told them, his huge sandy head bent over a stick of pale green celery. "Except the final Walter/Mary scene. Sacco's still nit-picking. He's driving me nuts."

"You and me both," Joe said. Chalice, chewing on olives, merely nodded agreement.

For all the abuse they were taking, Cantrel observed, his writers were glowing radiantly, and attacking their food like a couple of Olympic athletes.

"You two look starved."

"Sea air," Joe said, buttering another roll and digging into his plate of mulligatawny soup. "Writing's so sedentary, we like to break it up every once in a while and have a good workout."

"Jogging?" Oliver asked politely. "Good for you. Blows away the cobwebs."

They had risen from bed and dressed hastily for lunch. The love flush that had just begun to cool on Chalice's cheeks rose again in embarrassment, but it needn't have. Cantrel had too many problems of his own to speculate on their personal relationship. They were single, healthy, attractive, and thrown together all the time. He hadn't inquired into their sleeping arrangements; that was Dilly's responsibility. But he assumed they were getting it on. As long as they delivered the goods, it was immaterial to him who was sleeping in which bed. His only problem was a shooting schedule costing ten thousand dollars a day. For the most part, the weather was cooperating, although it was always chancy in this part of the world. For outdoor scenes, you just waited on the light and the sun, ready to shoot at a moment's notice. The cast and crew were rising to the occasion, and the two writers were delivering a tour de force of patience and perception. The headaches were all caused by his star, Tim Sacco.

Cantrel looked at Joe with sympathy. "You can't stand him, can you?"

"Frankly, no. Can you?"

"I have to, I'm the director. And I like what I see in the rushes." Cantrel reached into the cut glass dish for another stem of celery and snapped it in two, pointedly, then uttered one of the masterpieces of understatement for which he was famous. "His last two films have brought him a certain following, and he is rather too concerned now with his public image."

"Yes, you could say that," Chalice said, straight-faced.

"He's asked for a one-on-one script conference with you, Chalice," Cantrell continued.

He had asked for a one-on-one conference with Joe two days ago, and after pronouncing the revised lines, "Right on," had once again changed his mind. But she made no comment.

"You're the soul of tact," Cantrel went on, "so I agreed heartily. Told him it would solve all the problems. Anything to get the show on the road. He'll be on set all afternoon, so I told him you'd get together with him after dinner."

Cantrel looked down at his soup. "When you talk to him, remember that the idea is to leave as much of the scene as possible the way it is, and convince him the Sacco image won't suffer. Gentle persuasion. You're not offended to be left out of this, are you, Joe?"

"Gentle persuasion is certainly her bag more than mine," Joe said. "But is a woman safe alone with him?"

Cantrel's piercing blue eyes crinkled humorously. "Oh, come on, you guys. He's a womanizer, I'll admit. But he's not Jack the Ripper. Jeffrey York's daughter—that impresses him. He wouldn't manhandle the distaff side of our esteemed writing team."

Joe glanced at Chalice. "Do it, for pity's sake, Chalice. Anything to get that scene in the can."

"Amen," breathed Cantrel.

Chalice nodded. "Of course, Oliver. I'll talk to him after dinner."

"I'll tell him to expect you a little after eight," Cantrel murmured, visibly relieved.

The star of *Many a Man* had refused the guest house accommodations. He had arrived in Cornwall, as he did to all his location jobs these days, in an oversized custom-fitted trailer. The technical crew had dubbed it the Love Wagon. Right now, it was parked in a green patch beyond the castle compound. The luxurious mobile unit allowed Sacco to follow his vitamin-charged diet and afforded the privacy required for one so consistently engaged in amorous adventure, she supposed. At a discreet distance from the shiny cream caravan was parked a cluster of shabbier vehicles housing his personal makeup artist, his dresser, and his cook.

Everything she'd heard about the Love Wagon was true, Chalice decided, getting her first good look at the plush interior. A playboy pad on wheels.

"Look darling," Tim Sacco purred, "I hope your sidekick isn't going to get all ruffled about this. I know how you writers are." Capped white teeth flashed in a dazzling smile.

"Don't worry about it," Chalice murmured.

Chalice took a seat on the gray kid banquette at right angles from Sacco, and withdrew a notepad from the folder she carried. "I don't think Joe has any objections," she mumbled. "He's just as anxious to get the scene right as I am."

"Good. Your partner may be a heavy on Broadway, but he doesn't have film technique in his blood like you do."

The statement was emphasized with a smoky sweep of lashes over sea green eyes. With that long, elegant nose and flaring nostrils, there was no doubt about it, she thought. Sacco was gorgeous, lounging around in his buttery cashmere sweater and tight jeans. Gorgeous like a mannequin in a shop window, she decided. Only on the screen did he resemble a flesh and blood human being.

"You're a sensitive writer," he went on. "And I have enormous respect for your creative talent. You know what my public expects. And this scene—well it's such a minor problem really. I'm sure we can lick it."

"Where exactly do you have a problem with the scene, Mr. Sacco?" Chalice asked him, becoming restive with his spiel.

He glanced behind him at the window and treated her to the famous profile. "Has the rain stopped?"

"Why, yes. It was quite dry when I walked over here." Chalice poised her pencil. "Now, could we—?"

"Oh put that away, Chalice. I want you to listen. I don't think you'll need to take notes." Sacco rose to his elegant full height. "I generally go for a stroll after dinner. We can talk and I can walk you back to the compound."

"Fine." Chalice followed him down the steps, relieved at the thought that the script difficulties could be resolved in the space of the ten-minute walk. But they began to walk in silence, Sacco expressing the need to simply breathe and ponder for a while. They were entering the rose arbor in the castle gardens before he spoke again, a moonlit tangle of narrow footpaths with trellis arches on which climbing white roses still gleamed from the recent showers.

"Mary is a simple character who's never loved anyone but Walter," he said at last, one hand resting on Chalice's shoulder and one passing reflectively over his chiseled bronze jaw.

"And in this scene," Chalice pointed out, "she's discovered his betrayal, has passed through the hurt and shock, to anger."

"But she's always found Walter irresistible," Sacco offered.

"*Uncontrollable* anger," Chalice insisted firmly. "She's ready to kill him."

"For a moment only. I just don't think I should have to work quite so hard to get the knife away from her. All that cajoling. I can't possibly take that knife seriously. Mary would never harm me."

That was baloney. Hadn't he read the book? It was on the tip of her tongue to ask him, but she bit back the words. He might be insulted. Gentle persuasion, Oliver had said. She breathed in deeply to calm her irritation. "How exactly do you see it playing in your own mind, Mr. Sacco?"

He stopped and turned her to face him. "Let's run it through, and you'll see exactly what I mean.

You're Mary. You adore me and are therefore
terribly vulnerable to being hurt by me. You approach me, knife in hand, and you raise your arm
slowly. Raise your arm, Chalice," he ordered. "As
though you're about to plunge a knife into my
chest."

Chalice obeyed.

"And I catch your arm here, and voilà."

With one swift movement, her right arm was
helpless, and she was pressed against him with his
famous nose touching hers as he bent over her. He
laughed and released her. "You're supposed to
struggle furiously," he said.

"I couldn't," she said. "You had my arms
pinned." Also, she was not built like Carolee
Downs, the statuesque leading lady who stood five
feet ten in her stockinged feet. There was absolutely
no point to this. He was showing off like a child.

"I'm sorry. I suppose I took you by surprise. Let's
try it again, and while we do it, just run the dialogue
through your head, and see how impossible it is to fit
it to the movements."

And it was virtually impossible to dislodge him,
she discovered, caught in his embrace a second time.

"You don't really want to hurt me, Mary," he
breathed, his mouth a hair's breadth away from
hers. He began to stroke the curve of her breast.

Both the words and the gestures were straight
from the script, but she felt outraged. Her hands
clenched, and she would have been tempted to kick
him in the shins if he hadn't held her too off balance
to move her feet.

She staggered back, almost toppling over as he
suddenly let go. She blinked. The man had vanished
into thin air. A long drawn-out wail pierced the

night. Then she heard a muffled voice a few feet away.

"Oh my God . . . I think it's broken." Tim Sacco sat on the grass at the edge of the rose bed, a dim, crumpled figure with one hand covering his nose.

"I hope it is," Joe said, rubbing his knuckles. He turned to Chalice with a sheepish grin, then steered her back under the trellises towards the guest wing.

"Come on, York. We'd better tell Oliver."

X-rays of Tim Sacco's valuable face had revealed no bone damage, and he was resting comfortably in his trailer bed, alone for the first time since his arrival in Cornwall. The damage to his nose was strictly surface contusions, but that was serious enough for the production—an estimated seven days before he could face the camera. It would cost the project a minimum of a quarter of a million dollars, Oliver figured, and called for battle stations.

An emergency conference involving all the principals of the production went on through the night. The long dining hall became a war room with transatlantic phone calls bouncing back and forth, leading to minute-by-minute updates of the situation. Strategy was planned and revised, calculations estimated, then refined. And gallons of black coffee were consumed under a blue cloud of cigarette smoke.

Dawn was silvering the mullioned windows by the time Joe and Chalice went to their room. Joe sank into the armchair, shaking his head like a punch-drunk fighter. His voice was flat with exhaustion. "Is it over now?"

Chalice, who had just collapsed facedown on the bed, rolled on her back and murmured, "Yes."

"So what's the score? Am I the villain or the hero? Am I coming or going? At midnight, I was officially fired for assaulting a principal. Sacco was about to press charges for assault and battery. Pacifica was withholding the balance of my fee against legal settlement. Now, suddenly, I'm to be paid in full, and nobody's suing. Run it by me again, York. It doesn't make sense."

"It does in Hollywood," Chalice said. Adrenal energy seeped through her limbs, and she sat up straight. She was way beyond sleep now.

"It's all very simple, Joe. Sacco's dropping the charges for fear of bad publicity. As for the rest, you can thank Plato Kalamandris."

Joe kicked off his shoes, still caked with mud from the rose garden, and rested his feet on the bed. "That's what I don't get. Why the sudden magnanimity? Doesn't Kalamandris own Pacifica Studios?"

"It's a personal thing. From what I gather, Tim Sacco was named in Plato's last divorce. Anyone who belts Sacco is a good guy in his eyes; his only criticism was your timing. Plato just wishes you'd waited till the wrap party; he's not crazy about pumping in another quarter of a mil, but the insurance policy might be good for it. That's why your being fired was hastily rescinded. The official word is: accident. No one to blame."

Joe squinted at her, his eyes red-rimmed. "But I have to leave the production anyway?"

"As a concession to Tim Sacco. Actually, though, he's too vain to leave his trailer before the swelling goes down, so he'll probably never know. As far as he's concerned, you've been fired off the movie."

"You make it sound so simple," Joe said.

"It is, if you understand Hollywood."

He closed his eyes. "How do you stand this business?" When she didn't answer, Joe rose from the chair and began to wander about the room, ineffectually opening and closing drawers. He was too tired to sleep and too limp to organize himself.

"What are you doing?" Chalice asked.

"Packing."

All night, she'd been functioning on red alert, in the electric, overcaffeinated atmosphere of a major crisis. But as Joe dragged out his valise, reality began to settle on her like lead. He was leaving. Collecting his things. Puttering around the room like an unshaven ghost.

"Must you do it this minute?" Her voice was testy.

Yes I must, he thought. I must do something. Her face was wan in the harsh beam of the bedside lamp, a small bleached heart against the dark blue silk of the headboard behind her. Hollywood had stupefied him. He was in danger of saying something straight out of the movies. *How can I ever leave you? Marry me, my darling. I can't live without you.*

"I'm sorry," he said. "You must be exhausted. You can turn out the light and sleep. I won't disturb you. I'll pack later."

He closed the suitcase and dragged it off the bed.

"I can't sleep," she said. "It's about six cups of coffee too late."

He changed direction like a robot, opening the suitcase flat again. "In that case, just lie down and try to rest."

"Joe, will you stop that a moment and talk to me?"

He came to rest at the far side of the bed, hugging a stack of sweaters and shirts. "I don't know what to say, York."

"For a start, you could explain why you swung at Tim Sacco."

He shrugged sullenly, his face a blank in the shadows. "He was making a pass at you."

"I'm not sure he was, actually. He would have stopped if you'd said something. You didn't have to try to bust his nose."

"Yes I did, somehow," Joe said slowly. "It was just a gut-level reaction. He's been asking for it for days now."

It was a disappointing answer. She said nothing.

"Maybe it's my street origins coming out, princess. You wouldn't know about gut reactions. You're too civilized."

Oh she was, was she? She edged around the bed towards him, wanting to take him by the ears and shake his head until his teeth fell out.

"Or maybe I've just been in Hollywood too long," he said, his voice faltering.

"But we're not in Hollywood." She scrambled to her feet and attacked him bodily, pummeling his chest with her fists as hard as she could. "Damnit, damnit, damnit, we are not in Hollywood."

He didn't defend himself. He simply stood there, holding his folded clothes, accepting her angry blows as passively as a punching bag, until she wound down and dropped her arms limply to her sides.

He looked at her white, defeated face. "You want to hear me say it, York? That I minded him touching you? Of course I minded. I was furious, jealous. But it doesn't matter, because it wouldn't work between us. Would it?"

"No." Her lips pursed in an O, then froze that way.

The clothes fell from his grasp, and he left them

on the floor. "It'll go better for you with me gone," he said. "As a writing team, we just didn't work."

"As people we worked."

He kissed her for that, wrapping his arms around her in a tight hug, because it was the only truth that really mattered. As a man and a woman, they worked in a way that had made him feel the world was newborn every morning. They complemented each other as perfectly as their bodies fit together. The soft touch of her, her liveliness, her grace, her refinement, and her miraculous love, he thought. They were knitted into his very breathing now. How was he going to let go of all that without coming unraveled? His heart began to expand like an overinflated balloon, until he thought it might burst.

"Cupcake?" He could see anticipation in those warm, round eyes, and beneath his breastbone he hurt.

"Sweetheart, will you . . . ?"

His voice failed, just a glitch in his speech mechanism, informing him that it was useless. That this was the end of the line, and masochism wasn't in his emotional vocabulary.

"Will I what, Joe?"

"Will you . . . go on writing movies for the rest of your life?"

"Absolutely."

"Then I guess we won't meet again. I'm not likely to work on the West Coast after this."

She would get through this, she assured herself. Some way or another. "Then I guess you're right," she managed to say. "We won't be seeing each other again."

"Not unless you were crazy enough to marry me," Joe heard himself say.

"I love you, Joe, but I'm not a housewife type. I'd fail you as a wife if I had to give up my career."

"I had a housewife type. It didn't work. What I want is the late, great Jeffrey York's daughter. They do have typewriters in New York."

"Yes, I know, darling. But Hollywood's where it's at for screenwriters. And let's face it, you can't stand the place, and I need to be there physically . . . at least some of the time."

And I'm a self-educated jerk who still doesn't eat with the right fork, he thought, and she should be mating with some blond Harvard prince. But she loves me. She does. She does. And she's willing to make it work. "We could divide our time. Would six months of the year be enough?"

Chalice reached out and touched his wrist. He could smell the warm body scent of her as she spoke and thought this might be a good moment to die. "You'd hate it spending half your life in the West."

His voice was like a drowning man's. "Not nearly as much as I'd hate spending all of it without you, cupcake. It's not just having you in bed. I love what you are and everything you do. And the special thing you do is write movies. You're a wonderful screenwriter. Marry me, and I'll never want to take that away from you. And I'll never invade your territory again. The movies are all yours."

"There'd be changes, adjustments for both of us," she said fearfully.

"Wonderful changes for me. I'll adjust gladly."

He stroked her face, losing himself in it as he watched her color return . . . a feathery rosing from cheekbone to jaw. "It'll be busy for you my love, shuttling back and forth. I won't always be able to come with you. Will you mind that?"

"I'll hate it," she whispered. "But not as much as I'd hate—"

He touched her lips lightly, stopping her. "Supposing I got you pregnant?"

"I wouldn't mind a bit," she said, taking his fingers between her lips.

"Do you want children?"

"Only if they're yours."

He made an involuntary fist, remembering the sight of Tim Sacco, his hands all over Chalice. He had felt ransacked.

She saw the fresh bruises staining his knuckles and brushed them with her lips.

"They'd better be," he growled and pressed her against his heart.

READERS' COMMENTS ON
SILHOUETTE INTIMATE MOMENTS:

"About a month ago a friend loaned me my first Silhouette. I was thoroughly surprised as well as totally addicted. Last week I read a Silhouette Intimate Moments and I was even more pleased. They are the best romance series novels I have ever read. They give much more depth to the plot, characters, and the story is fundamentally realistic. They incorporate tasteful sex scenes, which is a must, especially in the 1980's. I only hope you can publish them fast enough."

S.B.*, Lees Summit, MO

"After noticing the attractive covers on the new line of Silhouette Intimate Moments, I decided to read the inside and discovered that this new line was more in the line of books that I like to read. I do want to say I enjoyed the books because they are so realistic and a lot more truthful than so many romance books today."

J.C., Onekama, MI

"I would like to compliment you on your books. I will continue to purchase all of the Silhouette Intimate Moments. They are your best line of books that I have had the pleasure of reading."

S.M., Billings, MT

*names available on request

Silhouette Intimate Moments

COMING
NEXT MONTH

MIDSUMMER MIDNIGHT
Parris Afton Bonds
Damon was a freedom fighter committed to a revolutionary ideal; Sigourney was a journalist who dreaded war. For Damon she would overcome that fear and stand by him…if only he would ask.

BOUNDARY LINES
Nora Roberts
Aaron was a Murdock. Jillian Baron had been taught never to trust a Murdock, but when rustlers began to endanger her family ranch, it looked like she would have no choice.

NINA'S SONG
Anna James
Ambition had driven Nina and Alex apart ten years before. Now fate was bringing them together again. He had the words, she the music; perhaps this time they could be united in perfect harmony.

STAR RISE
Pat Wallace
Dreams can be very fragile. Lt. Col. Mike Nesbitt held Lisa Heron's dream of the stars in the palm of his hand. What choice did she have but to trust him to handle her with care?

AVAILABLE NOW:

VALLEY OF THE SUN
Elizabeth Lowell

THE MALE CHAUVINIST
Alexandra Sellers

SOFT TOUCH
Möeth Allison

TIGER PRINCE
Erin St. Claire